TOD

AFTER 9/11 WE OFTEN

HEARD THE EXPRESSION

"IT'S NOT IF WE ARE ATTACKED AGAIN,

IT'S WHEN."

J.E. LOCKHART

ISBN: 0-9730041-4-2
ISBN-13: 9780973004144

www.TodayIsWhen.com

DEDICATION

*Not to those who stare up at the night sky, but to
those that reach up and touch a star.*

Chris

Thank you for ya Support

Joe Lockhart

4/12/2010

ACT I

1.

The house looked like any house in any suburban neighborhood in any city in North America. The street was full of children riding their bikes, skipping rope, and riding skateboards in the warm July sun. The sound of sprinklers watering the grass scorched from the heat and the hustle and bustle of automobiles and everyday life filled the air.

Fadi looked out the window into the wilderness of suburbia. A smile came over his face. He was gloating over the ease with which he got his team and the supplies he needed into the country—supplies that would allow him to stage the crime of the century.

Americans are a lazy people, he thought to himself. They have all of these wonderful possessions and have no idea how easy it would be to lose them all. They pride themselves on collecting as many possessions as they can, but then they foolishly trust other people to protect them. *This is going to be—how do they say it in America?—like taking candy from a baby,* Fadi thought.

Amman sat at the kitchen table putting the finishing touches on the timers that would be used the day the world would forget 9/11. The attack they were planning would be a newer and bigger attack—one the Americans could never conceive. It would make 9/11 look like a backyard fireworks display on the Fourth of July. Fadi and Amman were waiting for another man who was coming into the country for "the project," as it was called. Fadi decided not to go to the airport to pick up Jabbar. He did not want to draw any suspicion as they fit the terrorist profile to a T. Fadi sneered at this wonderful country, one that could have

1

a terrorist watch list but did not allow profiling. How Fadi loved liberal media busybodies always making it hard for law enforcement and easier for freedom fighters like him. Yes, the Americans called him a terrorist, but the ones who control the media make up the names for the combatants. If you're on the winning side, you're a freedom fighter; if you're on the losing side, you're a terrorist.

Fadi had waited most of his life to get back at the "Great Satan," the American infidels who had polluted and destroyed many great cultures so they could be forced to join their brand of democracy, their new world order. *I'll show them "democracy,"* he thought to himself. If Fadi and his team succeeded, they would change the course of history. Fadi knew that his people would not enter the new world order without a fight. He and his team were about to bring the fight to America, to the cowards who carpet bombed women and children from forty thousand feet so they could rape the country of its natural resources. *And they call themselves "righteous." The day is near.* He grinned and thought what an honor it would be to bring about the destruction of the infidels.

America is ripe for the taking, Fadi thought. He had enjoyed his many years here waiting for the day the phone would ring and it would be the call he longed for. July was a great month to be in America. The weather reminded him of home, and Fadi enjoyed being out in the fresh air—the air that would one day be filled with the smell of gunpowder, dead bodies, and burning buildings, reminiscent of his home, thanks to American imperialism. Fadi couldn't wait to put the plan into action.

2.

Special Agent Burton Anthony Davis of the Federal Bureau of Investigation was no stranger to law enforcement and intelligence gathering. Davis started at an early age in law enforcement working for the world-famous Scotland Yard. After years of hard work, he joined his father when he transferred to the Secret Intelligence Service, or better known as MI6, Britain's equivalent to the CIA.

In his years of service, Davis wanted to be more proactive in the fight against terrorism and not reactive, which was the manner it was presently fought. Davis wanted to be two steps ahead of terrorists; he wanted to catch them before they killed, and not after. Davis wanted to be assigned to the American taskforce as he wanted to work in the one country that had, for the most part, been immune to terrorism. America did not have the history of terrorism that his homeland and European and Middle Eastern countries had. America was becoming the target of more terrorism, and Davis wanted to be there to help prevent the carnage that he had seen in his lifetime.

Davis didn't want to leave the UK and his family behind. He had roots that went back many generations. His decision to migrate to America was made easier by a terrorist cell that killed many people celebrating at a New Year's Eve party. His parents were guests at the event, along with the prime minister. The prime minister survived; his parents did not. Davis asked permission to avenge his parents' deaths as MI6 knew which cell planted the bomb. His request was declined because it was a "sensitive" matter that had major ramifications worldwide.

The door that had welcomed Davis into MI6 was now slammed into his face. Davis felt that it was time to leave before he was asked to "retire." He decided to immigrate to the United States shortly after his parents' funeral.

Agent Davis recently celebrated twenty years with the FBI. Long before 9/11, Davis was considered a maverick, merging the tactics of MI6 and the FBI in his progressive manner of detecting espionage. As time went on, Davis found himself getting little response or the cold shoulder from his colleagues. Newer agents didn't want to rock the boat. Promotions and a fat pension depended more on how much ass you kissed than how many bad guys you caught.

Politically correct morons, he thought to himself on more than one occasion. If the official story of 9/11 was to be believed, it meant that the so-called intelligence community was asleep at the wheel. Maybe some were asleep—but not Davis. He was on top of Al Qaeda and kept track of them. However, the memos to his supervisors about several terrorist threats went unheeded. After 9/11, Davis asked why his memos were ignored. "What memos?" was the blank reply that he received from Agent Johnson, his supervisor and the biggest pain in his ass. Davis never asked again. He was later told that his memos were lost in the abyss of the computer's mainframe.

Davis thought often about early retirement from the service after 9/11, but he stayed on because he felt that he would be abandoning his watch if he left, letting his family and his adopted nation down. He couldn't just walk away with a golden handshake and the watch to match.

Davis thought that his twenty years at the FBI meant something. Because of his work, mothers could go to the grocery store to buy milk and not get blown up by some nut-job who hates America. Davis was the lead investigator on many past attempts to attack his adopted nation. His "team," as he called them, had stopped many major attempted attacks on America. The public never heard about that; all they heard about was how the intelligence community had dropped the ball on 9/11. Davis wasn't in America on that fateful day—he was on a mission in some country not even on the map. Since 9/11, there had been talk of prior knowledge of the attacks from within the government. Davis dismissed this but found it funny that he was out of the country on a bullshit mission when the attacks occurred. The attacks on 9/11 were something that he didn't even want to think about. Until he had any proof to the contrary, Davis considered Usama Bin Laden to be guilty of mass murder; he was still on the FBI's list of most wanted fugitives.

Each bright and sunny morning gave Davis cause to worry. He always wondered when he was going to get the call about more hijacked airplanes or buildings being blown up. His worst fear was that Al Qaeda or some other group would sneak in some of the missing Russian nuclear weapons. *What city would be the next target then?* It was enough to give him an ulcer. Davis ate more antacids than real food. It was going to kill him—that and the stress of waiting for the phone to ring or his pager to go off at the next attack.

Davis spent too much time at the office and the shooting range and not enough time at home with his family. It was the job that had destroyed his marriage—not the infidelity that his wife had accused him of. Davis's mistress was the Bureau. The job was in his mind every waking moment, and yes, he did take it to bed with him. It was in his dreams and more commonly in his nightmares.

Over the years, Davis had made some good friends and allies. One was his personal assistant, Grace. She had been with the Bureau almost as long as Davis had. She was more than a personal assistant to Davis—she was his rock and the person he went to for advice on important issues. When Davis wanted a second opinion, he often went to her for her pragmatic thoughts. Grace was more of a logical thinker than an emotional one. She was the woman Davis's wife had accused him of having an affair with, and Grace was the person he went to in his time of need. While the thought of having an affair with Grace had never crossed his mind, he often imagined it would have been nice to have married a woman like her.

Life, however, is strange. Susan had given Davis four wonderful children—that much he would never regret. It was his children and his grandchildren that he feared for the most. Where would they be in the next attacks? Would they be safe? It was to them and the millions of other free people that he dedicated his remaining years at the Bureau. Davis tried to stay one step ahead of evil wherever it reared its ugly head.

Davis needed to keep up on the latest information. He was about to check the FBI information center for the latest intel updates when Special Agent Monroe burst into the room, excited and nervous. He announced they were intercepting an enormous amount of chatter about an important event.

3.

Christmas is the busiest time of year for air travel. July is also a busy month as a lot of people are traveling for the summer holidays. Being an airport operations manager is a lifetime career, one that Randy Bergen took pride in. An airport is like a city unto itself. While it is plugged into city systems, it has its own water, gas, waste, communications, food, and electrical systems. Each airport is a self-sufficient city. It can function with its on-hand supplies if there is a major storm that closes the roads or shuts the power down.

Randy was the epitome of the micromanager. There wasn't a system in the airport that he was unfamiliar with. He could fix almost any system within the complex. The only area that he had access to but could not work in was the tower. Randy had picked up a few things in the thirty-plus years that he had worked in airports. A few times when he visited the tower to talk to Chief Controller Phil Wayant, Randy would catch himself mouthing the words of the air traffic controllers, or ATCs for short. "Westjet flight four-one, turn right, heading zero-five-zero, climb to flight level one-three-zero." Randy mouthed these words as he had heard the controller say it a thousand times.

Randy was on his last assignment before retirement. He used to command a seven-acre, four-terminal airport in the United States until he did what was typical for him—he pissed in the wrong pool. Randy was a straight-up guy who played by the book. Everybody was equal, no matter who they were. Sure, they gave special treatment to VIPs like politicians and rock stars, but when it came to the law, all were treated the same. At least when Randy was in change they were. The incident that proved some were more equal than others was when a senator's son was caught with cocaine in his carry-on bag. It wasn't the fact that he was the son of a senator that had made Randy give him a second look. It was the young man's attitude that needed addressing.

"You know who the fuck I am?" the young man had asked, half stoned. Randy had given the same reply each time he was asked that question, and the kid had asked Randy that question a million times.

"If you don't know who you are, junior, how am I supposed to know? Maybe check your passport if you're confused," he said. "For the record, I don't care who you are," he added in a sarcastic tone, looking the young, misled boy in the eyes.

"All I know is that you were caught with illegal drugs in my airport," Randy said as he motioned to officers to arrest the punk.

"You'll pay for this, old man…"

"I'll pay? I'll pay for this?" Randy said, looking up through his glasses. "Let me tell you something, junior. I've paid my dues. I went to Vietnam and watched many a good man die for nothing. I'm sure your daddy didn't go, did he? While poor and middle-class kids go all over the world, dying for your daddy's wars, what are you doing? You're just walking around in a three-thousand-dollar suit and snorting coke like the little spoiled brat that you are. You're lucky you're in America and not Turkey—there they would cut off your hands. All that's going to happen to you here is your little hands are going to get slapped." Randy said it in almost one breath. The guards always liked when Randy put someone like this in his or her place. They just stood back and smiled.

Randy, however, did pay a price. Shortly after the arrest of the senator's son went public, Randy was dragged on the carpet. It seemed that the senator had powerful friends who sat on committees related to aviation. But instead of forcing Randy into retiring, out of respect for his years of service, his friends at the Federal Aviation Administration passed on Randy's name to an airport in Canada that was looking for an operations manager. Randy knew where Winnipeg was only because he remembered the call sign of the airport: CYWG.

Walking through the terminal in Winnipeg was a lot easier than walking through four, but it was not an easy task. After 9/11, Randy found himself scanning the faces of many passengers as they walked about to and from their gates. *Which one is the terrorist?* he thought to himself. It could be any one of the three million passengers who used his airport on a yearly basis. *Is it that man? Is it that woman? Is it the tall guy with the dark shades and hat, or is it the bookworm geek sitting waiting for his flight while reading the latest adventures of his fantasy hero?* Randy just prayed that if a terrorist picked his airport, the security was on the ball enough to catch it. Randy made his way through the terminal, making eye contact with as many people and employees as possible. Just as he was concentrating on a passenger who looked out of place, his two-way radio came alive with a call about a problem passenger at the departure lounge.

4.

In a few short days, it will be vacation time, William thought to himself. It had been several years since William had taken his family on a well-deserved vacation. The last was the take-the-family-to-Disneyland trip. What a vacation that was, William remembered. Thankfully, this vacation would be a little longer and not so fast-paced.

William Maddock was the owner of a dot-com company that he started as a young lad even before there was a dot-com. William's early venture into computer programming started with his father's old Commodore 64. His father told him about the old days of programming in DOS. That was a long time ago and a few million lines of code between his beginning and where he was now.

Thankfully, he had avoided the financial problems that plagued most dot-coms. He never took his company public, so the vulnerability of Wall Street never bothered him. He kept it simple. He serviced each of his small, medium, and larger companies as if they were his only clients. Customer service was what he sold, and he was available to his customers almost any time of the week. The weekends were reserved for his family. They were the center of his universe. Looking back from middle age, William was proud of his humble beginnings. He knew that hard work, talent, and some blessings would one day lead him to his dream—to make a living programming. He reflected on his beginnings and where he ended up, and it brought a smile to his face. Each day he knew he had a family to go home to. That was what life was all about.

Even after 9/11 when many in his family were concerned, William never had a problem with traveling by air. He believed that the chances were slim that a terrorist attack would affect him. *God will protect us,* he thought, and he prayed often.

Being a pilot himself, William enjoyed the serenity of flying around on short trips in his Beechcraft Baron 58P. This upcoming trip to Europe, however, would be left up to the professionals in the flight deck of a Boeing 747-400. The closest William had ever come to the flight deck of a jumbo jet was on his simulator at home. This time, however, William was going to get a close look at the flight deck as he knew the captain personally. Not only was William an avid pilot, he also enjoyed the hobby of amateur radio. The captain of the 747 was a friend and fellow radio operator from Quebec. Marcel Laroque was a captain for Western Global Airlines, piloting a soon-to-be-retired Boeing 747-400. William had booked the flight to make sure he would get to meet Marcel and maybe get to sit in a seat in the flight deck of his favorite aircraft, even if was only to look and marvel at all of the technology.

William loved flying in his Baron from his hometown of Saskatoon, Saskatchewan, in Canada to cities where his relatives and in-laws lived. He looked forward to the upcoming trip from Saskatoon to Winnipeg to catch the flight to England.

William's wife, Sandra, wasn't much of a fan of flying in light planes. She didn't like to feel like the only thing separating her from the outside world was a thin piece of metal that was supposed to be a door. She also found it boring. However, William's children, Shawn and Zoë, loved to fly and went up with him every chance they could. Shawn rarely looked out of the airplane as his eyes were focused on the instruments and radio equipment from his right-hand seat. Zoë, on the other hand, loved the scenery and couldn't get enough of the view.

She hated it when her father had to fly "instrument flight rules," or IFR for short. That meant the sky was cloudy or snowy, and the view was not so good.

The portion of the trip in the Baron would be short compared to the flight in the 747 across the pond to England. The weather was supposed to be clear for most of the flight east of Saskatoon, but "weather is as unpredictable as women," William often chuckled jokingly, to Sandra's dismay.

Sandra—now there is a woman, William thought to himself. She not only was bright and attractive, but she was also independent and confident. For years Sandra was the main breadwinner in the family as William struggled to make his company profitable. She would give of herself without asking for anything in return. It was a blessing when William's business began to make money. Now both William and Sandra could breathe a little easier about the future of their children. Sandra could enjoy the little things in life that she loved, and William could dedicate more time to his children, ham radio, and flying—the three things that were his passion.

William would often sit back and reminisce of his training as a pilot. He was old for a student pilot as he didn't start training to fly until his early thirties. Most of the students were in their twenties when they started off careers in aviation. William, on the other hand, learned to fly to prove to his father that he did have what it took. The little Cessna 172 that he trained in was small compared to the Baron he now owned, but she was a rugged aircraft that was well designed and could take a lot of punishment from neophyte pilots trying to master the flare in a fifteen-knot crosswind landing.

Thanks to his lovely wife, William's training flight time was a Christmas gift. Sandra was always there to help him chase his dreams. The one day that all pilots remember forever is their first solo flight. William remembered his well. It was a warm spring Saturday morning when William went to take his flying lesson. His instructor was impressed with his progress and decided that William was ready to go solo. It was like William had flown a million times. As he climbed off the runway to circuit altitude, he was feeling humbled and a bit sad. He was thinking of his father, who had little faith in him. As a youngster, William remembered expressing his thoughts to his father about a future as a pilot. His father, who was from a generation that showed little affection to their children, could only say, "You don't have what it takes." William made a right turn on crosswind and continued to climb to circuit altitude in his Cessna 172P, all alone, except for the ghost of his father by his side.

But now it was time for William to prepare for the long journey ahead. He had to pull himself out of his "remembering the olden days," as the children called it, and get back to making sure all that needed to be done was accomplished before they departed. Sandra did not leave anything until the last minute, and that was great as William didn't have to worry about missing anything. The family would be leaving in a few days—just enough time to prepare and get everything wrapped up at his shop.

5.

Jabbar went through customs with the typical questions and responses that he had rehearsed answering days in advance.

"What is your business in America?" was the robotic question from an overworked and underpaid customs employee.

"I'm here on business," replied Jabbar in a thick accent, trying not to stare down the overweight infidel.

"How long will you be here?" she asked.

"I'll be here for two weeks," Jabbar replied, knowing in the back of his mind that the only way he was leaving was in a pine box. Jabbar was trying to be as polite as possible even though he knew he wasn't being profiled. Cameras were everywhere he walked, and there were more than a few other customs officers keeping an eye on him. Jabbar just kept thinking to himself that he had to be polite and act relaxed so as not to attract attention to himself.

"All appears to be in order," announced the customs officer, not even looking up from the papers. "Enjoy your stay in America," she added as she stamped his documents and handed them back. Jabbar thought to himself that he would enjoy his stay, indeed.

He walked through the exit doors of the airport into the warm summer air of New York. Jabbar could not believe how easy it was for him to enter the country. He knew he could never just fly into places like Israel—they know how to take care of potential problems. *Americans, however, have no conception of how dangerous their open border policy is*, Jabbar thought. *Soon they will. Soon they will regret being so trusting, so naive.*

The grin on Jabbar's face was rare as he seldom had a reason to smile. He walked over to a fellow Arab who was standing at his taxi, smiling back. The driver swung his door wide open. "Welcome to America," the cabdriver said. Jabbar sat in the cab in amazement at the simplicity of this great superpower that he, a simple farmer, was going to help bring to an end.

6.

A lot of intelligence gathering is listening. Agents scrutinize every form of communication there is: cell phones, faxes, radio, pagers, text messages, e-mail, Web sites, and even baby monitors.

Chatter, as it is called, is intercepted, interpreted, and if necessary, red flagged. Since 9/11, ears had been glued to the speakers to see if there was any talk about the next big attack.

For Special Agent Monroe to be excited, it meant this was more than normal chatter. It must be very important.

Special Agent Ethan Monroe was Davis's protégé and had been at the Bureau since he was out of high school. Monroe was often teased for his boyish grin and good looks; he was the all-American boy. He was a poster boy of what America was supposed to be. He should be out dancing with young girls and driving fast cars, not chasing terrorists. He should be enjoying life and not trying to prevent the loss of it.

Monroe was young, but he was far advanced in his wisdom. He had helped Davis crack a few leads in the past to bring about terrorist arrests. This was different—this was big. Monroe was more than excited about this, and he just couldn't wait to share this information with Davis.

Davis followed Monroe to the communications center, a secure floor in the building full of radio communication and computer equipment. Davis walked over to Monroe's desk. It was loaded with a bank of computer monitors and radio equipment that Monroe used to decipher chatter.

"So…?" Davis asked. "What's all the commotion about?"

"You have to see this. The chatter is off the chart," Monroe explained.

"What kind is it this time?" Davis asked.

Monroe sat at his computer and brought up a screen with a few mouse clicks. He started to explain, pointing at the data on the computer screen. "About eighteen months ago, Echelon put a red flag on some chatter coming out of the UK. After it was red flagged, MI6 started to monitor it and anything related to it. Then Echelon flagged similar chatter from Russia and the Middle East and linked them. MI6 started to monitor that too. A few weeks ago, Echelon linked all of this overseas chatter with that which is going to and from Canada and here in the United States." Monroe paused and looked at Davis, who was intently looking at the information on the screen.

Monroe continued. "The overall chatter that started about a year ago has intensified in the last few months, and even more in the last few weeks and days. The latest information is still being translated, but the info from last week indicates that something coordinated is being planned," Monroe said, looking between the computer and his notes.

"Is the current chatter we're receiving domestic or international?" Davis asked. Monroe pointed to some information on the computer screen.

"Most of it is coming from within the United States and Canada," Monroe said with urgency in his voice as he looked at Davis. He continued. "What's different is the way it occurred. First there was the overseas call, and then there were the relay calls to several cell phones in the UK, Canada, and here in the United States. It's like the instructions are coming from overseas, and then groups in the United States are retransmitting the information to people here," Monroe stated, pointing to a new page on the computer screen.

"What's the gist of the chatter?" Davis asked in a pragmatic tone, looking at some of the hard copies of the notes.

"Let me bring up some of the latest transcripts," Monroe said as he scrolled through pages of transcripts on another computer screen. He then found the printed transcript in the pile of paperwork on his desk.

"Oh yeah, here they are," Monroe said as he found the document he was looking for. "OK, here's some of the latest stuff. Keep in mind that when they would speak in previous intercepts, they would say months or weeks; now they're specifying a day. We're monitoring certain people who have come up in conversation. The other day our mark got a short call from overseas." Monroe quoted from the transcript: "Your relative will be arriving on Monday."

Monroe continued, saying, "Our mark on the other end of the line paused and then asked, *'For the visit?'* The caller replied, *'Yes, the visit.'* The call was over, and then the mark called several local contacts and said pretty much the same thing. 'The relative will be here next week. Allah be with you.' And that's the end of the conversation."

Monroe paused and then continued. "There's a consistency in the calls. The visit or the visitor is mentioned often, and the arrival of someone or something is a repeated theme." Monroe added, "This is the type of chatter that's been going on all over the UK, Canada, and here in the United States. A call comes in from overseas, and then the relaying starts. It's the same with the e-mail and text messages that Echelon picks up." Monroe explained the order in which the information was being transmitted.

"Any one of the marks important?" Davis asked.

"Most of the intercepts from our marks are from low-level types. The other conversations that we're intercepting are from either throwaway pay-in-advance phones or from anonymous e-mail accounts. Nothing traceable, but it was picked up by Echelon. It's the same type of chatter over and over, and it's getting more intense by the hour. A year or so ago they talked about a gathering, and then a few months back they started to plan dates, and then they went from that to when the visit was going to happen. All of this is around the Fourth of July or in the month of July," Monroe explained.

"Can you ascertain from it what they're planning or where they're planning for?" Davis asked, not quite sure what to make of it. Davis knew that chatter was a common thing and went on 24/7, three hundred and sixty-five days a year. The Bureau had a list of people who were considered potential threats to national security. Their bank accounts, phone lines, and just about every other part of their lives were monitored in some way. On this day, Agent Monroe picked up some of the transcripts from one of thousands of people on the monitor list.

"Typically, the chatter we get is from different marks and Echelon intercepts that are not connected to each other, but this is a consistent theme. Something or someone is coming into the country next week, and all of these people are being told to get ready for it." Monroe was trying to convince his boss he was not Chicken Little.

"Are they being warned, or are they being told?" Davis asked, starting to pick up the same scent that Monroe was on.

"I think someone or, perhaps, many people are bringing something into the country that is too sensitive to be transmitted or sent in the mail or through FedEx for fear that we'll intercept it," Monroe explained, looking at the transcripts.

"Like orders from the top, or plans—something that cannot be sent via communications," he added.

"Biological?" Davis said with worry as he looked over Monroe's notes.

"We know they've tried it before, and they'll try it again," Davis said.

"The last time we caught them because they stuck out like a sore thumb. This time they may be better prepared. Where's the latest chatter located?" Davis asked as he grabbed a pad of paper and a pen.

"It's all over the country—mostly in major American cities and into Canada as well," Monroe said with concern in his voice.

"Canada?" Davis asked while making notes on his pad, looking up through his glasses.

"Yes, and not just the large cities like Montréal, Toronto, or Vancouver as we would expect. There's similar chatter in Mississauga, London, Regina, and Edmonton as well," Monroe explained.

While Davis loved Canada and had friends and relatives who lived there, he was always concerned about the terrorist hotbed that Canada had become. The government of Canada was more concerned about looking good instead of closing the floodgate to criminals who abused its immigration system. There were more terrorist cells in Canada than any other country, and more than a few had tried to sneak into America to commit acts of terror.

Davis remembered when Ahmed Ressam snuck into America from Canada in an attempt to set off a bomb at Los Angeles International Airport during the Y2K scare. Davis and his team were lucky that they got to Ahmed by tipping off customs. Back then Davis remembered the Y2K chatter to be not as intense, or as coordinated, as this new chatter seemed to be. "Have you called our contacts at the Canadian Security

Intelligence Service or the Royal Canadian Mounted Police yet?" Davis asked, looking up from his notes.

"I sent CSIS and the RCMP our regular memos that included this information yesterday," Monroe said.

"Call them ASAP and make sure they've read it and don't put it on some shelf for some analyst to look at a month from now."

"You bet," Monroe answered. While Davis wrote notes, Monroe stood up from his desk to get his book of numbers. He paused to take a long, hard look out over the city. *Is this the big one we all have been waiting for? Am I ever going to get married and have children? Will they be able to live in the same country I grew up in?* There were so many questions running in his head—too many questions and not enough time to answer them all.

Davis, in his typical take-command role, stood up after he finished writing his notes and said to Monroe, "Call the Canadians and warn them. Call our people—CIA and NSA—and ask them what they have received from their confidential informants. Keep on top of this and make sure the Secret Service and the president are in the loop as well."

He paused and walked closer to Monroe. "You better be sure about this. Get all of your facts together before you make the calls, and tell them we're on top of it here." Davis knew if this was wrong, it would be the excuse his bosses needed to put him out to pasture. "I'll be in my office going over a game plan," Davis said as he walked away from Monroe.

Davis paused again and turned back toward Monroe. He was proud of Monroe—he was like the son Davis never had. "Ethan, once you get all of the information together and you've doubled-checked your intel, make the calls to the other agencies yourself. Don't leave it to anyone else. Make sure you emphasize urgency when you call, and call the FAA as well."

Davis walked out of the room and to the nearest lift. He knew that part of the problem with 9/11 was the fact that agencies didn't talk or share information with each other. After 9/11 that was supposed to change, and agencies were supposed to be more open with information. But did it change? He knew that the CIA kept him in the dark about certain operations that they were partaking in. The same went for the FBI and other agencies. When agents didn't trust a lot of people in their own offices, how could they trust other agencies?

Davis feared many things since 9/11. He left the office and walked over to the lift and pressed the button to go down to his office. Each time he walked into a lift, he thought about the people who had been trapped in them in the towers that day. Did they burn to death, as the story goes, or did they die when tons of steel and concrete came crashing down on them? *What a way to go,* Davis thought as the doors opened up and he stepped into the lift. Just as they were about to close, Davis heard a woman's voice from down the hall.

"Hold that elevator!" she said, sounding out of breath. Davis instinctively reached out his arm to stop the lift doors from closing. He was about to look out to see who was coming when a woman in a wheelchair came racing through the doorway. Davis stepped back, startled at how fast she was going. She wheeled herself in with a smile and a thank you.

Davis felt his heart start to beat faster as he asked her what floor she wanted. "Main floor please," she replied, trying to catch her breath. Davis tried to hide the fact that his hand was shaking as he pushed the button. Seeing the woman in the wheelchair brought back memories of the debriefing after 9/11. There were a lot of people who needlessly died that day. Davis knew that the names and faces of many of them would never be known. Several groups of people who died that day never received much news coverage. They were what Davis called the forgotten dead. Most of what was heard on the news was about those who were killed in the towers. Not much was heard about the 124 people killed at the Pentagon who were minding their own business when a 757 came crashing into them, killing them and all 64 passengers on the American Airlines plane as well.

Davis knew that much had been said about those who perished in the towers. But not much information had been provided about the people who had time to make it out of the buildings but were instead held in certain areas. Davis remembered that one such group was people in wheelchairs. They were held in staging areas below the fire floor. Due to the fire, the lifts didn't work and could only be used by the fire department. Nobody in their wildest dreams thought the buildings were going to fall. Those people sat helplessly as tons of steel and concrete came crashing down on them. Every time Davis saw a person in a wheelchair, it always brought him back to that awful day.

It was memories like these that kept Davis out of retirement and on the trail of scumbags who wanted to destroy his adopted nation. *Not on my watch,* Davis thought to himself. *Not on my life.*

7.

"What's the problem here?" Randy asked Rebecca at the departure lounge.

"We have a customer who won't let us check his notebook to see if it's operational," she explained with frustration in her voice.

"He claims he's being singled out because he's Arabic," the girl at the counter said as she turned her head in the direction of the passenger to point him out.

"He's already talked to my supervisor, but he wanted to talk to the airport manager too," Rebecca said, clearly upset by the accusation of the passenger.

"It's OK," Randy said with assurance. Randy didn't deal with passengers directly unless it was important. Ever since 9/11, everyone was overly concerned about not offending people with a permanent tan. Randy, on the other hand, didn't see color; he saw only a potential problem. To him, explosives were color-blind. He knew that they killed people of all colors and from every part of the world. It didn't matter who you were or where you were from. All Randy saw was a violation of the rules—a violation of the rules that had to be addressed. Randy walked over to the customer who was standing at the end of the service counter.

"Sir, I'm sorry to inconvenience you, but we have to check to make sure that your notebook is functional," Randy stated with firmness in his voice, trying to look the customer in the eyes.

"Would you be doing this if I wasn't a Muslim?" asked the man in a clearly agitated voice.

"Our policy is neutral. It doesn't matter what religion or color you are—white, black, yellow, brown, Christian, or Jewish. All I care about, sir, is the safety of this airport and the safety of the passengers," Randy said to the irate customer. Randy always made sure that he maintained eye contact with whomever he spoke with. Randy believed that you can tell a lot about people by looking into their eyes. The eyes are the window to the soul, and Randy could always tell when people were not telling the truth or were being evasive. They would not look him in the eyes.

During the whole conversation, the passenger didn't return Randy's gaze. He knew that some cultures see this as a sign of respect, not evasiveness. Randy also relied on body language. This passenger remained firm with an agitated tone in his voice. Randy was having trouble discerning if the passenger was legitimately offended or if he was trying to keep them from inspecting his notebook.

"Look," Randy started to say, but the customer slammed his notebook on the counter.

"If you must check it, then go ahead and check it!" the man said loudly enough that half of the terminal could hear him.

"There is no reason to yell, sir," Randy said as he called Rebecca over to the end of the counter. "This nice lady will take a quick look at your notebook, and then you and the rest of the passengers can be on your way," Randy said with a sarcastic grin.

Each time Randy had to deal with an irate customer, he just thought to himself that his day would get better, and it always did. Randy loved the airport and airport people. However, Randy was always thinking that one day, in some airport somewhere in the world, people who felt they had a score to settle would again hold his fellow citizens hostage, killing a lot of innocent people.

The day started out like any other; there were minor problems with equipment and passengers, but for the most part things would get better. Randy was an optimist and always tried to see the good in people, but he knew that for some people, there just wasn't any good. They woke up on the wrong side of life.

The air traffic was higher than normal. Randy knew it would get busier as there were flights scheduled to leave for Europe this week. It was overseas flights that caused the most congestion at the airport. It was also the time that Randy made sure his security personnel were on top of their game as this was when mistakes happened and potential problems were overlooked in the haste to load the planes. This was when Randy thought airports had to be extra diligent to ensure that no terrorist would sneak in and cause havoc. While Winnipeg was an unlikely target, nothing is unlikely in the mind of a terrorist who kills innocent men, women, and children.

8.

It was early on a warm July morning when Sandra went to wake the kids so they could be ready for their early morning departure. The children were so excited they were already awake. In July the sun came up very early, so there would be a lot of light. William wanted to leave a few days early so he and Sandra could visit friends in Winnipeg before their flight to England.

Summer travel was something that William loved, but he also had to be cautious. He loved to fly in his Baron 58P to and from cities all over North America. The only problem was that when the weather turned bad, he couldn't fly. He knew that while it's usually fine to drive in a thunderstorm, flying in a light aircraft in a thunderstorm is not a good idea.

It took long enough to get Sandra to even sit in the Baron, never mind fly in it. The first few times Sandra flew, she gave a whole new meaning to "white-knuckle." She gripped the seat so tightly William was sure she must have had cramps in her hands. Normally Sandra didn't complain. She wasn't afraid of anything, but if she were flying the plane, she would feel better, more in control. She was very independent, and not being in control was something she didn't care for. When flying, Sandra couldn't point out the window and tell William which way to turn as she did when they were driving.

One flight came to mind that William and his family had taken during a summer vacation to Bellingham, Washington. It was a normal warm summer day on the return trip to Saskatoon. According to all weather reports, the visibility was twenty-plus miles with thunderstorms to the northwest, far away from William's flight plan. Still, William filed an IFR flight plan in the event the weather went from good to cloudy and rainy. He knew that, in this part of the world, the weather was prone to sudden changes with little or no warning.

William had been flying the Baron northeast over the mountains at thirteen thousand feet when he noticed a large column of cumulous clouds left of his flight path, closing fast. They were the large, white, pillow-like clouds, and they caused little turbulence. What William couldn't see were the thunderclouds and storms that were behind them. Once he noticed the storm clouds, William asked for the latest weather reports and the highest clearance his pressurized Baron would go. He was hoping that he could fly over the storm. There were no airports in the mountains, so William had to fly either to his destination or to an alternate one just on the east side of the mountain range.

With skill, blessings, and a lot of luck, William had managed to avoid most of the storm; he ran into turbulence, lots of rain, and a little lightning along the way. The Baron suffered no damage due to the weather. The only exception was the new nail marks in Sandra's seat. As a precautionary measure, William changed his flight plan so he could land at Calgary International Airport and wait out the weather. Sandra was pale as a ghost and needed to get on the ground. The children slept like babies. Needless to say, Sandra was rather reluctant to fly long distances in the Baron again anytime soon.

The children, on the other hand, practically grew up in an airplane. William loved to take them up every chance he could. One day Shawn would make a great pilot. He knew all of the instruments and what they did, but he had a little problem reaching the rudder pedals and looking over the dash. He loved to read out the heading, air speed, and when the instrument landing system glide slope was intercepted.

Zoë, on the other hand, was like her mother in the beginning. The first time she stepped into the Cessna, she started to cry. When William first passed his exam and received his license, he surprised his children by driving them to the airport to take them flying. Shawn couldn't wait, but Zoë didn't want to go. She had it in her head that she was going to be sick. William didn't want to see her sad, so he left her safely on the ground with Albert, the dispatcher, and the hangar cat whose name was appropriately "Cessna." William waved bye as he and Shawn rolled down the taxiway.

After the flight, William sat down with Zoë and talked about doing something nice for her brother. Shawn loved flying. Zoë should try to fly at least once. She owed it to her brother to give it a try. When Sandra's mother came for a visit at Christmas, William took Zoë, Shawn, and their grandma up for a short flight around the city. Zoë loved it; she was instantly hooked on flying and went up many more times with her brother and father.

Zoë loved to take pictures while she was high in the sky. She was going to make a wonderful photographer and had mastered her father's digital camera by the time she was seven. When she was ten, she had already won awards for her nature photos. Flying was a good way for Zoë to shoot some great scenery.

"Are we ready to go, Sandra?" William asked, knowing that Sandra was packing her last-minute items for the trip. William often left the little details up to Sandra. He knew she was better at taking care of them. William spent too much time on detail. "Don't sweat the small stuff," Sandra always said.

"I'll be ready in five," Sandra shouted as she shooed Zoë from the master bedroom. Both children were always excited about a trip. William wasn't sure if they loved flying in the little plane or the big one better. Either way, after they visited friends and relatives in Winnipeg, he was going to try to get the kids a look at a 747's flight deck—if it was OK with Marcel—as they flew over the pond. But they had to get to Winnipeg first, and that meant a few hours of flying in the Baron, as long as the weather cooperated.

The drive to the airport was only fifteen minutes. In Saskatoon William could get anywhere in the city in fifteen minutes, and at six in the morning traffic was almost nonexistent. They parked the car, grabbed their luggage, and made their way on the wet tarmac to the Baron. William always did the preflight check while Sandra loaded the bags and buckled in the kids. The WX, as the weather report was called, was calling for rain and possible thunderstorms. The system was heading northeast and not southeast. Winnipeg was their destination and was supposed to be nice and sunny. This type of weather was typical of July on the prairies. William didn't want Sandra to think about it too much.

With each flight, there was a fight over who would sit in the copilot's seat. After the flight from Bellingham, Sandra always chose to sit in one of the more luxurious seats in the back. Zoë often liked to sit in the back and take pictures. She did, however, like to keep her brother in his place. Being the younger of the two, Shawn was often reminded of his place in the pecking order.

"It's my turn to sit up front!" Zoë stated with certainty in her voice.

"You went in the front last time, Sis." Shawn tried to put up a fight. William finished the external pre-check and was removing his wet raincoat and setting the radio to Saskatoon ATIS at the same time when he noticed two sets of eyes looking at him for direction.

"You know the drill, guys," William said as he returned to listening to the prerecorded message that detailed the latest weather and runway information. Over the years, ever since the children were young, they had solved most of their conflicts the old-fashioned way: rock-paper-scissors. It was a simple but effective way to solve most conflicts. It started simply enough when the children were young and in the tub. The fight was always the same: who was going to get their hair washed first. Rock-paper-scissors was still a tradition for the children.

"One, two, three, four," the children counted. William was finished with ATIS and tuned the radio to the Saskatoon airport's ground frequency.

"Everyone buckled in?" William asked as he looked to see the smiling face of Shawn in the copilot's seat. William took a quick look in the back at Sandra and Zoë, who had a sad look on her face. It didn't matter anyway as they would be flying IFR that day. The weather was not good for taking pictures.

"Next time, Zoë, next time," William said with a grin.

"Let's start her up." William finished the prestart checklist and then turned the key of the Baron as the first of two engines started up with a roar. Once it was purring like a kitten, William started up the second engine. Shawn looked at the instruments to make sure all was well with the engines.

Once all was checked and running, William picked up the microphone of the Beechcraft and called for clearance using the aircraft's call sign. "Saskatoon ground, this is Baron Charlie-Golf-India-Bravo-Hotel, with Charlie. Requesting clearance on an IFR flight plan to Winnipeg."

The controller responded in an almost robotic form. "Baron Charlie-Golf-India-Bravo-Hotel is cleared to Winnipeg International Airport as filed. Fly runway heading, climb, and maintain five thousand feet. Squawk three-four-seven-one."

William read back the instructions verbatim. He taxied the Baron over to the run-up area. Here he had a chance to check out the plane's engines to make sure they were running correctly before he took off. Shawn read off to William the items on the checklist, making sure he didn't miss any.

After they completed their run-up of the plane, William called ground to get clearance to the runway. The controller replied, "Baron Charlie-Golf-India-Bravo-Hotel, taxi to and hold short of runway niner via taxiway Alpha. Turn right at Bravo, hold short of runway niner, and contact tower on one-one-eight point three when ready."

William looked over to an unimpressed Sandra, who was trying not to look too upset. She did so much for William to make him happy; she was the best thing that had ever happened to him.

As the Baron approached the hold-short line of runway niner, Shawn tuned the radio to one-one-eight point three. His proud father looked on. "Do you want to make the call, Shawn?" William asked.

Shawn smiled and keyed the mic on the copilot's yoke. "Saskatoon tower, this is Baron Charlie-Golf-India-Bravo-Hotel, holding short of runway zero-niner, ready for IFR departure to Winnipeg." The controller on duty recognized the young voice on the radio as William's son as he had talked to him many times.

"Baron Charlie-Golf-India-Bravo-Hotel, you are cleared to take off on runway zero-niner. Climb runway heading and contact Saskatoon departure on one-one-niner point nine. Have a good flight." The controller sounded happy for it being so early in the morning. Shawn read back the instructions and had already programmed in the departure frequency before they took off.

Takeoffs and landings were not Sandra's favorite part of the flight. She was always a little reserved about them, especially in rainy weather. Her preference was bright blue skies. She had something against not being able to see where she was going. Sandra had more faith in William than in instruments or technology she didn't understand. When it came to computers or her BlackBerry, she was great, but when it came to flying, she preferred to be in a 737 in these conditions.

William loved technology and how it made life simpler. When he purchased the Baron, he made sure it was fully IFR equipped with autopilot and GPS. When he was hopping around under VFR, or "visual flight rules," for the fun of it, it was always by hand. When he flew longer distances either VFR or IFR, he used the autopilot, or "George," as it is called. The autopilot was easier on an aircraft, anyway, and the GPS made navigation a cinch. William always used VOR beacons—very-high-frequency omnidirectional range beacons—as a reliable backup in combination with the GPS and his stash of navigation maps.

On the flight to Winnipeg, William turned on the autopilot and climbed the Baron to eleven thousand feet on a heading of zero-nine-five degrees. At the same time, Shawn tuned the radio and identified a VOR beacon as a reference for navigation. William smiled with pride.

"The skies are clear over Winnipeg," William remarked to Sandra, trying to make her feel better sitting in the backseat.

She just grinned and wished she could see better out of the window. *Only another two hours of this,* Sandra thought to herself. Shawn was having a blast watching all of the instruments and setting the radio for the next frequency change to Winnipeg Centre. Zoë couldn't take pictures, so she pulled out her traveling computer and was unconcerned about the weather.

As William watched Shawn set the radio to a new Winnipeg Centre frequency, he was comforted by the joy on his son's face. How different he was with his children in comparison to the way his father was with him. William's father was what he called "old school" and never showed him affection or gave him praise. "I'm proud of you, son," were words that never escaped his father's lips. William thought of his father often when he went flying; it was as if his father was sitting in the copilot's seat. After all these years, William was still looking for his father's approval. Was being a pilot worthy of his father's praise? How about owning a successful business or having a great wife and two lovely children? Was that going to get an "I'm proud of you, son"? Not from his father, who was as cold as ice.

On one trip his father was not only on his mind, he was not far away. Just on the right of runway three-six was the graveyard where William's father was buried many years ago. As William climbed out on runway heading, the only thought that came to his mind was, *If only my father could see me now.*

9.

All over the country, men and women were traveling to their early morning meetings. They didn't know each other, and they didn't know what they were going to hear. All they knew was they were being called to finally put an end to their oppression.

There wasn't much talking on the way to the meeting, just a lot of deep thought and praying for deliverance.

As Basim drove past some children playing in a park, he thought of the children back home who couldn't play in parks. There was no such thing back home; children played in their yards, never too far away. It was too dangerous for kids to be away from their parents. How Basim wished he had been born in a country like America. He thought about stopping and just shaking people in the street, trying to wake up them up to what was really happening. He wanted to awaken them from the dream world of corporate-controlled TV.

But it was too late for that, too late to turn back, too late for America. On the way to the meeting, Omar asked Basim in a calm, pragmatic voice, "What do you suppose this meeting is all about?"

"I have many ideas of what it could be about, my brother. I only hope it's not what I fear the most," Basim said in a somewhat reserved voice.

"Would it matter what it is about, brother? Are we not here to bring down the infidels?" Omar asked with near annoyance in his voice.

Basim had been in America for almost five years, waiting for the call that would put him in action. In that time, he had become used to life in America. Basim had lived his life in seclusion his first few years in America. He always had a gun with him, and he always spoke softly so as to not offend those in charge. After some time, he realized that there was no reason to carry his gun as there was no danger. He could speak as loudly as he wanted to, and nobody turned him in to the authorities.

Life in America wasn't as bad as he had been told. Yes, the women here were not like the women at home, but they were not the harlots that he had expected. He even met a nice Muslim woman once at the local grocery store whom he would have liked to take out on an American-style date, but he was too shy to ask her out. The streets were relatively safe in most places, the air was clean, and the food was good and plentiful.

He wondered why they were here to destroy this wonderful country. Why was this country worse than his own? Back home he had lived in constant fear. His family was not one of influence; his family was from a line of peaceful people who lived off the land. Basim remembered the hardship of his life and the fear the ruling family instilled in the whole country. He remembered the story of his uncle, who was at the wrong place at the wrong time. His uncle had bumped into a member of the Hussein family while crossing the street. He apologized profusely, but Kaditula Hussein had reached into his jacket, pulled out his .45, and shot Basim's uncle in the head. Everyone had just walked away and laughed. That would not happen in America.

"I suspect that we are being called into service. A lot of people will die, my brother. I just hope it is the right thing to do," Basim said. Basim knew that back home even thinking like that could get him killed, never mind speaking those thoughts out loud.

Omar didn't look impressed as they pulled up to the location of the meeting. They walked in silence and entered the warehouse where the meeting was being held. As they walked through the door, Basim looked at some of the faces in the room and noticed some of the people he had seen at the mosque. "Assalaam alaikum," Basim said in a quiet voice as he gave them a smile and a nod along with the traditional greeting, which means "peace be with you." There were a lot of people there, but he could not tell the exact numbers as the room was poorly lit. Then the room went silent.

In walked a man whom Basim had never seen before. He was tall and walked with confidence; he was definitely a man of authority. Basim could hear a pin drop as the man looked around the room, surveying the faces of his people.

He smiled and said, "As-salaam alaikum." He paused, and Basim's heart started to beat really fast. The crowd returned the greeting, saying, "Wa alaikum as-salaam," which means "and with you be peace."

"The time has come, the orders are here, and it's time to strike at the heart of the infidels," he said, raising his arms in the air. The crowed remained silent. Basim thought for sure other people could hear his heart beating.

"Over the next few days, you will be teamed up with brothers and sisters from all over America and from home. We will show you the plans for each of you, and we will execute the plan at the same time all over the world." Sweat was pouring down the face of the messenger. Basim could see the fear and anxiety on the faces of the others.

"Now, let's pray for success," he said as he turned to the northeast, bent his knees, and started to pray the Sura Al-Fatiha. Basim followed his example.

The crowd chanted in Arabic, "In the name of God, the Most Gracious, the Most Merciful. All praise is due to God, Lord of the Universe. The Most Gracious, the Most Merciful. Sovereign of the Day of Judgment. You alone we worship, and You alone we ask for help. Guide us to the straight path, the path of those on whom You have bestowed your grace, not of those who have earned Your anger, nor of those who go astray."

Basim thought to himself as he prayed, wondering how they could be praying about compassion and mercy when they wanted to murder a nation. He was torn between two cultures, torn between two worlds.

10.

Agent Davis had a bad feeling about this. He knew the United States was due for another act of terrorism. He only hoped that it would be years from now and not on his watch. Over the years he had thwarted many attempts, but it was like the little boy and the leaking dike. It wasn't a matter of if—it was a matter of when.

Davis was already going over his contingency list, which had been prepared after 9/11. There was a protocol developed in the event of another attack. This time agencies were supposed to be connected and communicating. Davis knew some things did change; some, however, will always be the same. Some of the agents who had been at the FBI since the days of Nixon should have been put out to pasture after 9/11. Some had come around to a new understanding, but most were from another time. It was a time of complacency, a time of mass incompetence—a time that should have been forgotten.

The list was long, and the task was monumental, but Davis knew they had to be ready in case this was another event and not just a lot of talk. Davis hoped it was just more chatter and not another major event.

When he arrived at the office at seven in the morning, Davis picked up the phone to call his counterpart in Canada. He was going to leave a voice mail when Stephen picked up the phone. "Hi, Stephen? Agent Burton Davis from the FBI. How are you?" Davis wanted to dispense with the pleasantries, but it was part of the job.

"That's good to hear. Sorry for calling you so early, but I was wondering if you got the memo that we sent you about the latest intel. OK, you've spoken to Agent Monroe, then? Great to hear. Do you have anything else to add to our information?" There was a pause while Davis listened to the information the Canadians had. "OK, keep in touch. Thank you again; call me anytime, Stephen." Davis hung up the phone, noting how much time it would take to call every name on the contact list. He could e-mail them today, as was the norm, but that meant the e-mail might sit in the contact's in-box for days before it was read. Davis didn't want to take that chance.

He would have to activate the National Security Alert System from Homeland Security. That would take a lot of explaining, and he couldn't use the "I have a gut instinct" excuse. He had to come up with hard evidence that there was a potential threat. Davis sat down at his computer, typed in the e-mail address for the network-wide paging system, and then typed in the emergency code, 26811. To everyone who received that e-mail either via computer, fax, or pager, it meant that they had to be at the special communications building in their city for a conference call by eight o'clock the next morning.

This was the first time this code had been used since 9/11 for real. Davis hoped that this turned out to be just another drill and not the real thing. He would have to make sure. In the meantime, Davis did what he did best: research. He compiled as much information as he could and put it in terms that would be easy for everyone at the meeting to understand. The information all pointed to something happening. Davis hated to speculate; he wanted facts and only facts, not conjectured half-truths or outright bullshit. Never again would he or his agents get burned with "weapons of mass destruction." Davis knew that line of crap never came from any credible agency; it was pure politics. It was made up in some office by some bureaucrat who worried more about his job and getting his boss reelected than about the thousands of men and women who died predicated on lies.

Davis knew his time at the Bureau was almost over. If he lasted until the end of the year, it would be a miracle as he knew people were out for his head. Davis knew this was his last chance to vindicate the way he did his work. He didn't want to be right about the intel his team had gathered and what it inevitably would lead to, but on the other hand, he didn't want to be wrong and be called Chicken Little, either. It was a quandary for Davis; being right meant the potential deaths of millions of people, and being wrong meant one more reason for the headhunters to get rid of him. This meeting would be the most important meeting of his career. His choice was to gather info and prove that there was a credible threat, or he could clear out his desk and collect a pension. The meeting tomorrow was do-or-die for Davis.

11.

William was on the final approach to Winnipeg International Airport. Sandra was much happier now that she could see the ground. Sandra liked it when the sky was clear and the ride was smooth.

William had just received his hand-off instructions to tune his radio for Winnipeg approach. He looked at Shawn and said, "Sorry, kiddo, I'll have to do this one myself." Shawn understood as sometimes the sound of a child's voice confused the controller. William keyed the microphone and said, "Good morning, Winnipeg approach. This is Baron Charlie-Golf-India-Bravo-Hotel, with your latest weather report Uniform. Cancel my IFR flight approach as we are full VFR. Can you give me clearance for a full-stop landing?"

"Good morning, Golf-India-Bravo-Hotel. You are radar identified. Enter left base for visual runway three-six. You are number two behind a 737 on two-mile final." The controller did it by the book.

William and Shawn always played a game to see who could spot the traffic first. William looked out the window and then to the right just as Shawn piped up. "There she is, two o'clock." William was beat again, but he was proud of his son.

"Winnipeg Tower, we have the 737 in sight," William reported.

"Baron Golf-India-Bravo-Hotel, you are ten miles northeast. Turn right and head one-eight-zero. You are cleared left base for runway three-six." The controller gave William the instructions he had anticipated.

"Roger, I'll head one-eight-zero degrees and join the pattern for left base runway three-six, Golf-India-Bravo-Hotel," William said, acknowledging his instructions. As he reached to retune his autopilot, Shawn's little hand was there turning the autopilot to the new coordinates. William smiled with pride.

Within a few minutes, the Baron carrying William and his family landed on the runway and headed toward the parking area for light aircraft. After unloading the plane, William and his family went off to pick up their rental car for their few days in Winnipeg before their trip to England.

12.

From the time the orders came in, cells all over America, Canada, and Europe met to cement the plans that would alter the course of history. This was not some simple suicide bomber who was going to blow himself up in a crowd of innocent women and children; when this was over, the Americans would think this was a sinister plan conceived in the bowels of hell by Satan himself.

Each cell had three members who were from different parts of America. It was important that each person in the cell didn't know the other as it kept them in fear that one of the three may be a spy sent to the cell to make sure they fulfilled their mission. Each cell worked independently of each other, and none of them were aware of the number of people or cells involved or the location of the targets. This time civilian targets were many, and there needed to be as much terror created as possible.

The equipment for the project was either smuggled into each country or purchased on the black market over many years. It was hidden in container trailers driven past overworked security and police forces up and down unprotected North American highways. This equipment was not just firearms and explosives. This time they managed to smuggle in a few misplaced Russian nuclear weapons as well as thousands of pounds of conventional explosives. The finest in American technology was going to be used to destroy the American way of life.

The orders were given, the equipment was in place, and the weather was going to be warm and the skies bright blue—great conditions to hijack airplanes and crash them into selected targets. By the end of the mission, those bright blue skies would be black from the plumes of smoke and smoldering rubble that used to resemble cities.

* * *

Jumah, who'd been in America for only a few weeks, was feeling restless. He hadn't been in a good firefight in a while, and his trigger finger was getting itchy. It was just after four o'clock in the morning, and he was awake and ready to start his mission even thought he wasn't scheduled to execute his operation for a few more days.

Numair, on the other hand, had been in America for a few years doing surveillance on many potential targets. While he found most Americans strange in their behavior, he thought Jumah was acting even stranger.

"You should get some sleep, Jumah," Numair said, still half asleep. Jumah just grinned as he checked over his AK-47 for the third time.

"We will sleep for an eternity, my brother," Jumah said with pragmatic realism, knowing that he would die soon. To be a martyr had been his goal ever since he was a child. While American children concerned themselves with Barbies and baseball cards, Jumah thought about the day he would ascend to heaven to be with Allah. That day would be soon.

13.

Davis awoke at his regular six o'clock in the morning. He normally tried to get six hours of sleep, but the previous night he may have slept for two. This was going to be the most important day of his career—the most important day of his life. He needed to convince his bosses and the heads of the other agencies that the threat was real, that the threat was credible.

Davis along with his team, led by Monroe, gathered at the office shortly before seven o'clock. Before the meeting, there was the typical banter about the latest football scores and how the wife and kids were. It was time to call the meeting to order and put all of the cards on the table. Just as Davis was about to set up the network-wide conference call, in walked the deputy director of the Bureau and his team, as well as agents from the Central Intelligence Agency. The office was rather crowded.

Davis was surprised by this. As his new unexpected guests found themselves seats at opposite ends of the table, he could feel the tension in the air.

"Hold off on that call," his boss, the deputy director of the FBI, demanded as he sat at the table. "Burton, I'm sure you and your team have done your research and that there is a lot that can be gained by this, but are we not jumping the gun here a little?" He was trying to defuse the issue. The way the deputy director saw it, it was an election year, the economy was good, and the country was safe. People were starting to travel in good numbers again, and there was no need to panic the American public.

Davis was in shock. "Jumping the gun, sir?" he said, standing at the head of the table and trying to understand where this was coming from.

"What exactly are you going to be saying here? Let's cut the bullshit and get to the meat and potatoes."

"With all due respect, sir, I'm not sure why you're here today, but I think we have credible intel that something is up. We invited the other agencies here to exchange information and see if we have something to worry about," Davis added, trying to bite his tongue.

Davis paused for a moment, still stunned over his meeting being overtaken. He asked, "Is there something you'd like to share with us, sir?" Davis sat down and let the director have the floor. This took the deputy director by surprise.

"All I can say, Davis, is we have information as well, and the president wants me to assure you that what you think you're receiving is nothing to concern yourself with." The deputy director smiled as he sat back in his chair.

Davis looked over the table to the CIA deputy director and asked, "Do you concur?"

"As of now we do," the CIA deputy director said, looking over to his counterpart from the FBI and trying not to make eye contact with Davis.

"Then I think we're done here," the deputy director of the FBI said as he began to get up to leave.

"What about the conference call? They're all waiting," Davis said, pointing to the phone.

"I've cancelled it; I told them it was a drill, nothing more."

"Wait one second here!" Davis said as he stood up, looking at the people in the room. "That's not it. We have credible information here, and I think this is going to lead to something big." Davis was looking at all of the faces of people who were too scared to say anything because of office politics. Nobody wanted to stick out their necks.

"When is this supposed to happen, Burton? We don't have any credible information that there is an immediate threat," the deputy director said, trying to downplay the intel.

"Soon—" was all that Davis had time to say before he was interrupted.

"Soon? All you can give me is soon?"

"Look, we all know that there will be another attack. It's not if, it's when," Davis said, looking at the director with an exasperated stare.

"When? That could be a month, a year, or ten years from now. All I know is it's not in the immediate future," the deputy director said, closing his briefcase and preparing to leave.

"What if you're wrong?" Davis asked. "What if today is when? What about tomorrow or the next week?" Davis stood up. "Don't just turn your back on this. Lives are at stake here," Davis said with a plea in his voice.

"The president thinks otherwise. I'll let him know you disagree," the deputy director said as he started to walk out of the room, followed by his staff.

"Then share your information with us," Davis said with a loud, demanding tone.

"You will be fully briefed when the time is right. Until then, take a few days off—"

"A few days off?" Davis said, interrupting his boss. "We don't have a few days left. We think they have and are about to sneak dirty bombs, biologicals, or even nukes into the country. If this goes off as we think it will, we won't have a country left for the president to preside over."

"You may have had a great career with MI6, and your work here has been great, too, but I think you're overreacting. I'll let the president know you disagree with his assessment, Agent Davis. I'll also let your supervisor know," the deputy director said as he walked out of the room, leaving Davis with a thinly veiled threat. Davis looked at Monroe, and Monroe returned his glance. They were both in a state of shock and disbelief. Burton Davis had spent his life waiting for the time to put his boots to the bad guy. He had walked into the meeting thinking that politics would be left at the door. He was sadly mistaken.

Davis leaned over to Monroe and said, "There's something going on here," whispering so the other men in the room would not hear.

Monroe didn't want to believe it. "What are you saying?" Monroe asked.

"I don't want to speculate right now, but let's take a closer look at some of the transcripts and at what's happening here at home…" Davis never finished his statement because in walked his supervisor, Jeff Kowalski, almost taking the door off the hinges.

"Davis, my office—now!"

14.

After a few days of visiting friends and relatives in Winnipeg, William dropped off Sandra and the kids for a bite to eat. William headed off to meet his old friend Marcel.

William had first met Marcel many years ago on the radio waves. Both were ham radio operators and had spoken to each other on many occasions from their homes in Saskatoon and Montréal. William was delighted to find out that Marcel also shared his passion for flying, but he was jealous as Marcel did so from the captain's seat of a Boeing 747-400.

Marcel was the pilot of the 747 that William and his family were scheduled to be on for their flight over to England. It was the last 747-400 in Western Global Airlines' fleet. It was being replaced with the newer 747-800. William was happy that he could get a close look inside and out before they retired her.

William met Marcel in the pilots' office at the Western Global Airlines terminal. He did as he had always done—he greeted Marcel in an attempt to speak French. *"Bonjour, mon ami. Comment allez vous?"* This was the first time they had met in person, and William was surprised how young Marcel looked.

"I'm well, my friend," Marcel said in a thick French-Canadian accent with a chuckle in his voice.

There wasn't much time for conversation, so Marcel cut to the chase. "We don't have too much time, Wil. Do you want to take a look at her, my friend?" he asked. All William could do was smile as they walked out toward the 747.

* * *

As she was moving boxes about in the hold, Hilary Graham glanced over her shoulder through the open cargo door and noticed two men on the tarmac. One of the men she recognized as Marcel, the captain of this flight, but the other man she had never seen before. He was tall, about six feet, thin, and appeared authoritative. As Hilary was looking over the man, he looked back and they gave each other a smile. Being the observant person that Hilary was, she made a mental note and carried on with the task at hand.

To prepare for the flight to England, Hilary was in the cargo hold of the 747 making sure that they had all of the supplies they needed. She made it a habit to make sure all of the supplies were where they were supposed to be.

Hilary Graham was the chief flight attendant on the upcoming flight to England. She was Western Global Airlines' number-one senior flight attendant, and it was not because she was the bimbo-Barbie-doll type. Hilary was a pragmatic, no-nonsense woman with a good head on her shoulders. Not only was she attractive, but she could also outthink most troublemaking passengers before they even realized it. Her specialty was men who thought they were still in the seventies—the ones with a look and chauvinistic attitude right out of a disco movie.

Hilary was tall, and at five feet and nine and a half inches, she could see over most of the passengers. She was great at remembering faces, often visualizing the passengers in their seats as they entered the plane.

Hilary's style and her British propensity for doing things by the book helped her to excel. She concentrated on getting her job done without being involved in its politics. She was the envy of many flight attendants who had been there longer but didn't get the promotions as quickly. Hilary was the prize of

Western Global Airlines and was a consummate professional. She loved to fly and put in more miles than most flight attendants. She had it all—or so people thought by looking at her.

That was what she wanted people to think, that she was happy and in control. Her schedule was full, but her life was empty. She covered many flights for the other attendants who had families. She, on the other hand, had nothing but her career. Each mile she flew was one mile further away from her problems.

As a younger person, Hilary had been a victim of violence, and as a married woman she had been victim again. Not only did she suffer bruises and a broken arm, she also suffered from a broken heart. Her wall was up, as she put it. Never again would she let someone into her space. Her mistrust of people—and of men in particular—would not change until she could love again. It had been a long time.

One day she thought she would meet the man who would respect her for who she was and not what he wanted her to be. Until then, she would keep flying.

"All up to your specifications, ma'am?" the cargo worker said in a thick accent, trying to use as much sarcasm as he could in his voice.

"As good as it's going to get," Hilary replied with her British tone of authority as she moved the final box of supplies to the lift so she could bring it up to the galley. She didn't get a good look at the worker in the cargo hold, but she made a note of his distinctive European accent.

Hilary had a simple philosophy: if you want it done right, you have to do it yourself. She was lucky, however, that there were other flight attendants who had the same "get it right" attitude as she did. On this trip she would be traveling with several who were in her class. Of the seventeen flight attendants on this flight, five of them were top-notch. They also possessed the skills and the maturity that went with age. The other eleven flight attendants were the younger types who were flying for various other reasons. Some liked the travel, some were escaping, and some just loved to serve people and make good money along the way. Hilary thought that every mile she flew was one mile closer to meeting her soul mate.

With all of the supplies in their proper place, Hilary was satisfied that this would be a trip that should go well—as long as all the members of the team did their jobs as well as she did hers. Hilary took one more look around and then at her watch. It was time to put on that famous smile and greet the passengers.

15.

The airport was a buzz of activity. This was always the time when the hair on Randy's neck stood on edge. He often thought that if a terrorist wanted to try to hijack an airplane, a smaller airport like Winnipeg International Airport would be the perfect target. While Winnipeg International Airport was small compared to JFK or LAX, what it lacked in size it made up for in volume. Over three million people used the airport for their travel. There was never a dull moment, as Randy put it.

The conventional thinking was that a smaller airport had a smaller security force and therefore was easier to penetrate. Randy was not a conventional thinker. Randy was a think-out-of-the-box guy. His security force was top-notch, well-trained, and always "on duty." It was not a place for the donut-eating stereotypes; his airport was one of the safest in the world. Randy slept well at night knowing that his airport and the people who used it were secure.

Randy was on his way to check out a small problem with the baggage carousel when he noticed several men sitting in the passenger waiting area. They were not together, but they looked like they should be. What caught Randy's eye was the fact that these men were wearing clothes almost from the same rack, yet they looked like they were purposefully trying to blend in and not be noticed. Randy always ran a checklist in his head. He wanted to make sure that he was not just singling them out because they were from the Middle East.

These men certainly appeared suspicious. Randy was trying not to profile, but it was sometimes a necessity. Randy made a mental note of this as he looked up at the flight number in the lounge they were sitting in. It was Western Global Airlines two-niner-one-five, the flight to England.

Maybe it was nothing, maybe it was something. He had to check it out for his own mental health.

After he took care of the problem at the baggage carousel, Randy headed back to the departure lounge to check out the situation. Randy scanned the departure lounge, looking at the faces and giving a smile. The men he had seen earlier were nowhere to be found. Perhaps they were already on the plane, or maybe they were somewhere in the airport.

"Randy, this is control. Can we see you in the office please?" was the call from his radio.

Randy reached into his vest pocket and keyed the microphone. "I'm on my way." The walk to the control room was not far, and Randy looked at the faces as he walked by.

* * *

The control room was quite dark with a wall full of TV and computer screens. There was a large computer desk in the middle of the room facing the TVs and computer screens. The chief of security, Mike Harper, sat at this desk, viewing as many screens as he could. He also typed a few e-mails.

Mike stood up after the last e-mail was sent out.

"Todd, what's our status?" Mike asked his number two in command.

"All systems are operational," Todd reported to his boss.

"Nothing out of the norm?" Mike asked, wanting to make sure everything would run smoothly on this busy day.

"As far as security is concerned, we're in perfect running order," he answered, sounding proud of his team. "The only things we have are some minor maintenance issues that won't cause any security concerns."

Mike was pleased that all was going well, and he was confident that the day would run smoothly.

Mike Harper had come a long way from being a lost little kid in a northern reserve to the big city. Winnipeg was big enough for him, and as far as he was concerned, the safety of the passengers in this airport could be compared to any airport in the world. Mike looked at all of the people in the room that he was in charge of. Who would have thought that this aboriginal man would be the chief of security in a large airport?

Mike always found it amusing when he was asked by a passenger what tribe he was from. Some even referred to him as a Native American even though his people were from Canada long before there was a Canada. When passengers asked, he said he was a Saulteaux. He told them it was easier to just call him an aboriginal as it was easier to pronounce, and it set him apart from Native American tribes in the United States.

Mike never looked at the color of his skin as a stumbling block to get in the way of his success. He often mentored aboriginal youth. He told them that no matter how the world saw them, they had a duty to excel in whatever they did and be perfect examples of how aboriginals should live. Mike thought of himself as a positive role model for his people.

It was tough for him, and he never tried to get by on programs and handouts. What he earned was on merit, and none of it was given to him for free. When he started to work in law enforcement, he refused to check the box on the application marked "aboriginal." He thought of himself as just like any of the other people who worked at the airport. Maybe he had a tan that never faded, but that was the only difference. His scores on his tests and his marksmanship were top-notch, and he was proud of the fact that he did his job just as well as anyone else. When management started to notice his success, he received promotion after promotion until one day he became the chief of security at the airport that he had started out at. Mike smiled and thought to himself, *Now I don't mind when they call me chief.* He looked at the door as Randy entered the room.

"What's up, Mike?" Randy asked as he walked to the center of the room.

"Well, as you know, we receive these bulletins from the RCMP and Transport Canada regarding possible threats. While most of them are based on the United States, this one is for both the United States and Canada," Mike said as he handed the document to Randy. Randy scanned the document and remembered it being mentioned in a meeting he had attended.

"Yes, is there something to be concerned about?" Randy asked, looking at Mike.

"We have some people here now who fit the profile," Mike said as the hair on Randy's neck was at full attention. Randy was wondering if they were the same guys he had been trying to keep an eye on.

"Do you have them on surveillance right now?" Randy asked as Mike motioned him over to the monitors.

"We've been watching them and running their names through CSIS and Interpol, so far with no luck; it's a long process," he said in frustration.

"Have you looked at their bags?" Randy asked, covering all the bases.

"We went through them with a fine-tooth comb. We even had Rusty take a sniff at them, and they're all clean. No evidence that anything has been exposed to any drugs or explosives." Mike paused and then added, "They just look out of place. They're alone, but they look like they should be together. They look like they shop at the same store and get their haircuts from the same barber." Mike echoed Randy's thoughts as they watched them on the TV screen.

"Where are they from?" Randy asked.

"From their passports they look like they're from either the UK or the Middle East. They're heading home, but nothing connects them together like being from the same city or town," Mike said with concern in his voice. "Should we hold them?" Mike asked, knowing it was his call. He wanted to make sure that airport management was on his side. The politics of the boardroom sometimes made life for Randy and Mike difficult.

The board of directors had made it clear that there would be no racial profiling. The airport was profitable, and they didn't want any stigma that the airport was racist. That could lead to lawsuits and loss of revenue. The bottom line was money and not safety.

"How many do you have under surveillance?" Randy asked, remembering the several that he had noticed.

"Right now we have eleven," Mike replied.

"Eleven?" Randy said, mentally scolding himself because he hadn't noticed that many. "Until we get reports of anything substantial, keep an eye on them. Are they all heading to England?"

"England it is," Mike said, looking at one of the suspects on the TV screen.

16.

Hilary liked to greet passengers with Melissa, her second in command, on international flights. On domestic flights, Hilary left it up to the junior girls to greet them. She thought if she was going to be stuck with these people for up to eight hours or longer, it was good to look them in the face and get a good feel for them. Hilary had the ability to get a good idea about someone's personality by looking him or her in the eyes. The eyes told a story, and Hilary could read them like a book.

"All ready to bring the passengers on board, Melissa?" Hilary asked.

"Ready as you are," Melissa said, grabbing her flight manifest and heading toward the door.

"Looks like we have a few coming on board here," Melissa said, looking at her lists.

"How many?" Hilary asked.

"Looks like about one hundred and fifty; that makes three hundred and twenty-one total on this leg," Melissa replied.

On this flight she had seen a lot of the same emotions: nervousness, excitement, and apprehension. As she was greeting a passenger, her eyes drifted toward another passenger in the queue. Their eyes met for a microsecond as he turned away. It was as if he knew she could read his mind. A chill went down her spine. After 9/11, she looked a little closer at people, Middle Eastern men especially. Hilary wasn't a racist, but the track record of some men from the Middle East was not good. Perhaps they were also in her bad books because of the way some of them treated their women. She not only looked a little closer, she looked a little longer into their eyes. Most often they would try to stare her down. Hilary would never back down. She would never lose.

She couldn't put her finger on it, but there was something about this man that was different. She made a mental note and carried on with her job. As he approached the door, he made it obvious that he didn't intend to have anything to do with her.

"Welcome aboard," Hilary said to the man, trying to look at his boarding pass. He handed the boarding pass to Melissa, the other flight attendant at the door.

Hilary kept in mind that being five feet and nine and a half inches tall was intimidating to most men. Hilary reached for his boarding pass and took a quick look at where he was sitting. She also noted that he was boarding alone. This was odd but not unusual for a flight across the pond. She handed the boarding pass back to the man and pointed in the general direction of his seat. She would keep an eye on him.

As Hilary looked up at more passengers entering the plane, she noticed a familiar face. "Long time no see," she said to William as he entered the plane. William caught on as he remembered seeing her in the cargo hold.

"Yes, it's been a while," William said with excitement. Sandra looked at him, not knowing what was going on.

"You always get a close look at the plane before a flight?" Hilary asked William with a chuckle.

"It helps if you're a pilot and a good friend of the captain. I'd never walked around the outside of one before. Marcel was giving me a tour while he did his walk-around," William said as Hilary looked over their boarding passes and pointed toward their seats.

"Great to hear we have a spare pilot aboard, just in case," Hilary said in a joking manner. "You're just over there on the left. I'll talk to you later. Enjoy your flight," Hilary said as she turned to greet more passengers.

Hilary's heart almost skipped a beat as she greeted another passenger. It was another man from the Middle East, and he had the same look and the same attitude. He also was traveling alone and would not hand his boarding pass to her. Hilary took a quick look at where he was sitting and noticed that it was in the not in the same area as the other man. Perhaps she was overreacting. She'd had hundreds of Middle Eastern men on her flights, and most of them had been courteous.

She needed someone to take her mind off of things. She needed a man, a lover, a friend. She looked over at William and his family as they got settled in their seats with somewhat of a sad smile. Hilary always wished she were the one on vacation with her family instead of being the single woman on the run, looking for love. One day she would find her love; one day she would find happiness.

By the time the last passenger entered the cabin of the 747, Hilary had made mental notes of several men from the Middle East who were sitting in different areas. *This is most likely nothing*, she thought. Still, it was always good to be able to remember where people were supposed to be.

"Melissa," Hilary called out, "what's the final count?"

"Right on the numbers, according to the manifest and the head count: three hundred and twenty-one," was the answer from the bubbly flight attendant.

Hilary looked up and down the plane, taking one last look at the passengers and making sure the entrance was closed and secure. She then picked up the intercom to call the captain.

"*Oui*," was the response.

"Boarding is complete, Captain. All present and accounted for, sir. We are ready to go here." Hilary waited for any last-minute instructions from the captain.

"*Merci*," the captain responded.

Hilary motioned to Susan to begin the standard safety announcements in both official languages. As Susan began her safety announcements, Hilary did a walkabout to get a better look at the men who gave her chills.

ACT II

17.

A few hours had passed since the sun crept over the eastern United States. The sun warmed Fadi's face as it never had before. He stood looking out the bay window in his rented house in suburbia. In a few hours the project was to begin. Fadi knew it would be the last time he would ever see the sun rise. He was enjoying this moment in reflective thought. He knew he would not see it set this day; he knew it would set on one of the greatest superpowers the world has ever known.

Amman emerged from the hallway as he was heading toward the door of the garage carrying what he called his "bag of death." This bag carried his weapons, explosives, and timers. He paused for a second and made eye contact with Fadi, who was still standing at the bay window. They said nothing to each other. Nothing needed to be said. They were both committed soldiers on a mission.

They finished loading the van with their supplies, and Fadi opened the garage door. The van rolled out of the dark garage and stopped at the front door, where Amman was waiting. Amman inhaled the warm, fresh air. He knew in a few hours it would turn into the smell of burnt flesh. Fadi looked over to Amman and was feeling the same emotions. He left the van to join Amman in a few minutes of prayer. When that was done and all of the prayers were said, the men entered the van and started their drive to destiny.

The roads in the morning hours were full of travelers on their way to work. Little did the travelers know that the van driving beside them was the author of their destruction. Fadi was careful not to drive too fast or slow. He had to drive consistently and not raise suspicion on his way to his target.

Power plants were an easy target. They were, for the most part, unprotected. Many relied on the skills of underpaid and undertrained security guards. Americans called them "rent-a-cops" as they were not real police officers. They did carry a radio and a gun, which could cause a potential problem. If Fadi had to engage one of these rent-a-cops, it could jeopardize the timing of his attack, which was to set the pace for all of the other ones.

When they arrived at their target, Fadi and Amman pulled the van up as close as they could to the building. So far they had raised no suspicion. Fadi began to sweat. He looked at his watch; it was almost time. If all went as planned, it would awaken the sleeping giant. He only hoped that their attacks would mortally wound him so he could not retaliate and fight back. Fadi looked at his watch again and checked to make sure the timer was accurate. This was to be a suicide mission. They were to stay and protect the contents of the van. This bomb had to go off and start the project off right.

Trying to ease the tension in the van, Amman turned on the radio to listen to the morning news. "What a wonderful, warm day it is today," said the overpaid harlot reporting the weather. Fadi and Amman smiled; they knew it would be a wonderful day indeed. The day started out as any other beautiful day—warm, clear, happy, and productive.

This scene repeated itself in cities and towns all over Canada and the United States. Dedicated men and women would be doing their part to bring down the Great Satan.

* * *

Back in New York, Jabbar was on a high as he remembered how easy it was to get into the country. He was sure that the rest of the mission would be just as easy. *The Americans are a selfish people,* he thought, *all too concerned about football, beer, and MTV. Yes, they are a "free" people,* Jabbar thought to himself. *Free to destroy themselves.*

The early morning July sounds of chirping birds would soon be replaced with the sounds of explosions and gunfire. The day would start off peacefully, but it would end up in death and destruction. The world would never be the same.

* * *

The New York sky was clear and sunny. The time was 8:43 a.m. when Yusuf walked down the stairs with his package. Over the last few weeks, he and other men had made the same trip each day with the same box heading for the same train. This time, Yusuf would never catch that train. He would do what he had to do to bring down the Great Satan.

This is just the start, Yusuf thought as he was reflecting on the plan. He was what the American media would call one of the "masterminds." Yusuf had instructed other men and women who had been all over America planting their boxes. This time, not only would they hijack American airliners, they would also attack countries that supported America.

The intent was to bring down the infrastructure by destroying the supply of water, electricity, and gas and then let society implode. Remove any of these three necessities, and problems would arise, Yusuf knew. Remove all three, and chaos would ensue. *If some innocent people get killed in the process, so be it,* Yusuf thought as he stood waiting for the right time to flip the switch. These people supported the oppressor, and they were going to pay. It was better they die now than die suffering after their society collapsed.

Specific targets in each city were chosen. This was where they would plant the bombs. Some were infrastructure, and some were symbolic. They were also going to hijack airplanes and crash them into buildings as they did successfully on 9/11. However, there would be more men like him on each plane to make sure there were no American heroes. The planes they didn't hijack would be in trouble, too. They planned to destroy as many airports as they could along with the navigation aids that guide the airplanes. With no place to land and no way to get to any airport, thousands of commercial jets would crash. If they were successful, these coordinated attacks would kill more civilians in one day than the Americans had killed in all of the years they'd been in Iraq.

Yusuf was proud of their plan. To top it off, they had also snuck Russian nuclear weapons into the country along with some radioactive material that was made into dirty nukes. If America survived this day, there would be some cities that they couldn't reinhabit for many years.

If all went as planned, America as the world knew it would no longer exist as of five o'clock eastern time. Yusuf took one last look at his watch; it was almost time.

18.

Every time Captain Marcel Laroque sat in the left seat in the flight deck of the 747, he still was amazed at how impressive this bird was. The 747 had been in service for over forty years and had flown countless millions of miles around the globe. The 747's fuselage was an amazing 231 feet long, and the tail was as tall as a six-story building. The 747-400 rolled into service in 1989 with a wingspan of 212 feet. She had a range of over seven thousand miles.

Marcel started flying 747s when Air Canada first purchased them back in the seventies. He loved the bird and everything about her. He had flown millions of miles in them with a perfect safety record.

Marcel was a stickler for doing things by the book. He never skipped anything on the checklist. Each item, no matter how minute, was checked and rechecked. The only time Marcel didn't go through a checklist completely was many years ago when smoke started to fill the cabin at the back of his DC8.

His first officer at the time had wanted to go through every checklist and dump fuel before they made an emergency landing. Instead, Marcel turned off the autopilot, did a quick calculation in his head, and knew the remaining fuel onboard would not make the aircraft overweight. He decided to perform an emergency landing at the nearest airport. Marcel knew how a little smoke in the cabin could lead to a major in-flight fire. With over 220 passengers onboard, he wasn't going to take that chance. He advised his chief flight attendant to prepare for a fast emergency landing and have the passengers ready to use the evacuation slides. He called in a mayday and did a quick emergency landing. As he was landing the plane, smoke had started to overwhelm some passengers in the back. With the quick response of the flight attendants, all of the passengers made it down the escape chutes as smoke poured out of the open doors. After making sure that all passengers were off the plane, the chief flight attendant went down the chute. She was followed by Marcel, who was the last off of the plane. His first officer was in awe.

"Captain," he said as he looked back at the burning DC8, "how did you know it would be this bad, and how often do you fly the DC8 like it was a Cessna?" In many years of flying, the first officer had never seen a plane that size being flown so elegantly without autopilot.

Marcel was taken aback by the question. "Well, *mon ami*, autopilots help you fly the plane, but if you use them too much, you can get lazy. I fly with it off so I can feel how the plane is responding. By the time you get to be a captain, you will understand that you don't let the plane fly you—you fly the plane. You feel it; if it doesn't feel right, you get it on the ground."

Marcel was the epitome of French elegance and was at the top of his game. He had been offered on more than one occasion the chance to fly the French Airbus A340. Other pilots often teased him as to why a man such as himself with such class and style would fly the American Boeing and not the French Airbus. Marcel took it in stride as he knew it was just in fun. He loved flying the Boeing 747 and would soon retire as a captain with his last flight being in the Boeing. When Air Canada retired their last 747 in 2004, Marcel was offered the captain's position in either Air Canada's A320 or the long-range A340. Marcel declined and submitted his resignation. He headed south to fly for Western Global Airlines. Western Global Airlines was one of only two airlines that were still flying 747-400s in North America.

"Get us clearance to the active runway," Marcel told his first officer, Brent Ducharme.

"Winnipeg clearance, deliver; this is Western Global Airlines two-niner-one-five requesting IFR clearance to the active runway, and we have information Kilo," Brent said as he had his pen in hand, ready to mark down his clearance from the air traffic controller.

"Western Global Airlines two-niner-one-five, you are cleared to Halifax International Airport as filed. Fly runway heading, climb, and maintain eight thousand feet. Squawk three-niner-seven-five; contact ground for taxi clearance on one-two-one point nine."

Marcel was going through the last pre-taxi checklist items. In his thirty-plus years of flying, he had never missed an item on this checklist. He wasn't going to start a few weeks away from retirement.

"Winnipeg ground, this is Western Global Airlines two-niner-one-five requesting taxi clearance to runway three-six." Brent knew in advance which taxiway the controller was going to give him clearance for. He had been in Winnipeg many times.

"Western Global Airlines two-niner-one-five, you are cleared to runway three-six via taxiway Victor-Hotel-Foxtrot-Papa. Hold short of runway three-six. Contact the tower on one-one-eight point three. Keep an eye out for a Cessna on taxiway Victor. Have a good flight." Brent made a note of the Cessna on the taxiway and called for the airplane to be pushed back.

The longest part of pre-flight was taxiing. The captain never taxied the aircraft as that was left up to the junior officer. Brent thought one of the benefits he was going to enjoy when he was a captain was that he wouldn't have to taxi anymore. Marcel was a great teacher, and Brent looked up to him. Often Marcel would let Brent line up the 747 for the takeoff roll. That was something Brent just loved—the feeling of fifty-eight thousand pounds of thrust from the Rolls Royce engines pushing over eight hundred thousand pounds of aircraft was a feeling that couldn't be understood without experiencing it firsthand.

* * *

In the lower level, Hilary was in her seat. She loved the takeoff roll. She always looked back at as many passengers as she could. She could tell by the looks on their faces if they were frequent flyers or if they were going to be nervous, always pushing the attendant button.

* * *

Brent received clearance and rolled the 747 onto the runway. He turned on the takeoff lights and checked that the flaps were set to ten degrees. "Let's roll," Marcel said as they both moved the thrust levers forward. The sound of the engines winding up always thrilled Brent. The 747 rolled down the centerline of runway three-six with ease.

"Eighty knots," Marcel called out to his first officer. This was the do-or-die speed. If they had to abort the takeoff, they could do it before they hit eighty knots. After that, there was no stopping the 747.

"Eighty knots," repeated Brent. The 747 was picking up speed fast.

"V-one," Marcel called out. Then a few seconds later, he said, "Rotate."

"Rotate," Brent replied, with his heart beating fast. He eased back the yoke of the 747, and the nose started to lift off the ground. Brent often wondered if he would ever be as calm as Marcel during takeoff. Perhaps that came with age and experience.

* * *

In the passenger section of the plane, the passengers could feel the landing gear lift off the ground as the plane took to the skies like a bird leaving the nest. William often said that the 747 was the ultimate achievement in aviation. Sandra thought he was a little biased. There were bigger planes now, but the 747 had been the biggest and the best for almost forty years. William looked out his window with his GPS in one hand and Sandra's right hand in the other. He looked over to her to give her a reassuring smile. Sandra felt better in the 747 than in the Baron. She thought she would never get over her fear of flying. The kids, however, were having the time of their lives. Zoë had won the right to sit in the window seat this time by beating her brother at another round of rock-paper-scissors.

19.

Special Agent Burton Davis of the Federal Bureau of Investigation wore his title well. He was proud of his accomplishments. He and his team had saved countless lives by stopping terrorists all over America. The general public had no idea about the commitment of the men and women who worked with him. The public never heard of the successful operations because they were classified. They only knew of the failed operations—when they were accused of dropping the ball.

Davis was often asked where the FBI was during 9/11. It had been implied many times that the FBI was asleep at the wheel. Agent Davis resented that question; he seldom slept, never mind being caught asleep at the wheel. Davis wanted the Bureau to be vindicated in a big way. He wanted to stop the next big one and retire with dignity. Davis held his breath as he walked into the office of his boss.

"You wanted to see me, sir," Davis said with a sarcastic tone as he walked into his supervisor's office.

"Close the door and sit down, Burton," Department Chief Jeff Kowalski said. He seldom, if ever, called Davis by his first name.

Davis never fully sat down before Kowalski got into it.

"Look, Burton, I've given you a lot of latitude in this department; you should have called me before you pushed the panic button," Kowalski said, sounding like a man who had just had his ass handed to him on a silver platter.

"The chatter was getting more intense, and we were just making sure that no rock was left unturned," Davis said, trying to defend his actions.

"Look," Kowalski said, giving a big sigh, "I just had the deputy director of the Bureau tear me a new one. My career is on the line too, Burton."

Davis was rather confused. *Is the FBI not supposed to investigate and stop terrorism?* he thought to himself.

"Jeff, we have credible intel that says something is going to happen. By the amount of chatter we're intercepting, it's going be big. I think that's a cause for concern," Davis said in a tone of annoyance.

"That could very well be, but you should have asked me first. You should have followed protocol." His volume was increasing.

"Protocol? I should have followed protocol? Just what the hell is that supposed to mean?" Davis was a stickler for protocol. "Are we supposed to sit back and wait for another attack, or are we supposed to be proactive here?" Davis was rather pissed off at the accusation that he didn't follow protocol.

"Burton, you know as well as I do that politics plays a major role in everything we do. You just can't call an emergency meeting when there's no emergency. What if you're wrong?" The chief paused for a moment and then continued, saying, "We'll end up looking unprofessional, and the next time you push the panic button, nobody will give a shit because they think we're trigger happy." The chief was under a lot of pressure from above.

"But what if we're *right?*" Davis asked, standing at the end of the desk. "If we're right, there will be an enormous loss of life. This will be a nation brought to its knees. If I read the intel right, this could be a worldwide attack." There was a long pause, and the room was silent. Then Kowalski, not being a man of few words, looked up at Davis standing at the end of his desk.

"I've been assured that the chatter you're talking about is nothing to be concerned about and that the people at Homeland Security and other appropriate departments are on top of this. Everything is under control." He said it in one breath. The chief wouldn't look Davis in the eyes.

"Now, it's time to take a few days off and relax a bit," Kowalski said in a quiet, condescending tone.

"Is that all, sir?" Davis said with disdain in his voice. He was not even looking at Kowalski.

"Burton, you have a family and a pension to think about. Don't bark up the wrong tree again," Kowalski said as he waved Davis out of his office.

Davis was aware that Kowalski mentioned his pension as a threat. That was the problem with the Bureau; they worried about a pension and not about the country or the safety of the people in it.

Kowalski yelled at Davis as he walked away from his office, saying, "You're on vacation, Davis. Go home!"

While Davis would go home, he wouldn't be on vacation. He knew that something big might be in the works. Luckily for him, he had equipment at home that would help him make a clearer assessment of this latest threat.

20.

Marcel leveled off at thirty-five thousand feet. The Boeing 747 operated flawlessly. She flew smoothly and steadily.

"Cruising altitude checklist, please," Marcel asked, and Brent was already holding it in his hands. They went through the checklist, making sure not to leave out a single detail. Over the years Marcel had memorized the checklist, and on a few occasions other first officers would intentionally leave out or skip an item to see if Marcel caught it. Brent never had the guts to do this, but he heard stories of other first officers getting the cold stare from the captain—one that they would not soon forget.

"Looks like a smooth ride to Halifax, Captain," Brent said as he put away the checklist.

The one thing that Marcel would not miss about flying eastbound early in the morning was having the sun in his eyes. It was a minor annoyance. For the long trip overseas, they always left early and stopped at Halifax to pick up more passengers, fuel, supplies, and a relief flight crew. Then it was a hop across the ocean to England.

* * *

In the lower cabin, Hilary checked on passengers and made sure that her attendants were doing a top-notch job of keeping them happy. Between Winnipeg and Halifax, they were going to be served breakfast. All had to be right as this was going to be a long flight for some of the passengers. Long flights made people tired, and when they were tired, sometimes they got cranky. On this flight, Hilary also made it part of her routine to check up on the men from the Middle East. They made her uneasy. There were several of them who had boarded the plane. She found it odd how they were sitting in every section. They were spread out in the airplane so as to not be noticed. Two of the men were in the upper level between rows twenty-one and twenty-six, and the rest of the men were between rows thirty-one and sixty-nine. Just as she was approaching galley eight, a passenger, who was a nun, stopped Hilary.

"Can Sister and I get a chance to look at the flight deck and take a few pictures for the parish scrapbook?" she asked, looking up at the towering Hilary. After 9/11, normally people were not allowed in the flight deck. Ultimately, the captain had the final say, and these were a couple of nuns. *What harm could they do?* Hilary thought to herself.

"I'm going to talk to the captain soon. I'll ask him then," Hilary said with a smile as she turned toward the galley to pick up the phone and call the captain.

Marcel answered the phone. *"Oui?"*

"All is OK down here, Captain. We're starting to serve breakfast." Hilary turned and looked toward the nuns. "By the way, Captain, there are two nuns here who would love a quick tour of the flight deck to take a few pictures—if that's OK with you." Hilary thought, *How could he say no?*

Nuns, Marcel thought to himself. As he was a devout Catholic himself, he thought it would be great to have the nuns in the flight deck—a bit of good luck, if you will.

"Sure, in about half an hour it will be OK," he said. Hilary smiled and gave them the thumbs-up. The nuns looked at each other with big smiles.

21.

Mike was at the top of his game. He scanned the information that was coming in from all over the globe about the men they had been watching.

All of the information, all of the data, and they may have let them slip through their fingers. If this was the case, he needed to know as soon as possible so he could react and prevent the terrorists from reaching their target.

Information was slow and sometimes inaccurate. He had to make sure he was right before they diverted the plane away from any potential targets. *What would the targets be?* he asked himself, keeping it in the back of his mind that they might be overreacting. Just as he was looking at the latest e-mail, the phone rang.

"Yes," he said, already sure he knew who it was on the line.

"Any leads?" asked Randy.

"Nothing yet," Mike said as he was scanning his monitors and e-mails for clues.

"I want to be sure about this. I don't want egg on our faces," Randy said. "Do you know the cost and the embarrassment it would be to divert a 747 because we saw a bunch of guys who looked suspicious?" he added, wanting to make sure he emphasized how important it was to be accurate.

"I know what you're saying. We need to be sure, and so far there's nothing but speculation and e-mails with alerts for people with similar names," Mike added, hoping to find a clue.

"Keep on top of this, and anything you think is important, call me right away. Keep off the radio and call me on the landline or cell phone. If I'm out of the office or don't answer, send me an encrypted text," Randy said. He was feeling like the walls of his office were closing in on him. "I hope we're wrong," Randy said and bid Mike good-bye.

As Mike went through reports, e-mails, and database searches, he couldn't help but reflect on when he was young. Life for him was tough, and he grew up with a rough crowd. He was smaller than most, and on more than one occasion he was the brunt of the jokes and the teasing. He also remembered being in the big city and getting the "look," as he called it. He would hear people close by say it loud enough for him to hear: *"Dirty Indian."* As he got older, he didn't want to be the guy who was a bully, and he didn't want to assume what a person was all about because of the color of his or her skin. Many candidates for his security team failed because they were nothing more than a combination of both, racists or bullies on a power trip. They were easy to weed out, for the most part. Some of them hid it very well.

His team was the best in the business. They were great at what they did, and they were always fair in the way they treated people from all over the world. Maybe this was one time when he was fooled because he didn't want to stereotype. Being fair and treating everyone equally was an attribute that may have been used against him. Maybe he and his team should have been more aware and more aggressive in determining who walked in his doors and onto an airplane.

Mike was looking at the information on his computer screens, and it was becoming more and more apparent that something was wrong with these guys. They were almost too clean.

His eyes left the computer screens and scanned the room. If there was going to be an attack, this was the team that he wanted to be with. They gave hard-working and dedicated a new definition. Mike looked back at the computer screen when he received an e-mail with important new information.

22.

Yusuf looked at his watch. It was on its final count to the last minute of his life. He took one more look around and walked a little closer to a group of people in suits talking about stocks or something irrelevant.

He looked at his watch again as the train loaded with people pulled into the station on time. The doors opened, and people flowed out of the train like water down a waterfall. Yusuf closed his eyes, said a silent prayer, and pushed the button. It was over in a microsecond.

* * *

At the same time, the same scenario occurred in New York's hundreds of subway stations. Those passengers not directly affected in the subway could hear the echoing of the explosions from within the tubes. The sound was getting closer and louder. Passengers started to panic and put two and two together. They started to head up the stairs, but they were met at the top by a dark figure wearing a long coat and a smile and with the explosive force of C4.

* * *

Outside the AirTrain JFK Airport Station, Abdul sat watching the police. They were running about with their walkie-talkies glued to their ears. *Looks like there is a little panic in the air,* he thought. JFK was one of the busiest airports in the world, and this little man with his little black box was going to destroy it. Not only was he carrying C4 on his body, there was a truck parked in the lot containing a dirty nuke. The explosives would take out most of the airport and a few city blocks. What the explosives didn't take out would be useless for a very long time. Radioactive material would be spread for miles.

Abdul could see the panic in their eyes; he could smell their fear. *It is just like it was at home,* he thought. Just like it was after the Americans bombed Iran. He pulled the trigger device out of his pocket, flipped up the safety switch, and paused to savor the moment. In another second he would be with Allah and he would be a martyr. It was over before the sound of the click of the switch reached his ears.

* * *

Lieutenant Chris Donahue of the New York City Police had known this day was coming, but he had hoped he would be long dead and gone before it did. He had been a beat cop longer than he liked to remember and was blocks away that fateful day in 2001. This time they were not attacking by air—they were attacking by ground. He scanned all of the faces and listened to his radio at the same time.

This time Donahue was outside Brooklyn Bridge Station, watching the chaos unfold. So far there had been no explosions close by. However, he could tell they were getting closer by the chatter on his radio.

Just as he was about to call his partner on the radio, he noticed a person who stood out in the crowd. As Donahue scanned the faces, he looked for anyone who looked out of place. This man did because he seemed rather calm considering the panic all around him. He also stood out because of the large, bulky backpack he was carrying. Donahue was making his way through the crowd toward the suspect when he took a turn toward the station. Donahue wanted to yell, but the words would not come out of his mouth. He walked closer to the man, keeping an eye on his backpack. Just as he was about to walk into the station, Donahue yelled, *"Police! Freeze!"* The man kept walking, reaching for the door.

Donahue felt the man was one of them, and if he didn't act fast, a lot of people would die. Donahue, with his gun at the ready, made his way through the stampeding crowd and pointed his gun at the man's head.

"I told you to stop!" Donahue again yelled. "Put your hands in the air, *now!*" he ordered. The man stopped and started to turn around to face Donahue. He started to reach into his pocket. Quicker than a heartbeat, Donahue pulled the trigger of his service revolver, and the bullet struck the man in the chest. People screamed and ran in all directions.

Donahue's partner came up the stairs of the train station. "What the hell is going on?" he asked. Donahue didn't say a word as he walked over to the man lying on the ground, bleeding. Donahue reached down and pulled a 9 millimeter handgun from the injured man's jacket. Donahue could now see the top of the backpack. It was packed with explosives. Donahue rolled the man over so he could see his face.

"Too late, pig," the man said. Donahue was shocked because the man was not Arabic—he was white.

"Where's the trigger?" Donahue asked him.

"There is no trigger; it's on a timer, pig," the man said as he coughed up blood.

"But you're not Arabic. What the hell are you doing being a terrorist?" Donahue asked as he searched the man for the timer.

"I'm not some imperialistic pig living off the backs of the poor people in the world. I hate you as much as they do. You deserve to die." He spouted rhetoric that Karl Marx would have been proud of.

Donahue found the timer—twenty-two seconds left. He then looked at the man with the blood-soaked, smiling face. He was dying right in front of him.

"No time to run, pig." Those were the last words that he said before he died.

Donahue began yelling as loudly as he could. "Run! Run!" he yelled to the people watching nearby. *How much ground can I cover in less than twenty-two seconds?* he thought to himself as he and his partner ran as fast as they could.

Please, Mother of Jesus, don't let me die like this, was the thought that ran through his mind. Just as he thought there was no hope, he spotted two armored car guards panicking to keep people away from their truck. Donahue yelled at them to hang on as he and his partner ran as fast as they could towards the armored car. The driver saw the two police officers running towards him and swung the door open wide. He waved them inside. Donahue and his partner leaped into the back of the armored car just as the driver pulled the door shut. The sound of the door slamming was louder than he thought it should be—or was that the sound of the exploding bomb he heard? He knew that he was in the hands of Mother Mary, and whatever happened was meant to be. The explosion took out a city block, killing many people, but not as many as would have died if the bomber had reached the intended target of the subway.

Lieutenant Chris Donahue opened the door to the overturned armored car and looked at the carnage outside. He and his partner had survived the explosion. But he knew he had a long day ahead of him. New York had survived 9/11. *If New York survives today, it will never be the same again,* he thought.

23.

Since 9/11, Washington, DC, resembled a military zone more than a city. There were more military police and soldiers there than anywhere else in America. That's why this was a special mission for a special team of terrorists. Asad and his team had trained for this mission the last three years. It was important that this one didn't get messed up.

Asad was a man reaching the peak of his life, and he was chosen for this mission because of the coldness of his demeanor. He killed people like Americans barbeque steak. He had little left to live for as the Americans had bombed his village and killed most of his family. This mission was personal.

Asad assembled his team from a group of young and impressionable men who would do what they were told without asking questions. This strike was going to be different. Not only did they need to take out as much infrastructure as they could, they also needed to take out all of the military personnel who were on the streets. The bonus for Asad was that this was a mission that deliberately targeted politicians. Asad considered them just as guilty as the illegal invaders of his sovereign nation. Politicians who gave the orders to send young men and women to die for their war would now become causalities of it as well.

The four trucks were placed outside the protected zone but close enough to cause the damage they intended. As Asad waited for the right time, he made sure that all of his men were in place and ready. He could see from his hiding space that the people in the streets were unaware of what was happening in New York.

With all of his teams in place, he raised his transmitter and looked at the little red button. It reminded him of a little bug about to get squished. His thumb covered the button, and he gave it a gentle push. Even though Asad wore ear protection, the sound of the explosions was deafening. He could also hear the screaming of people as the streets erupted.

Asad had to wait the right amount of time before his teams made their move. All this time he kept his eyes on the chaos in the streets. He had to time his move, or the most important aspect of his mission would fail.

Five minutes passed, and Asad called Mansur and his teams to move into position. This would be easy as the teams were camouflaged—not in military fatigues, but in the uniform of the District of Columbia Fire Department. With a few old fire trucks purchased on eBay and repainted DCFD colors, Asad's team drove right past military checkpoints and down Pennsylvania Avenue to the United States Capitol. Asad thought it was amazing what you could buy in America, as long as you had enough money. With buildings burning all around them and people running amok, Asad's team jumped off their fire trucks with gear in hand and headed right to the front doors of the Capitol Building. Asad thought there would be some questions at the door as the building was not on fire. Instead, they got a big smile and a wave in by the U.S. Capitol Police, letting them right in the building.

"The senators are in the secure room," the police officer said as Asad's team headed in that general direction. As Asad walked down the corridor, his team took off their breathing apparatus and placed them strategically in their correct places.

This didn't look out of the norm as there was no fire and no smoke.

Asad was at the end of the corridor, close to where the senators and congressmen were in hiding. He may not be able to get to them directly, but the explosives he and his team brought with them would bring down the building and bury them alive.

It is done, Asad thought to himself. The same scenario was playing out at the Pentagon. This time the amount of explosives brought into the Pentagon would make a 757 crashing into the building look like it was a Cessna. Asad removed his breathing apparatus and looked at his team with pride. They had accomplished their mission and stood three feet away from a room full of men and women who had brought them so much sorrow and pain. Asad and Mansur embraced one last time, and then they began to pray to Allah.

* * *

Even though he had only been on the job for a few weeks, all of the activities of the firemen down the hall were beginning to look suspicious to the police officer at the entrance. His eyes scanned the faces of the men, and he noticed that they were all Arabic. The police officer felt that something wasn't right about these men, and then he saw them go to their knees and begin praying. "Control, this is three-eleven from the United States Capitol Building. Ah, we have a bunch of firemen here who are all Arabic, and instead of securing the building, they are all on their knees praying, over."

There was a pause that seemed to last forever. The radio came alive with the loud, screaming voice of the commander on the other end of the radio. *"Clear the building! Clear the building, now!"*

The police officer reached for the big red emergency button and was about to press it when he noticed one of the firemen had walked up to his booth and had a button of his own. The rest of the impostor firemen finished praying and stood up and yelled, "Praise be to Allah."

That was the end of the United States Capitol Building and many of the world's most powerful men and women.

24.

Davis sat in his car at a streetlight a few blocks away from FBI headquarters. He looked in his rearview mirror only to see the FBI Building collapse. *"Shit!"* was all that Davis had time to say before his car was hit by the shockwave, knocking it out of control and crashing it. Davis was trying to get control of his senses as a million scenarios were going through his head. *Was it because of the chatter I heard? Where else would they attack? Did anyone get out of the building?* All of these questions would be answered in time. But first Davis had to worry about getting out of what was left of his car.

Davis was confused. As he was trying to get out of his car, Davis kept hearing what he thought were more explosions. *Must be echoes,* he thought to himself. As he got out of the wrecked car and looked around the city, he could see smoke plumes coming from many locations. *Echoes don't produce smoke,* he said to himself. This was a big deal. Monroe was right; he was vindicated. It was a big price to pay to be right. A sinking feeling hit Davis. *How big is this going to get? This is going to be one long day,* Davis thought as he started to walk towards what was left of the FBI Building to look for survivors.

25.

Jason Ingersoll had served as a mechanic for twenty years for a small, fixed-base operator at the airport. He never felt like the rest of the men who worked there or anywhere in the airport complex. Jason was a communist. He was a closet-case communist, but he was a communist nonetheless. His father was a communist, and his grandfather was a communist. Jason never understood American imperialism. He learned from his grandfather that if he were an open communist, he would have lost his job years ago. He kept his opinions to himself and made plans for the day he would be proud to prove that he was a communist and to show his hatred for America.

After what McCarthyism did to his father and his comrades, Jason knew he had to keep his beliefs to himself. He didn't mingle with the people at work. While they were top-notch at what they did, like most people, they thought small. They worried about weekend sports and alcohol more than they worried about the future of their nation. They often teased Jason for not mixing in and for being less talkative. He just ignored them.

Everything changed for Jason after 9/11. He remembered the thick smoke rising from the Pentagon only a few miles away. Since that day, he planned to be involved in the next strike. He would make the world a better place for the working man.

Jason not only maintained aircraft, he also was a pilot and owned a twin-engine aircraft. After 9/11, he quietly retrofitted his twin-engine aircraft into a flying bomb. His twin was always ready to fly, and Jason had the highest clearance available to airport employees. He would have no problem implementing his plan when the time was right. The twin was ready, and so was Jason. He listened to the radio all the time for the first hints of any attack.

On this warm July morning, Jason arrived at the airport an hour early. He performed his ritual of checking the news and his twin to make sure it was ready to go. Thankfully there were many trusting people. Jason never had any problem with nosy people asking too many questions.

Jason was about to start his shift when the first reports of bombs going off in New York came over his portable radio. He dropped his cup of coffee, grabbed a few supplies from his locker, and ran to his ready-to-go twin. On his way out of the shop, he ran into a person whom he would be only too happy to see die—his boss, Jim. Jim was a loudmouth fool who put the letter "M" in macho.

"Hey, where the hell are you going in such a hurry?" Jim asked as Jason went out the door to the shop. Jason ignored him and just kept on walking. Jim was right on his heels.

"I asked you a question, asshole," Jim said as he grabbed Jason and swung him around. Jason didn't even hear the gun go off, but he knew he had hit Jim in the chest. He kept a 9 millimeter hidden in his locker and had stuck it in his jacket as he was leaving. Jim was clutching his chest and trying to catch his breath.

"Why?" he asked as he fell to his knees.

"Better you die now than when the big one comes," Jason said. He just walked away. He wouldn't miss Jim. He had always given Jason a hard time. Jason thought that Jim knew he was a communist. Jim often talked about his hatred for commies when Jason was within listening distance.

Jason hopped in the twin. His hands were shaking; he took a deep breath. His voice cracked as he asked for clearance to the active runway, hoping there weren't any restrictions imposed as of yet. He received his clearance, and luckily it was for runway three-three. That would save him time as all he had to do was head almost directly north to his target.

The twin was rolling down runway three-three, full of explosives and fuel. Jason was still listening to the controller's instructions to avoid restricted airspace as his twin lifted off. The plane only had to climb a few hundred feet to clear some buildings. Then he would make his move.

In the control tower of Ronald Regan International Airport, news of the attacks in New York was coming in slowly. The controllers were waiting for instructions as to whether or not to close down the airport as had been done on 9/11. One of the controllers was trying to concentrate on the traffic and the news; he noticed the twin that had just taken off was no longer on the radar screen.

26.

Hilary had a soft spot for people who had religious convictions. She also had a soft spot for the grandmother types. She paid them the same respect she would pay her own mum.

"Ladies," she said as she pointed to the stairs leading to the upper deck, "follow me."

The nuns left their seats and headed towards the front, pausing to smile at the passengers and nod at two Middle Eastern men watching them. The nuns said little as they climbed up the stairs and into the flight deck of the airplane.

* * *

Back at the Winnipeg airport, Randy was in his office, sitting at his computer and waiting for any information on the suspicious passengers now on their way to England. He received a special e-mail alert about the attacks in New York and Washington on his BlackBerry. Randy didn't have to read the message twice to make the connection. He grabbed the paging system phone to make an airport-wide announcement.

"Attention passengers, attention all passengers. Please remember to keep an eye on your luggage at all times while in the airport. Thank you for your cooperation." That was all he needed to say. That was the code phrase for possible terrorists on the grounds.

* * *

"Thank you, Captain, for letting us see the flight deck," one of the nuns said as they fumbled in their handbags, looking for what Marcel thought was a camera. Hilary left the flight deck to attend to her duties because she knew the nuns were in good hands.

"No problem, Sister," Marcel said as he waited for the nuns to get their cameras out. "What parish are you from?" the captain asked.

* * *

Mike Harper heard the page and was about to call Randy on the radio when he remembered that he had said the radios could be monitored, so he picked up the phone instead and called Randy. Randy answered the phone immediately.

"It's bad news, I assume?" Mike asked on the other end of the phone, still reading the new e-mail.

"I'm not sure if you know. New York and Washington are under attack," Randy said in a clam voice.

"We have CNN on one of our monitors here, and they just started to cover it live," Mike said, with worry in his voice.

"I think there's a connection with the men we were watching. What do you think?" Mike asked, not sure if he wanted to hear the answer.

"Let's not take a chance. Let's recall flight two-niner-one-five. Get on the company secure line and call them now; let them know they may have a potential problem." Randy's mind was playing out many possible scenarios.

* * *

In the flight deck of the 747, Brent turned to see a light flashing on the control console. This light indicated that there was a call on the secure encrypted channel. He turned his eyes away from the nuns long enough for them to pull out syringes—the kind used to give insulin shots. This was a bit confusing to Marcel, and it took him by surprise when one of the women stuck the needle into the top of his arm. There was a little prick, and his arm went numb. Marcel looked over at Brent as the second nun did the same to him. Brent watched the little light flash on the console as he lost consciousness.

Marcel slumped back into his seat. He was held in place by his seatbelt. His whole body was going numb, and he was finding it hard to breath. He could see out of the side of his eye that Brent was convulsing. Then he realized that they had been tricked. These ladies were not innocent nuns, but terrorists taking over the plane. *Too late,* Marcel thought to himself as he felt the life leave his body. Marcel's thoughts centered on his wife, his children, and his grandchildren. He would not make it to his retirement party. The last thing he saw was a vision of Mother Mary coming to take him home.

The imposter nuns made sure they did their jobs. They checked the pulse of both the captain and the first officer to ensure they had given them a fatal dose of potassium chloride. The nuns turned, left the flight deck, and motioned to two men sitting in the upper deck. They slowly moved out of their seats and into the flight deck, closing the door behind them.

* * *

The phone rang in Randy's office; he picked it up, not expecting what he was going to hear. "Randy, it's Mike. We've tried to call two-niner-one-five a few times, and there's no answer on the secure channel."

Randy was a seasoned airport manager of twenty-plus years of service. He had seen it all and had his share of problems. Having terrorists waltz right through his terminal and onto a jumbo jet was something that he had prayed would never happen. It looked like it had, and it was too late to stop them. They were already in the air. His only hope was that whatever they planned was to occur between Halifax and England and not between Winnipeg and Halifax.

"Have the tower try to call them on the regular channel and see if they respond," Randy said, reading information on his computer. "Call me back after you talk to the tower. I have some information about the men coming in now. I'm getting something from Interpol right now; I'll call you back," Randy said as he hung up the phone and started to read the information about the men coming in from Interpol. He hadn't even finished reading the first paragraph when he hit redial. "Shit," he muttered to himself.

Mike answered the phone. "Do you want the bad news first or just the bad news?" Randy asked, trying to emphasize the gravity of the situation. "Here's what we have, according to Interpol. These guys have been moving around the UK and the United States for the last few months. They fell off of the radar a while back, and all of a sudden they showed up in Winnipeg last week. As you know, today they're off to England."

"So there is a connection," Mike said, sounding concerned.

"Looks like they're the real deal. Let the guys in the tower know," Randy added with urgency in his voice.

"If we can't get a hold of them, we'll have to advise Halifax International what's coming their way. Also contact Transport Canada and the RCMP. Tell them we may have a hijacked airliner, and lock this place down tight." For the first time in Randy's career he sounded scared.

"We're on it now. I'm calling every person into work, and we're going to protocol red," Mike said as he typed in the orders that would be paged to all security personnel: emergency 911. As one of his guards approached him, Mike added, "Hang on a sec, Randy." Mike held the earpiece of the phone on his chest as Tim whispered into his ear. Mike had a look of worry on his face. "Damn," he said in response to Tim's news. He then put the phone back to his ear. "If the news wasn't bad enough, just so you know, the tower can't reach flight two-niner-one-five on the regular channel, either."

There was a pause. Randy was momentarily at a loss for words.

"Keep me in the loop," Randy said before he hung up the phone and headed toward the door. He stopped just long enough to make sure his gun was ready as he picked up a few extra clips of ammunition from his desk.

27.

It was far simpler than Jason had expected. So far the Pentagon was still standing, but he assumed there were a lot of people ducking for cover. He kept his eye on I-395 as he turned north toward the Jefferson Memorial. The radio came alive with the worried-sounding voice of the ATC.

* * *

"Six-four-Yankee, can you squawk ident?" There was no response. The controller tried again. "November-seven-eight-six-four-Yankee, we have lost you on radar. Can you say your location?" The ATC was starting to sound nervous. This could be his worst nightmare come to life. He looked around the room to see if anyone else had him on radar. "Hey guys, do you have that twin that just left on radar?" he asked, still looking north. There was no answer.

The controller picked up his binoculars and looked out of the tower in a desperate search for the twin. He keyed his microphone again and asked for a pilot report from the aircraft that were in visual range. "Can anyone give me a pirep on a Piper twin north of the airport?" he asked all pilots in the area. There were no responses.

* * *

Back in the twin, Jason reached over and turned the volume of the radio down and pointed his twin straight north. He passed the Washington Monument and pushed the throttles as far as they could go. He was low enough that he could see people pointing and scrambling to take cover. Just as he passed E Street NW, he started taking small arms fire. They caused little damage to the fortified twin.

Jason was only feet away from his target, the White House. He noticed lots of smoke coming from either the IRS or the FBI Building and realized that there were others who wanted to bring down this evil, capitalistic government. A barrage of automatic gunfire started peppering his twin. It was too late. He had enough momentum to take him right to the front door. Jason grabbed the microphone and yelled, *"Power to the people!"* before he became paint on the walls of the White House.

* * *

The controller in the tower was looking through his binoculars. He noticed two large plumes of smoke in the direction of the White House.

"I think we found the twin," he said in a whisper.

28.

Davis walked toward the pile of rubble formerly known as the Federal Bureau of Investigation, wondering who else had survived. *"Monroe,"* Davis whispered. The training that was supposed to kick in hadn't. He was still in shock, and his ears were still ringing. A million thoughts went through his head. He needed to figure out what to do next, and it looked like it was going to be on instinct and not the training as he was having a problem clearing his head.

He instinctively reached into his jacket to make sure he had his 9 millimeter in its holster. The Beretta was there, and it was something he could always count on. That was another thing that made him different from most other FBI agents. They carried the standard Glock 22 or the 23. He liked the Beretta and its Italian style, and he liked the fact that it had never let him down when he needed it the most.

I need to slow down and think. He walked past what was left of a car and looked around at the destruction. *What did I miss?* he asked himself as he surveyed the damage all around him. Davis looked at what he thought was the box of a cube van. *Is this where the bomb was?* he asked himself as he was trying to get his thoughts straight and the ringing in his ears to stop.

"Help, help!" Through the ringing in his ears, Davis thought he heard a cry from a short distance away.

Davis stopped in his tracks and looked around to see where the cries for help came from. The sound was coming back to Davis's ears, and he could hear the sounds of emergency vehicles, shifting rubble, and a woman screaming for help.

"Where are you?" Davis yelled, looking in the area he thought the scream came from.

"I'm over here! Please help me!"

Davis had a problem trying to tell where the plea was coming from. Now that his ears were clearing, he was having a hard time focusing in on the pleas for help.

"Yell again," Davis called to the woman. There was a bit of a pause, and then Davis heard a man call out for help.

"I'm over here! Can you help me out, buddy?" the man called out. This threw off Davis. Now there were two voices calling him. *I'm sure there will be more,* he thought to himself.

"Just a second, mate. I'll be with you as soon as I free this woman trapped here," Davis said. "Ma'am, yell one more time so I can tell where you are," he said, wanting to focus on the sound of her voice.

"I'm in the car over here," she said, with excitement in her voice. "Please come and get me out of here. I'm claustrophobic."

Davis understood that feeling, and with the woman's last statement, he could tell what car she was in. It was almost completely buried under rubble. He walked over, looked at the pile of debris, and started to dig out the helpless woman.

"Thank you," the woman said as she heard Davis begin to dig her out. Within a few seconds of him arriving at the car, a few more survivors came over and started to dig her out as well. Davis was happy to see other survivors. Not only were there more survivors, there were also more cries for help now coming from all around.

29.

Kameel was on a special mission. He was to take out the mouthpiece of America: CNN. Kameel had a special loathing for CNN. They were nothing more than the government's unofficial department of propaganda. Millions of Americans watched CNN and were spoon-fed the government's anti-Arab line, 24/7.

Kameel thought the Americans were cowards. He also thought this was a coward's way of getting back at them. Sitting in a truck and pushing a button was effective, but he wanted to cut the throats of Americans in a real fight, not in some cowardly way. He also wanted to attack military targets instead of civilian ones. It was the military that killed his family. He thought innocent people should not have to pay the price for the actions of the military. But it was not up to him. He was a soldier in a holy war, a jihad. He must follow orders.

His orders were to wait until the parking lot was full of the "reporters," with their mouthwash and hairspray. The time had arrived to push his button and end it all. He said a prayer to Allah and was about to push the button when he noticed one more car pull into the parking lot at high speed. *This must be someone important,* Kameel thought. He was driving fast and racing by the security guard like he wasn't even there. Kameel waited until the car stopped to see who it was. The car screeched to a halt, and out popped a man on a mission. He didn't even park the car correctly; he just jammed it into park, opened the car door, and started to run for the entrance to the building. Kameel could see the face of the man. He had seen the man on the air many times, but Kameel couldn't remember his name. He recognized his messy hair, his signature bowtie, and the arrogance in his demeanor. This was one American pig he was glad he was going to kill.

Kameel was ready to push his button. It would be like changing the channel on his remote control, except he would not be changing the channel—he would be changing the future. *Click.* The reporter never made it to the front doors, and CNN was off the air.

30.

After leaving the flight deck, Hilary had resumed her duties and began walking around the cabin again to check on the passengers. Then she noticed out of the corner of her eye the nuns at the bottom of the stairs heading for the nearest lavatory. Before they entered, one of the nuns looked over and gave a nod to one of the passengers Hilary was keeping an eye on. It was odd, she thought, that both nuns would need to use the lavatory at the same time. She made a mental note of this as she made her rounds.

* * *

William loved technology. Tracking the flight with his computer fascinated him. Zoë was reading a book, as usual. Shawn was playing with his newest portable computer device. Sandra, on the other hand, was concerned about some of the passengers. Sandra had the blessing—or curse—of having a photographic memory. She could go into a room and know what had been moved or changed, even if it had been years since she'd been there. She could also look once at the faces of the passengers in a plane and remember what seat they were in hours later. When she was returning from the bathroom, she noticed that several men had changed seats. She tried not to let this bother her. It was most likely nothing more than her overactive imagination. William gripped Sandra's hand, trying to reassure her. He had no idea what she was concerned about.

Since 9/11, Sandra had been more concerned about body language and behavior that stood out. She noticed these men.

They seemed to be looking at each other for a signal—it was strange behavior. The flight was going to be a long one, though, and until she had something more concrete, she had to keep her mind busy. Then Sandra noticed one of the men walking up to the tall British flight attendant and motioning her to the back of the plane. As they passed her seat, another man had moved to the back of the plane from the other aisle. Sandra looked back as the flight attendant and the two men disappeared behind the curtain. Her heart started to race. Her eyes met the eyes of another man heading to the back. They were black, cold, and empty. She squeezed William's hand hard just as she heard a scream.

31.

This is not going to be easy, Randy thought as he left his office on the way to meet Mike. He was stopped in his tracks as he noticed passengers packed into and looking in through the windows of a restaurant that had a TV in it.

All eyes were on the TV screen, and then it went blank. "What the hell," was the comment from a man sitting and watching. "Just like CNN to go off the air when you need them the most," he added. People in the restaurant started to talk, and the chatter was getting louder.

"Turn the channel then, man!" a man yelled over the chatter in the doorway. The waitress fumbled for the remote and turned the channel. The first one she turned to was fuzzy, but they could see New York in the background. She changed the channel again, and there was New York, smoke, and a Spanish announcer.

"Oh c'mon, lady, turn it again, eh," the sitting man said, sounding frustrated.

She gave him a dirty look and pushed the button one more time to change the channel. The TV was clear, and the room went silent.

New York was ablaze, and some of the people were starting to become concerned that this day would be just like that one so many years ago. They were witnessing the new attacks taking place.

Randy knew that he had to lock the airport down and not cause a panic. He walked into a sea of confusion. Some people were starting to cry as they were huddled around every TV in the terminal. Others were in shock, and some were in denial.

He took out his phone and called his wife to make sure she understood the gravity of the situation. Randy had been married for a long time, and he had told his wife that if he ever called and told her straight out that she needed to get to the safe house, then she should do so without hesitating. Randy didn't have to worry about his children as he knew his wife would call them and tell them to do the same thing. No matter where they were, they would all meet at the safe house. Randy's children were all grown and had families and lives of their own, but when Randy called, they knew it was bad.

For now, he had to evacuate the airport and secure it from any potential threat on the grounds. That could take some time as it was not a small airport and there were always lots of people in various stages of arriving and departing.

Randy was walking towards the command center when his radio startled him. "Stand-by, we're about to set off the evacuation alarm," the voice on the radio said.

He couldn't reach his microphone fast enough. *"No, wait! Do not sound the alarm!"*

32.

Right down to his last name, John Smith was as typically Canadian as a man could get. He was an average young adult who had just turned twenty-one and, like many others, felt he had no purpose in life.

He was a son of the times. His parents both worked and had little time for him. His mother was around more than his father. John's father spent more time with his cell phone than his son. He was unlike those fathers who made every attempt to be with their sons.

As a teenager, John had yearned to understand the ways of the world and to belong. However, he had no one he could hang out with. He did have some friends, but they were few and far between. John felt empty. He found his purpose the day he stumbled across an Internet Web site. John felt good when he visited this site. The people on it expressed the same thoughts he had. The content of the Web site was dark and about death.

Through the site, John made friends. Eventually he met a man who helped him understand issues that he had questions about. John met this man at the local mall with his friends. John, like many lost teenagers, fell into a cult and started to believe the rhetoric and lies told by his newfound friend. This was not a religious cult that preached love and obedience. This cult preached one of the world's oldest emotions: hate.

John's training taught him to hate his family, taught him they didn't understand him. John received a lot of attention from his new teacher, praise and attention that his father never gave. John, like a flower blooming in the sun, enjoyed the attention. He blindly believed and followed the words of his newfound, adopted father.

The words that came from John's new father had disturbed him in the beginning. He was so filled with rage and hatred he would have believed anything just to get the attention he so desired. When John was told about another attack being planned all over the Western world, he was afraid, but he was also glad. John would be a part of the bigger picture—destruction of the infidels. For the first time in his life, he felt like he belonged.

The idea of participating in the destruction of the city of his birth seemed terrific to him. John was an Anglo in a city that was predominantly French. Even though he was fluently bilingual, his last name was Smith—not a French name. He was a minority in a world of minorities, trying to fit in. If they wouldn't accept him, he would get back at them in a way that would make them remember how badly they had treated him.

John was being tutored for a new assignment. This time the terrorists were going to punish Canada for helping the Americans on September the 11th. The Canadians permitted airplanes heading to the United States to land in Canada. If no major airports remained in Canada, they would not be able to land any airplanes. The terrorists planned to target navigation and landing systems. In some cases, they would take out the entire airport.

John's mission was to cause as much damage as he could to the airport and the nearby rail yard and rail lines. With no air service, they would certainly try to use the rail system to rebuild infrastructure.

John was taught how to drive a truck for the mission, and he drove it well. He parked the fifty-three-foot semi truck at the end of Rue Harry-Dubreuil, just off of Thirty-second Avenue

East in Montréal. It was a great spot. It was between the airport and the rail yard. The area was swarming with semitrailers. It was the transportation district. His truck would blend in nicely and not be noticed.

John simply jumped out of the truck and looked at his watch. He could have escaped, but he wanted to be a martyr. *Almost time,* he thought as he walked down the street. It almost seemed surreal, but soon it would be over. "Society sucks the big one," he said. The streets were quiet in the early morning as he walked to the corner. As he stood waiting for the end, he was approached by one of the harlots he'd been told about.

"Want a date?" she asked with a big smile, walking toward John in her hot-pink miniskirt.

"A date?" John paused, looking at the hooker. "I'll give you a date you will not soon forget," John said with a smile as he looked at his watch for the last time and then looked into the eyes of the prostitute. She had no idea what would happen next.

It was over in a flash of light. The airport, rail yards, and transport trucks were all one in a mangled heap of smoldering metal and ash in this newly formed crater that was once the city of Montréal.

33.

It happened so fast that there was no time to even think. The man with the cold eyes came up the aisle, and at the front of the cabin, he grabbed a female passenger. "If anybody moves, she will die!" were the words out of his mouth. The plane went silent. This was the cue for other men to spring out of their seats and go into action taking hostages.

William thought it was a dream. Sandra looked him in the eyes as if it were the last time they would see each other. As if they were speaking to each other telepathically, they both reached over the seats in front of them and grabbed Zoë and Shawn. The children were confused and scared. Sandra wanted to protect them, but it was too late. One of the passengers Sandra was watching became a hostage-taker. He was sitting a few rows behind and gave Sandra a cold stare as he walked by and grabbed Zoë by the hand. He pulled her out of the grip of her screaming mother. It was almost in slow motion. This was the ultimate nightmare coming true; William and Sandra were helpless while their child was being kidnapped. William stopped Sandra from leaping at the hostage-taker when he noticed a knife at little Zoë's throat.

* * *

Hilary was trying to remain calm with a makeshift knife held to her throat. Her first thoughts were, *Is the flight deck secure? Have they taken control of the plane?* Then she remembered the nuns. The man took hold of Hilary and walked her towards the front of the section. What to do now was the question running through her mind as the terrorists were rounding up the rest of the flight attendants and placing them in the upper deck. It looked like women and children hostages would be used by the terrorists for insurance.

* * *

Back in the passenger cabin, all hell was breaking loose. By now it had sunk in what was going on. The passengers were starting to panic. They grabbed for cell phones, just like on 9/11. The hostage-takers held up what looked like sharp plastic knives or box cutters to the necks of some of the hostages. It wasn't too long before the hostages found out how sharp they were.

"Passengers of this flight!" yelled the terrorist Sandra thought of as "Cold Eyes." He looked like he was in charge. "Stay in your seats, and do not fight us!" he said, looking around while holding a passenger by the hair and waving a knife in the air.

"We have taken control of this aircraft, and if you resist us, you will end up like this infidel pig." Without even blinking an eye, Cold Eyes cut into the throat of one of the only passengers who had stood up to them. The passengers started to scream as Cold Eyes held up the passenger with blood gushing out of the open wound. He looked like he was enjoying himself. He let the passenger go. The plane went silent. There were no more screams, just crying and stares of disbelief. The man with his throat cut slumped to the floor as the blood that carried his life spilled onto the carpet next to the coffee stains. His life was over in minutes.

"Anyone else try to get funny, you will end up the same!" Cold Eyes yelled, waving the blood-soaked knife in the air. "We've taken some of your women and children, and we have them upstairs. If you try anything, they will all die." He paused, looking around with hatred and sweat all over his face. "You don't believe me?" Cold Eyes screamed. Without blinking an eye, he reached over and grabbed one of the remaining female flight attendants and placed the blood-soaked knife to her throat. "Then watch me as I cut the throat of this pretty pig, too."

34.

Americans are a special people, Davis thought to himself. No matter where in the world there was a disaster, the Americans would be there. They loved to help in times of need. It was one of the many things he loved about being in America. He felt pride knowing that even though the city was in ruins, here he was in the middle of the street, and complete strangers were helping to dig out survivors.

"There she is!" proclaimed one of the people who was digging through the rubble. The woman was stuck in her car, which had been buried.

"Get that wood off of the door," Davis said in command mode. The woman in the car started to cry in relief, knowing that she was going to be saved. Three men moved the wood and brick from the car, giving them access to the door.

Davis stepped back and let the stronger men pull the door open and free the woman. She was covered in dust, and the only place he could see her brown skin was from where her tears had washed away the dust. There were high-fives all around. Davis was pleased; this was one moment of pleasure in this day of hell.

"OK, people, on to the next one," he yelled as the woman came over and gave him a hug. Even covered in dust, Davis welcomed the hug and embraced her, trying to reassure her that things would be alright.

35.

Naheed sat at her desk. Her eyes were fixed on the picture of her family. She had come to Canada years ago as a student and fell in love with another East-Indian student studying at the University of Toronto. They decided to live in Canada and live the American—well, the North American—dream. They were married and had a house with a two-car garage. They even had the proverbial white picket fence. Naheed worked for a large financial institution as an accountant in a large office tower in Toronto. She had three children and was planning a vacation in a few weeks to Disney World.

It didn't surprise her that the building she was in was targeted. The building was the home to the financial institution she worked for and also home to many Canadian government offices, including a branch office of CSIS. All she could do was cry. The office was abuzz with people running around with the news of the devastation that was unfolding all over America. Her coworkers were in a panic, trying to call their loved ones to find out any news. Some were packing up their stuff to leave the building as a safety precaution.

Naheed was crying at her desk when a coworker asked, "Why are you crying?" Kathy had worked with Naheed for several years and considered her more than a friend. "Is there something I can do?" Kathy asked, with a concerned tone in her voice. Naheed just ignored her.

A few weeks ago, two East-Indian men whom Naheed didn't know had approached her. They knew her, and they knew of her family back in India. They showed her pictures of them and told her they were safe as long as she did what they told her to do. If she called the police or didn't comply, they would kill her family back home, one by one. If she did as she was told and became a martyr, her family would live like kings for the rest of their lives.

To Naheed, it was like living back in India. When she came to Canada, it was like coming to a whole new world. There were laws and order—not like what she was used to. There were no secret police, and people didn't just disappear. She had thought her life was going to be great until she was stopped on York Street a few weeks back. She knew that if she didn't do as she was told, the men who had stopped her would kill her family. They had killed people for a lot less. She had no choice.

Naheed smiled at Kathy as she cried. She liked Kathy, and they worked well together. "Kathy, you better go home to your family while you can," Naheed said with a whimper.

"But what about you, Naheed? What are you going to do? Why are you so upset?" Kathy asked, a little puzzled.

"I'll be OK! Just leave while you can. *Please,* Kathy, just leave!" Naheed pleaded, with panic in her voice. She knew that there was no stopping what she had to do.

"I can't leave now. I have to wait for my husband to pick me up, but he's stuck in traffic," Kathy said. The tone in Naheed's voice was worrying her.

Kathy was looking at Naheed, who was looking back and crying. She reached into her vest pocket and pulled out what looked like a remote car starter. Naheed took one last look at the picture of her family, and then she looked at the clock on her desk. It was time.

Kathy felt a lump in her throat as she saw the device in Naheed's hand. She assumed the worst. In a panic, she turned away from Naheed and ran for the exit.

Naheed knew it would be over in a second. She took a deep breath, hugged and kissed the picture of her family, watched the clock roll to the exact time, and pressed the button as she had been instructed to do. The explosives that she had smuggled into the building over the last few weeks took out two city blocks. Kathy never made it out of the building.

36.

The passengers watched in horror as Cold Eyes held the knife up to the neck of the young flight attendant. He was about to cut her throat when a woman dressed in traditional Arabic clothing stood up and yelled, "*Stop!*" This took Cold Eyes by surprise.

"Why should I stop? She is just an infidel pig like the rest of them," he said.

"We cannot hate all Americans for the actions of a few. Allah would not approve of this," the woman said, pleading with Cold Eyes. "This woman could be your sister," she said, trying to get through to this man.

Cold Eyes got even madder. "This *pig* my *sister?*" he yelled as he dropped her on the floor and spat on her. He then casually pointed the knife at the Arabic woman and said, "Foolish woman, you have only delayed the inevitable. All of you will die for what you have done. Allah will be pleased." He walked away into the next section, tossing the curtain out of his way.

The woman sat down and started to weep. "This is something that Allah would not want," she said as she cried and started to pray.

One passenger who was watching the terrorists, waiting for the right time, was Air Marshal Cleotis Johnson. He was looking around and trying to rationally ascertain the situation. Years of training all came to this. This was not a drill. This was the real thing—a real hijacking. Cleotis was trying to keep calm, but his heart was beating fast, and he was beginning to sweat. Cleotis decided he would wait and see how this played out before he acted. First, he would study the terrorists. So far he had counted five. *There must be more,* he thought. He knew the plane had not changed course, so he hoped that maybe the flight deck had not been taken over yet; it would only be a matter of time before they tried. He had to act before the terrorists took over the flight deck; if they did that, it was game over.

Cleotis had years of experience in law enforcement. It had been hard. Cleotis was as good if not better than a lot of men who had received promotions before he did. The difference was that Cleotis was black, and most of the promotions went to people who looked like the bosses. It was frustrating, but Cleotis had done well for himself. He had a life that most people would envy and did not let the ignorance of others hold him down. Cleotis had started working in security and then soon found an opportunity as a police officer with the Portland Police Bureau. It wasn't long before Cleotis made a name for himself, proving that he was as good as any other man. His arrest record was top-notch, and he had received many awards for his service. These awards came both from the police service and from civilian organizations for his volunteer work.

Cleotis's drive was to make society a better place for all people, and most importantly for his family and friends. He was a gentle and compassionate man. He loved to take his family on vacation, and even there Cleotis was on duty. He always carried his off-duty revolver in the event he needed it. His wife often teased him that there were no bogeymen in the bushes. Cleotis loved to prove his peers wrong, even if it was his wife. One time Cleotis and his family were asleep in their cottage at Cape Meares State Park in Oregon, when there was a commotion on the beach that woke him up. Cleotis went down to see if he could lend a hand. He had no idea he was stumbling onto a small boat of refugees.

Most of the teenagers on the beach were welcoming the new arrivals to America. Cleotis, however, was suspicious. Some of the men didn't look like refugees, and the women on the boat all looked too much like slaves. Only Cleotis would have noticed that. He called for backup on his cell phone and then noticed some of the men looking around the beach like they had lost something. Cleotis also noticed a young kid standing on the beach, looking on. The kid was either seven feet tall, or he was standing on something. It was hard to tell in the dark, so Cleotis walked over to the kid and noticed he was standing on a crate that was half-buried in the sand. It was a crate of AK-47s.

Cleotis had suspected that these men were not refugees—they were snakeheads with some of their slaves with them. He thought that they might also be connected to the Chinese Red Army, judging by some of the equipment they had. They had landed with their slaves on what they thought was a deserted beach. Even at three o'clock in the morning, a lot of teens gathered to skinny-dip and drink. Cleotis noticed that they were starting to leave. All it took was one shot in the air, and the slaves sat down on the beach with their arms up in the air. The snakeheads tried to run, but the kids on the beach put a stop to that. It looked like the slaves were interested in a hot meal, so some of the people on the beach started to feed them. It was like they hadn't eaten in weeks. One of the female slaves, who looked about fifteen, raised her half-eaten burger in the air and said in broken English, "I'm loving it!"

Afterwards, the Chinese government denied that the men were connected to the Red Army or that they were snakeheads, for that matter. Politicians in America trying to uphold relations with China wanted the incident to go away. Cleotis was given his choice of jobs in law enforcement as his reward—his wife called it a bribe. Cleotis was not getting any younger, and being that this was not too long after 9/11, he thought of slowing down before his retirement. He took on the challenge of air marshal. He had worked for Western Global Airlines for a few years and decided to fly some international flights for them. While WGA was based out of the U.S., they used many Canadian airports for their international flights such as this one since there was little competition in Canada.

To date he had helped with many drunken passengers and even a few cases of air rage, but this was the real deal. These guys meant business. If only he could get a chance to get his weapon out and take out a few of them, then that would improve the odds. Cleotis knew he had to get to the flight deck before they did. But in a plane that was 231 feet long and not knowing how many terrorists there were, that would be quite a feat. All of his planning went out the window when he heard a thick Arabic accent on the intercom.

"We have this plane. If you try to take it back, we will crash it. Stay in your seats." As the plane went silent, Cleotis looked around and thought to himself, *It's time for plan B*.

37.

Azeem was looking at his watch as he sat in his truck in the arrival parking lot listening to his radio. The news of the attacks in New York was all that was on. *This is really happening,* he thought to himself. He looked at his partner sitting in the driver's seat, holding his gun and smiling. Not much was said as they both waited for the appointed time to take on the Great Satan.

* * *

Inside the airport, people were coming in and leaving the airport terminal as Mohammad wheeled his suitcase toward the front door. Mohammad had a special hatred for America. America was more than the Great Satan to him. America was hell on earth. Mohammad believed America was to blame for all the ills of the Middle East. He hated the way the people were so self-indulgent, so arrogant. The world revolved around America, and Mohammad was going to do his part to make sure he blew it back into the Stone Age.

Mohammad could hear the people nervously talking about the attacks in New York. He wheeled his suitcase toward a large group of people waiting for their luggage at the carousel. The sound of chatter was filling Mohammad's ears.

"We're safe now that we're on the ground," one man said while hugging his wife, who was upset over the radio reports. Another couple embraced with tears. They were hoping their children back in New York would be OK. Little did they know that their children might survive, but they would not. Mohammad wheeled his "terror" right past security.

He was supposed to just walk in and set off the device and become a martyr. But Mohammad wanted more; he wanted to see the terror in their eyes. As he wheeled in as close as he could to the middle of the baggage carousel, he noticed that the people were looking at him and moving away.

Mohammad used this as an excuse to vent his hatred toward America. "Why are you backing away?" Mohammad asked, looking at the people. "Yes, all Muslims are terrorists." His voice was getting louder, and the crowd was getting quieter. All eyes were on Mohammad. He scanned the faces of the people and slowly raised his hand, gripping the trigger. He could feel their fear. The people started moving away faster, bumping and tripping over each other as they started to scream and flee.

"How do you Americans say it?" Mohammad yelled in a thick accent. *"You can run, but you can't hide!"* he said as he mocked America with his hand held high like the hand holding the torch on the Statue of Liberty. *"Praise be to Allah!"* were his last words, and then he pulled the trigger.

* * *

The explosion took Azeem by surprise. He could see glass and body parts fly out of the windows, and he could see the people fleeing.

Azeem's partner opened the door of the truck and pulled out his AK-47. "Wait a few minutes before you set it off," he said to a praying Azeem. He walked past the bushes between where he was parked and the driveway toward the fleeing passengers. He lifted his AK-47 and started to fire on them. The bomb would have killed most of these people, but this was his bittersweet revenge for American imperialism.

As Azeem finished praying, he could hear the gunfire and the screaming of the people. He closed his eyes, and then squeezed the trigger of the truck bomb. It was another dirty nuke that had been snuck into the country courtesy of a politically correct and overworked immigration system.

38.

Randy keyed his microphone again. "Did you get my last message, over?" He was almost at the command center.

"We're standing by," the perturbed voice replied from the command center.

"I don't want you to sound the evacuation alarm as that would cause a panic, and we would have a lot of injured passengers," Randy said, letting the microphone go and hoping the person he was talking to understood. There was no reply.

Randy reached the doors at the command center and had to think of a way to safely evacuate the airport. Mike was standing at his desk giving orders to his officers.

"What's the plan?" Randy asked as he reached Mike's desk.

"I'm getting reports that the passengers are getting wind of what's going on and are starting to leave on their own. We'll get the boards to display that the flights out are canceled. I'm setting up my officers at every door to stop people from entering, and we're letting them know there will be no flights today. We're also getting officers to start to tell the passengers who are waiting to leave that there are no outbound flights."

"No system-wide page?" Randy asked.

"No, we don't want a panic," Mike replied looking over at Tim. Randy was happy that he and Mike were on the same page.

"If there's one thing we don't need, it's a panic," Randy said, scanning the computers and monitors in the command center.

"Officers are showing up, and we're starting to secure the airport and the grounds," Mike added.

"How long will it take to secure the perimeter?" Randy asked.

"Once we get enough officers here, we can start on that. Right now I want to make sure there are no threats in the airport or on any of the planes that are arriving," Mike said as he looked at his computer screen.

"We also might be getting unexpected visitors from the United States," Randy added. "What are we going to do about that?"

"That's one of the things I'll need your help on," Mike said as Randy listened. "We need to unload the scheduled arrivals that are heading this way, and then we need to find room to move the airplanes. Once that's done, we're going to have find space to put the planes and passengers that may be coming this way."

"I'll get on that and talk to all of the airlines. We'll have to get as many tugs going as possible to move these planes around and have places to park them." Randy pulled out his BlackBerry and started to type an e-mail.

* * *

The passengers in the terminal held onto their luggage and children tightly. Some stood in one spot looking around, and others headed for the nearest exit.

"Where are we going, Mommy?" a young child asked. The mother had too much on her mind and ignored the question from her child. "Are we going to Disney World?" he asked, giving his mother some resistance once he realized they were leaving the airport and not getting on the airplane.

"One day, Anthony, one day," she said as she held him tightly and pulled him and the luggage out the doors of the airport. *Just not today*. She kept that thought to herself, not wanting to upset her son. At least they were safe on the ground. She knew this day wasn't going to be a good day to fly.

39.

Texas was to be a special target for the operation. Texas was the home state of a few past presidents, and Texas has a lot of oil. *If the Americans are going to take our oil,* Abbas thought, *then we will destroy theirs.* Abbas and Samir were the leaders of three different cells. The cells did not know of each other; only Abbas knew of their existence. Samir was Abbas's assistant, and he was the only person Abbas could trust. This was a project that was important to the cause. Destroying what little oil the Americans had would bring them to their knees.

The targets for these attacks were oil fields and oil refineries. Each cell was to deliver explosives during the early morning hours and wait for the right time to either set them off manually or by timers. Abbas had the trucks equipped with GPS trackers so he could see when they were in place. He just loved American technology.

The teams were in place, and he was ready to go. He was waiting for the right moment to set off the devices. Abbas watched CNN go off the air on his portable TV; he knew it was time. He opened the switch of his trigger and pushed the button. The three blips that represented his teams were gone. He could feel the rumble of one of the explosions close by. He and Samir were left all alone.

Abbas and Samir embraced.

"It is done," Abbas said to Samir. Well, it was almost done. Samir and Abbas had personal missions that needed to be fulfilled.

Abbas waved good-bye to Samir as he drove away to complete his own personal mission. Abbas drove his van full of explosives down Monroe Road, close to William P. Hobby Airport, which was close to a nice suburban area of Houston. Fire trucks raced past him. He parked his van, and all that was left was to wait for the timer to set off the explosives. His mission was complete, and now he could indulge in a longtime fantasy: killing Americans face-to-face. He wanted to see the fear in their eyes. The memory of his desolate village was all the motivation he needed to even the score.

This will be like an American turkey shoot, Abbas thought to himself as he checked the timer on his bomb. Ten minutes left. He stepped out of the van and loaded his jacket pocket with ammunition magazines. He took a long look around at the nice houses and started to walk toward the first house he saw with a car parked in the driveway.

The sound of sirens in the distant background served as music to Abbas's ears. *Payback time,* he thought as he reached the first house and kicked in the door. There was no one home. Abbas looked around at all of the nice things they had, and he knew he would never live like a king, an American king. In a jealous rage, Abbas emptied a clip into the furniture and the plasma TV. *Americans are spoiled brats,* he thought to himself.

Abbas walked out of the house, leaving it a wreck. He changed his clip and walked across the lawn to the next house. He kicked in the door. A woman screamed. She was dressed in a bathrobe and crying hysterically. "Don't kill me!" she screamed. Abbas didn't even aim; he just pointed the gun in her general direction and fired. The AK-47 cut her in half. Her blood splattered all over the furniture, soaking the walls, floor, and expensive leather couch. Abbas just laughed and walked out the door. From the corner of his eye, he spotted another woman running away from the house next door. *This is too easy,* Abbas thought as he ran toward her.

The clock in the van was ticking down as Abbas shot the woman in the back. "American whore!" Abbas yelled over the dead body of the suburban soccer mom.

Abbas looked at his watch and knew the time was near. He lifted his AK-47 into the air and emptied out the clip. He then started to yell as loudly as he could at the top of his lungs, *"Death to America!"* Then the bomb in his truck went off, taking out the airport and a few blocks of American suburbia.

40.

Marcel! William thought to himself. *Did they kill the flight crew like they did on 9/11? Maybe they didn't this time.* However, William knew the chances of that were slim as these guys seemed to be following the terrorist handbook.

He calmly put his notebook under the seat as he shielded Shawn as much as he could. The terrorists had taken most of the children, but they never noticed Shawn hiding at William's feet. William and many other passengers were looking around to see how many terrorists there were. He could only see two; both were standing at the entrance of their section. He could not see where they had taken Zoë, and he was trying to keep Sandra calm. So much was going through his mind. It was 9/11 all over again. He was wondering what their target was, where they were going to crash this plane. William looked over at another passenger; he was a big man who could have taken up two seats. He was agitated and looked like he was going to pop out of his skin.

"We're not going down this time!" he said under his breath. "I'll kill these fuckin' wankers meself if I have to!" he said in a Cockney accent as he looked around for support from other passengers. Some were nodding in approval, others were shaking their heads, and some were crying.

"We can't wait too long for them to settle in, or we're all goners. Who's with me?" asked passenger Nigel Bowen, looking for support. William was not much of a fighter, but he wasn't a wimp, either. He changed places with Sandra so he could get in on the conversation. Sandra scooped up Shawn and held him tightly.

"What's the plan?" William asked the burly man who was wearing his team's rugby shirt with pride.

"As far as I can tell, all they have are some plastic fucking knives. All we need are some pillows or blankets to put in front of us as we mow the fuckers over. I have six of my mates with me from my team; I'm sure we can get to the front and take her back before they crash the bloody thing." He sounded like a coach talking about the game's big play.

"We only need another five or six men to kick the shit out of them wankers." He was getting the rest of the male passengers in an uproar.

One passenger whispered, "Yeah, we can't just sit here and let them kill us off like before." Other passengers started to agree.

"OK, OK, we need a plan," William said to the other men. One of the men sitting a few rows ahead was trying to put his two cents in when his crying wife told him to mind his own business.

"We need a diversion to keep them busy so we can take them out," Nigel said in his thick accent. William was having a problem trying to understand him.

"OK, we need to slow down a little bit here." William was at his best when the information was coming in a form he could quantify. "Sorry, what was your name, by the way?" William asked, reaching out his hand to shake the hand of the Englishman. Nigel took a deep breath, realizing that he was talking too fast.

"Sorry, mate. I'm Nigel, and I'm here with my mates on the way home from a rugby match," he said, looking about the cabin and using his chin to point to his fellow teammates.

"We need to do something and do it fast," Nigel said.

It's easier said than done, William thought to himself. "I'm William. And I agree—it's worth a shot. We need to take out these *bastards* before they reach their intended target, and we need to save the hostages," William said with all eyes upon him.

"What do we do?" asked another passenger. Nigel piped up with the suggestion of getting the crying wife to make more noise so they would come over to see what was wrong. That didn't go over too well.

One of the men sitting in one of the middle seats of the four looked up to see where the terrorists were.

"I have an idea," he whispered. Nigel and William were all ears. "I can pretend that I'm having a seizure or something like that. My wife will call them over, and then you guys can do the rest," the man said, looking at Nigel and William for approval. They both loved the idea.

"OK, whatever works to get them fuckers in me reach. Now let's put it into practice." Nigel pointed to his mates to move to empty seats. The terrorists yelled for them to sit down. "Get some pillows or a coat or something to block the knives," Nigel whispered to his teammates.

Nigel looked over to the man who was going to pretend to be sick and said, "You get their attention, and when they come over, me and my mates will landscape their beaks." William and the rest of the passengers had no idea what that meant, but it sounded effective.

Nigel waited for everyone to be in their places. "OK, that's it, lads. Are you ready?" Nigel's eyes were on fire as he looked at the other passengers.

Many passengers, including his teammates and William, gave a nod of approval. Sandra was not impressed with William putting himself in harm's way.

"Wil, let them do it. You can't get hurt," Sandra said through tears. But she knew William wasn't going to let other people take a chance and get injured while he did nothing.

"I just can't sit and watch," William said.

Sandra was trying to explain to William what she meant and hide Shawn back on the floor at the same time.

"They say they've taken over the plane. You know that means they've killed the flight crew. And that means that if the passengers get the plane back, we'll need someone to fly the plane. That someone is you."

That was a thought that had not yet entered his mind. She was right—if the passengers got the plane back, he would likely be the only one who would have a chance to land it. William reached over and kissed Sandra on the forehead.

"You're the best thing that ever happened to me," he said. "Always thinking two steps ahead of me," William added. "OK, once the crap hits the fan, head to the back of the plane and hide Shawn until I tell you all's clear."

"We have to get Zoë, too," she said with tears in her eyes.

"Yes. We'll get her, too. One thing at a time, hon." William looked back at the burly Englishman.

Nigel nodded at William, realizing it was time. "I'll say it the way we would say it back home: let's *fuckin'* roll, mates," Nigel said, remembering the words of passenger Todd Beamer on Flight 93.

The passenger who was a part-time actor played the best role of his life. With a little help from some stomach medicine and water, he started twitching and foaming at the mouth. His wife stood up and screamed, "My husband is having a seizure." The terrorists looked for a second, not knowing what to do.

Nigel, not being a patient person, piped up, saying, "C'mon, man, can't you see he needs some fuckin' help?" The terrorists appeared highly agitated as they walked over with knives pointing at the passengers. They looked to see the man foaming at the mouth. They had no idea what this was all about.

Just as they were close enough, Nigel yelled, *"Now, lads!"* He and his teammates jumped to their feet, grabbing the nearest terrorist and beating him into submission. The other passengers did the same to the second one. Just as the passengers were enjoying the success of their mission, the curtain that divided the cabin flew open, and in walked two more terrorists along with Cold Eyes.

Nigel looked up and said, "It's time for a field goal, lads."

41.

Lionel Ferguson was top-notch as far as your local neighborhood conspiracy theorist goes. He could tell you who shot JFK and about the dangers of drinking fluorinated water. He also had a habit of being in the know with his satellite TV and his many police radio scanners. Lionel liked to keep a close eye on his neighbors and anyone who wasn't supposed to be there.

On this warm July morning, he had just turned on the TV when reports were coming in about explosions in New York. He tried to tune to CNN, but it was off the air. He instinctively reached over and turned on three of his police scanners. The scanners were rather active with calls for officers to report to their stations, and a call was in for SWAT. Lionel had an uneasy feeling about this day, and he suspected it would only get worse. He reached for his portable scanner and went to the basement to get what he called his "life insurance policy." It was his favorite 9 millimeter, his Beretta.

He was in his basement when he felt his house shake. He was trying to analyze the sound. Train crash, airplane crash, car crash? No, not the right sound. It could only be one thing. Explosion. He started to become nervous as he loaded the clip of his Beretta. The portable scanner came to life with the sound of a distressed police officer calling for backup. *"Officer down, officer down. I need assistance!"*

"This is it. I knew this was going to happen. I just knew it," he kept repeating to himself. This was vindication for Lionel as he had been telling friends and coworkers all along that Texas would be a target and that they had better be prepared. They had all laughed at him, and finally his so-called friends stopped calling. His coworkers shunned him, too. He was right, and who was laughing now?

* * *

Samir drove his van and looked for the perfect target. His main mission was over, and he was going to take the fight to America in a way he knew all too well—the street fight. Samir had heard about Americans and their love for guns. He was hoping to meet a few and show them there was a difference between shooting at a defenseless animal and a soldier.

Samir stopped his van in what he thought was a great example of America. The suburb that Samir stopped in was a paradise compared to what he had lived in back home. He opened his door and stepped out onto the street. There were people outside as the sound of the explosions brought them out to investigate. He paused, took a deep breath, and reached over to his AK-47. He felt good as the adrenaline was starting to flow. He walked away from the van, not even closing the door, and headed toward the first house he saw. The people in the street who saw him started to run for cover. Samir cocked his gun, and he was ready for battle.

* * *

Lionel finished loading his gun and had started to bring supplies upstairs when he thought he heard the sound of a woman scream and gunfire. *This can't be happening,* he thought. But it was; not only was it happening in the state of Texas, but it was happening right on his street.

Lionel crept to his front window and slowly pulled back the curtain. What he saw horrified him. In his little suburb of Houston, Texas, on a warm July day, people were running and screaming for cover from a man with a gun. This was too much for Lionel's brain to process all at once. What was he to do?

He was about to close the curtain when he heard the familiar sound of an AK-47. He had heard that gun fired at his local firing range many times. This time it was not shooting at paper—it was shooting at people. This time it wasn't being used by a member of his gun club. This time it was being used by a man who hated every fiber of the people he was shooting at.

Lionel had to act as the terrorist was crossing his grass towards a frightened neighbor woman who had fallen against a car while trying to escape. The terrorist ran out of bullets and was changing clips when Lionel decided to make his move.

It was like it was all in one motion. He pulled the slide back on his Beretta, putting a bullet in the chamber. Then he opened the front door and walked out onto his manicured grass. The terrorist's back was turned to him as he yelled, "Hey, bastard, welcome to America."

The terrorist had started to turn around when Lionel pulled the trigger and put a bullet in his chest. Lionel kept firing as the terrorist faced him, now blindly firing his freshly loaded AK-47. It was in slow motion. Lionel kept squeezing the trigger. Each shot hit the terrorist until he was on the ground in a pool of his own blood. It spilled out of his body like Texas oil. The AK-47 was silent, as was the woman leaning against the car. The neighborhood returned to the silence of midmorning.

Lionel looked over to the woman to see if she was injured. Their eyes met in a silent stare. Lionel found it ironic. He had saved the life of his neighbor, the same neighbor who had always seemed to have an endless amount of time to talk about how crazy he was.

He looked over at the terrorist to make sure he was dead. He then walked over and offered the woman his hand. She reached up, her eyes never leaving his. So many emotions and thoughts went through Lionel's head. One of them was that being vindicated was bittersweet.

42.

The moment of victory was dashed by the appearance of Cold Eyes and two more terrorists. "We told you not to fuck with us!" Cold Eyes said with anger in his voice. He reached out and grabbed a female passenger who was trying to get out his way.

Nigel wasn't going to just stand there and let another passenger get her throat cut. He tossed the terrorist he had just killed into a row of seats, reached down, and grabbed a discarded jacket. With one hand holding the jacket, he punched it with the other and called to the terrorists. "OK, fuckers, think you're tough?" He started to walk towards the terrorist who was about to kill the passenger. The terrorist tossed her into her seat.

"Oh, a tough guy. I love to kill British pigs, too," the terrorist said in broken English. He then added, "How do you say it—bring it on!"

He lunged toward Nigel with the knife pointed at his throat. To Nigel, it was in slow motion as his ears filled with the sound of the crowd at a rugby match as they chanted on their favorite hero to score a point. Nigel wouldn't disappoint them as he took the jacket that in his mind was a football and blocked the advancing knife attack. As he blocked the knife with the jacket, Nigel reached out with his other hand and grabbed the terrorist by the throat. In his life, Nigel had felt rage and hatred; all of it was focused on his fingers, squeezing the life out of this man.

The terrorist dropped the knife and tried to remove Nigel's hand from around his throat. Nigel backed up a few feet with the terrorist hanging on like a rag doll. The other terrorist tried to run to his aid. Nigel tossed him into his advancing friend. With the momentum, he bounced him back towards Nigel. In true form, he kicked him in the crotch like he would a rugby ball.

"Field goal!" Nigel yelled. Cold Eyes dropped the passenger and advanced towards him. Cold Eyes didn't realize that other passengers were now surrounding them. Nigel, who was in a fighting stance, saw the other passengers surround them. He stood up and smiled. "You better give up while you can, assholes," Nigel said as he pointed toward the other passengers getting closer to them. The terrorists realized their mistake. It was too late. The passengers pounced on their captors and beat them into submission.

"Time to move," William said to Sandra and Shawn. They both moved out of their seats and towards the back of the plane.

William looked over as a fourth terrorist came to the aid of his comrades. Realizing the futility of trying to help on his own, he turned to run toward the front of the plane to get help. That's when he met the butt of the gun of Air Marshal Cleotis Johnson. The terrorist slumped to the floor, and Cleotis quickly closed the curtain behind him. He peeked into the next section to see if there were any more terrorists heading his way. The terrorists were busying themselves with the passengers. When Cleotis turned around, all eyes were staring at him. He pulled out his badge and identified himself as an air marshal.

Nigel smiled and asked, "What took you so long, mate?"

43.

This is just too surreal, Davis thought as he made his way back to what he thought was the FBI headquarters, also called the J. Edgar Hoover Building. He looked around to make sure. There was so much dust he couldn't really tell if this was the FBI or one of the surrounding buildings.

Davis spit out the dust and was finding it hard to breathe. He needed some water. What was on his mind mostly was finding survivors. There were sounds of jets in the air, emergency vehicles, and people screaming everywhere.

"Hey, buddy, put on this mask." Davis was caught by surprise as an EMS worker was handing out breathing masks.

"Remember what happened after 9/11," the EMS worker said as he gave Davis the mask and went on to look for more survivors. Davis remembered all of the EMS workers who had died or developed major health problems after breathing in a concoction of toxic chemicals in the dust that was generated after the Twin Towers collapsed. He put the mask on and hoped that he would find other survivors in time.

All seven stories of the front part of the building were in a pile of rubble. Nothing more. *That must have been one hell of a bomb,* Davis thought. "How did they let this happen?" he said under his breath. The north part of the building, the part that looked like it was resting on top of the first seven floors, looked like it was undamaged. *There must be survivors in there,* Davis thought. The problem was that his and Monroe's office was in the south part of the building.

The dust started to diminish, and Davis could see clearer and a little bit further. There were people all over the place. Some were EMS, some were employees. Most were in shock, including the young agents who were walking around in a daze.

"Davis!" He heard his name being called from across the street. Davis turned in the direction of the voice, not knowing who it was.

"Over here," Davis called out, removing his mask. He was hoping it was someone from his floor, someone with information. The person was getting closer, and Davis recognized her as one of Monroe's technical assistants.

"Where is Monroe?" Davis asked, not realizing he should be happy that Kimberly had survived.

"Yes, Burton, I'm fine," she said sarcastically.

Davis realized his mistake. "Sorry, too much going on right now," he said.

"That's OK, Burton. I understand," she said, happy that she had found another survivor from the same floor.

"Monroe is fine. He got out as well," she said, much to Davis's relief. "How did you get out?" she asked, sounding confused.

"I wasn't in the building at the time. I was down the street," Davis said as he pointed in the direction he thought his car was in.

"I'm not sure where Monroe is right now," Kimberly said as she looked around for him.

"I'm sure we'll find him," Davis said, putting his arm around her and walking towards a group of survivors.

"Have you seen Grace?" Davis asked, wondering about her. Kimberly shook her head no. Davis looked back at what was left of his building and wondered how anyone had survived.

"How did you make it out?" he asked Kimberly.

"There was an alarm, and we had made it out to the north of the building when there were several explosions. We were all knocked to the ground," she explained.

"Monroe was with you at that time?" Davis asked.

Kimberly chuckled and said, "Monroe threw his body on top of mine to protect me from flying debris. I guess I was in shock because when it was all over I teased him that he should be careful that lying on top of me could result in me charging him with sexual harassment."

Davis chuckled too. *With all that's going on,* Davis thought, *we need to have some humor. It's what keeps us human.*

"When did you lose track of him?" Davis asked.

"Once we got up, there was so much dust, confusion, and people running around that we got separated. I haven't seen him since," she said.

Davis stopped an EMS worker and got a mask for Kimberly.

"You should put this on," he said, offering her the mask. She took it with reluctance, but she realized the significance of it. It brought it back home to her how much danger they were in. She began to shake, and Davis held her tightly.

"Let's go and sit down," Davis suggested, and they walked over to some broken trees and sat down.

Before Kimberly put on her mask, she said, "I'm sure he's somewhere digging out people. You know Monroe—always there to help."

Kimberly was about to go into shock, and Davis knew he had to keep her warm. He looked around for an EMS worker and called her over.

"Can you help me with her, please? I think she's going into shock," Davis said as he pointed to Kimberly, who was slumped over. The EMS worker was about to attend to her when Davis heard a familiar voice.

"Just what I suspected—alive and kicking." Davis didn't even have to look as he recognized the voice. It was Monroe. Davis stood up and smiled. It was odd to see Monroe covered in dust and bits of insulation.

Monroe reached out his hand to his boss. Davis reached over and gave Monroe a hug. It was odd, but well deserved.

"What now, boss?" Monroe asked as they broke off the hug.

"It looks like there's not much more we can do here. And besides, we need to find a vehicle and get to the safe house," Davis said, looking at Monroe and reveling in the feeling of survival.

44.

All his life Peter Knoll had lived within the boundaries of the law. Being a third-generation cattle farmer in western Canada was tough enough without the problem of being politically correct, which was an expectation of eastern cities thousands of miles away.

He said little when the government took his hard-earned money in taxes and gave him little in return. He said little when the eastern government raped his province of its natural resources during the oil boom. The least the government could do was keep his family safe from harm. He said nothing when the government made him register firearms that had been given to him by his great-grandfather. He thought it was his duty to follow the law. Peter assumed the government should know what they were doing.

Even after all the guns were supposed to have been registered, crimes still were committed with guns, and the country was no safer. Finally the government decided that all guns should be confiscated and that the only people who should have them were the police and the military. That was when federal agents from the RCMP came to take his guns, his family history. They had said he wouldn't need them anymore and that they would protect him from harm.

Peter thought like millions of people all over Canada and the United States. A government that couldn't trust its people with guns couldn't be trusted. He was right.

It was only a matter of time before the overseas wars came to North America. If Al Qaeda, or whomever, decided to attack his small Alberta town, Peter would not stand idly by. This was his home. No one was going to take that from him.

The day had started off nice and peaceful. Peter was driving his truck when he heard a call over the CB radio. The voice on the CB sounded familiar, so Peter turned up the volume. *"We need help!"* the voice yelled. *"The town is under attack!"* Peter sat in shock for a few seconds, trying to digest what he had just heard. He could tell this was no hoax. The voice on the other end of the CB was scared as hell.

The voice on the CB sounded out of breath. *"They've taken out the RCMP, and now they're going up Fifty-Third Street, killing everyone. Help us! Please help us!"* Peter could hear gunfire in the background as the man pleaded for help.

He did what he had thought he might have to one day do. He just wished it wasn't today, or in his lifetime. He wished his children would grow up in a safe country, safe from terrorist scum like this. He turned on the AM radio in the truck to hear of the news of attacks all over America, and now it was happening in his own town.

Why Ponoka? *Who knows why people do what they do,* Peter thought. He didn't understand why they had chosen his small town. He would leave that discussion for another time. He stepped out of the truck, closed the door, and as calmly as he could, walked back to the house. He went in the basement to his special place where he kept the guns and other supplies that the government didn't need to know about. He had a bag of supplies already packed in the event he ever needed them. He grabbed the gun bag and his belt of ammo. On his way back to the truck, he met his wife's eyes; she had a look of panic and concern. She had been listening to the base station CB radio and knew what was going on.

"Grab the kids and head to the storm shelter. I'll be back as soon as I can," Peter said to his wife, remembering the many arguments they'd had about the guns. She had always said to get rid of them. Peter always said that he may need them one day. "It's better to have a gun and not need it, than need a gun and not have it," Peter's father always used to say. He was right. Peter's wife gave him a hug before he left. She knew that to argue now would be futile.

"Be careful," she said as he walked back to his truck.

The CB was alive with people calling into town to say that help was on the way. He put the bag on the seat beside him and took one more look at his wife. He put his Ford pickup truck in gear and headed into town.

45.

Once Cleotis knew the area was secure, he huddled with a few of the passengers. They needed to decide on the next step in their plan. Cleotis, Nigel, William, and the other passengers formulated a plan to take out the remaining terrorists and take back the plane.

"OK," Nigel said as he looked over to his mates, who had dragged the bodies of two terrorists to their makeshift jail behind row sixty-nine. "What's next?" he asked.

Cleotis looked at the other men as a courtesy. Taking control would not be a problem as he was a natural leader; the other men knew it and looked to him for direction. He took out a floor plan of the aircraft and showed it to the other men. "We are here, in zone E. It's now secure, but we need to get through and secure zones D and C. Once we've done that, we need to pass galley G4 and head up the stairs."

"Let's get on with it then," Nigel said.

William piped up and said, "We have to be careful. There are hostages upstairs, and my daughter is one of them. If they panic, they might start killing them or just crash the plane."

Cleotis looked at William and the other men, trying to think of a way to break the news to them gently. "If we wait too long, they will reach their target and crash the plane anyway. If we act now, we have a better chance of taking the plane back and saving the people upstairs." He was right, and the other men knew it. It was a long way to go, and they didn't even know how many more terrorists there were.

"There could be several men in the lower deck, and then there are the ones in the upper deck with the hostages. Never mind the two or more in the flight deck, for sure," Cleotis said.

"You're right," William added, understanding the gravity of the situation. "If we have any chance to succeed, we need to take the plane back soon."

"OK, so let's go toward zone D and see what's going on there. We better do it soon before they realize their friends are missing. Make sure you grab pillows or whatever you can to protect yourself," Cleotis added.

"Why can't you just shoot them?" Nigel asked.

"If I did that, they would know it was over, and they'd just crash the plane; we would never have a chance. We need to do this discreetly. OK, are we ready?" he asked, looking at the brave men under his charge. He received nervous nods from them.

The men armed themselves with pillows, blankets, and anything they could use as shields to protect themselves from the terrorists' makeshift knives. They slowly walked towards zone D.

"Looks like it's all clear," one of the passengers whispered.

"Just a lot of shit-scared people," William added.

"On to zone C." Cleotis motioned to the men as they moved toward the front of the plane. Some of the passengers who had seen them joined in behind. There was a line of passengers crouched down low, heading up both aisles towards zone C.

It seemed all of the passengers had 9/11 on their minds. This was not going to be a sit-in-my-seat-and-wait-to-die situation. This was going to be a do-or-die situation. It didn't matter if the passenger was white or black, American, Canadian, or British—this was their Battle of Gettysburg. They were going to show these terrorists what real men and women were made of. They were not going to sit back and wait to become entangled in the wreckage of some skyscraper.

Cleotis had no idea how many terrorists there were on board, but as far as he was concerned, all Arabs were suspects. Cleotis peeked through the curtain that separated the cabins. "Looks like we have two or three more in this section," he said in a whisper. "And there's one standing right in front of the stairs to the upper deck," he added. Cleotis also noticed a blind spot that the terrorists could not see. "If we send a few people down the aisle crawling on their stomachs, they would never see them. What we'll do once they're in place is cause a diversion. When they come toward this area, we'll surround them."

Cleotis pointed to Nigel and a few other passengers who looked like they could handle themselves in a fight. They would crawl down the aisle. Nigel took his pillow and the makeshift knife that he had taken from the terrorist. The other passengers followed.

"OK, men, get ready," Cleotis said as a few of the men prepared for the moment of attack. Nigel stood up at the end of galley G4 and gave the signal. On cue, the passenger started to scream and yell. Predictably, the terrorists headed toward the commotion.

As soon as the terrorists ran down the aisle, Nigel and his group followed. The terrorists opened the curtain to find all of the passengers not in their seats. The next thing they knew was that Nigel was tackling them in classic rugby style. The other passengers joined in the pile.

"How many of you fuckers are there?" Nigel asked while pulling the terrorists off the floor. One terrorist spat in Nigel's face. That was a mistake. With one headbutt, Nigel knocked him out.

Cleotis asked Nigel to make sure the terrorists were secure in the back of the plane. "Tie them up and make sure they don't get loose," he added. "Search them for any weapons or electronic devices, and have someone watch them," he said.

"I'll watch them meself," Nigel offered.

"No, I'll need you with me," Cleotis said as he smiled at his new six-foot-two best friend.

46.

By the time Peter reached the edge of town, there were several trucks in the convoy, all filled with good ol' boys from nearby farms, little towns, and even from the local First Nations band. They all had the same look on their faces as they gave each other a nod. They knew what had to be done; they were all "loaded for bear," as they say. The problem was there was no bear to hunt. They were going to hunt an animal far more dangerous.

The men said little to each other as they got out of their trucks with their guns and started to walk down Main Street. In the distance was the sound of automatic gunfire. Peter looked over his shoulder to see his friends, neighbors, and fellow farmers with the guns the government hadn't found. Peter thought it was ironic that some of the men who stood alongside him were the same men who were in favor of registering long arms. Peter, being the man that he was, didn't believe in rubbing it in their faces. He just gave them an I-told-you-so grin and walked alongside them.

Peter, like most people in town, liked to fish and hunt. They hadn't been on a hunt for a while as all of the guns were supposed to have been confiscated. This was going to be like old times. But this time they were not hunting deer, elk, or bear. They were hunting terrorists.

The group of men and women reached the corner of Main Street and Third Avenue. Some of them were on the north side of the street, and some were on the south. All of them were looking at the carnage and dead bodies belonging to people who had been fleeing the terrorists. It was hard to look at. What was even harder to look at was the terrorists backtracking up the streets with their AK-47s over their shoulders, laughing and mocking the dead people.

"Where's your Jesus now, lady?" one terrorist screamed as he spat at the corpse of a dead woman with a cross around her neck. It all happened like it was in slow motion. Peter never had a bad word to say about anyone. He never hurt a fly, yet he felt himself slide the bolt forward in his .308 and looked across the street at the same time. His fellow townspeople did the same. At least ten men and a few women fanned out in the street and pointed their guns at the enemy. The terrorists stood and stared in disbelief. Peter was going to give them a chance to surrender. Paul Friesen—the town's preacher, pacifist, and lover of all things—raised his handgun and shot the leader in the center of his forehead. The twenty-two-year-old neophyte terrorist fell where he stood, two feet from Paul Friesen's dead wife.

The other terrorists were caught off guard and tried to raise their guns. It looked like the gunfight at the OK Corral. The townspeople took aim and fired. It would be a while before the ringing in Peter's ears went away. Needless to say, the men and women from a small town in Alberta showed these imported terrorists that "gun control" is a good thing. They made each shot count.

47.

Basim received his instructions from the leader. He pretended to be happy and enthusiastic about his assignment. He wasn't. Deep down he loved America, and he had gotten used to living in a safe country and breathing fresh air. He was assigned two other team members. He met them a few times at meetings or at the mosque. He didn't like them, and he was glad he wasn't allowed to associate with them on a regular basis. That would have been against the rules. The leader didn't want them to become too close with people. *They could be planted spies keeping an eye on me,* Basim thought to himself.

The team met as planned and loaded their truck with the supplies that had been brought in for the project. Basim also kept a loaded .45 under his jacket for protection. While he hated what America was doing to his homeland, he couldn't blame the people. Killing civilians wasn't a good idea. Killing innocent people was a coward's way, not a soldier's way.

Ghazi, on the other hand, was a good example of what years of being taught hate could do to one's mind. He couldn't wait to push the switch. The look in his eyes was the look of a crazed man. He seemed almost aroused.

"We are really going to pull this off, my brother," Ghazi said with much excitement in his voice. Basim tried not to engage in conversation because he was afraid he might say something wrong. Hassan remained silent as he sat in the back of the truck, smoking his American cigarette.

Ghazi was annoyed that Basim wasn't enthusiastic and that he didn't respond. "Why are you so quiet? You should be rejoicing," Ghazi said, looking at Basim as they drove to their destination.

"I have a lot on my mind; I don't want to get distracted," Basim said to deaf ears. Ghazi was irritated.

The team reached their destination on Perth Street on time. They parked the van at the end of the crescent. They were a few miles from the airport. At an elevation of over five thousand feet, this nuclear device would do much more damage—not just from the blast, but also from the radiation. This part of Colorado would be uninhabitable for many years to come.

As they stepped out of the truck to take their last breath of air, Ghazi again asked Basim, "What is wrong? Why are you acting so cowardly?"

"I'm just in silent prayer," Basim said, trying to avoid a confrontation. Ghazi enjoyed berating his team leader.

"You are going to push the button?" Ghazi asked with skepticism in his voice. Basim just walked away.

"I not only think you're scared, I think you're weak—too much living in America, too much living like an infidel," Ghazi said. Basim had to react; he couldn't let him talk to him like this. Without even thinking twice, Basim pulled his .45 out of his belt, turned around, pointed his gun at Ghazi's head, and pulled the trigger. The sound of the gunfire echoed in the peaceful crescent.

Basim thought of many things. He loved life and wanted to live. He didn't want to kill innocent people, and he didn't want to die. He wanted to one day have the chance to invite that nice girl who worked at the grocery store out on an American-style date. What was he to do? Could he stop it in time? He knew that the bombs not only had a trigger, but they also had a backup timer. In the event the team either had cold feet or were killed, the timer still could set off the explosives.

Basim looked at the house at the end of the crescent. A light turned on, and the face of a man appeared looking out at them. The sound of the gunshot must have awakened him. He was not going to let the bomb kill this innocent man. His mind was made up; he was going to stop it. As he turned to walk back toward the truck, he was met by Hassan with his loaded AK-47.

"Wait!" Basim said as he felt the sting of hot lead entering his body. Hassan, standing in front of the truck in silhouette, fired his AK-47 while he puffed on his cigarette.

Basim felt the life begin to leave his body. His legs gave way, and he fell to the ground. He lay on his back in a pool of his own warm blood. He looked back towards the house to now see the man in the background talking on the phone. In the window was the little figure of a child. The child had no idea what was happening on his street, the same street where he and his friends had played roller hockey the day before.

Hassan walked towards Basim, his gun still smoking. Basim mustered enough energy to pull his arm from underneath him with the .45. Basim could see Hassan's eyes open wide as he didn't expect this. Basim emptied the remainder of his clip into Hassan.

Basim needed to get up and stop the timer, but there was little energy left in his bullet-ridden body. He was becoming cold, and his mind was wandering. He remembered his childhood, playing back home in the desert heat, as he felt the warmth of his blood. *Must get up*, he kept thinking.

Basim managed to get up and walk over the body of Hassan, stumbling onto the front seat of the truck. The sound of sirens was filling the air. Basim reached in the truck to find the detonation device. It was under the seat. He pulled it out as the timer counted down—003, 002, 001. He said a silent prayer to Allah. In a microsecond before the explosion, Basim had an eternity of memories flash before his mind. He hoped that he would be forgiven and that the girl in the grocery store would survive.

48.

Sandra's thoughts were focused on getting to Zoë. She bolted out of her seat to follow William.

"Stay calm. We'll find her, and she'll be alright." William looked over to Nigel and Cleotis as Cleotis motioned him to the front of the plane where the stairs were. Just as the men went around the stairs, an Arab man got out of his seat and turned toward William. Cleotis pointed his gun to the man's head and cocked the hammer.

"I can help you get your daughter back," he said in slightly accented English. "Trust me—I'm not one of them. I'm with Interpol. I'm an American." He paused. "It's a long story. I speak the language, and I can help you get up the stairs where they are holding all of the hostages." He then extended his hand out to William. "My name is Haydar. My friends call me Harry."

The name Harry was about as America as you could get. William thought that perhaps that was a good sign. William was unsure of his new friend's motives, but it was worth a try. William looked over at Cleotis, who lowered his gun, checked Harry's ID, and then looked back at William, giving him a reassuring nod. They moved forward toward the stairs with a few passengers behind.

* * *

Hilary, meanwhile, was trying to keep the other hostages calm in the first class upper deck. She had heard the commotion from down the stairs and tried to cover it up by talking loudly to the passengers and crew. It was hard to do in such a cramped area. There were twenty-four seats in the upper deck and about fifty hostages there. The bodies of the flight crew had been placed in front of the stairs as a warning. The hostages couldn't help but see them.

Hilary was trying to figure out a way to get past the two rather chatty men who were endlessly talking and not paying too much attention to the goings-on downstairs. She knew there was an air marshal on board. She hoped that he had somehow taken action in the lower deck.

* * *

Cleotis, Nigel, William, and Harry crept to the bottom of the stairs. Harry was trying to listen to what they were saying. William asked him to translate.

"Well, they're talking about how easy it was to take over the plane and how it will be just as easy to take over America." Harry was having some problems hearing the terrorists as they were too far away.

"We'll assume that there are only four left—two in the upper deck and two in the flight deck. We need to keep one upstairs so we can get Harry to get them to open the flight deck door. Without that door open, we're all dead," Cleotis said as he was trying to get a look up the stairs.

Harry piped up and said, "Oh, we're in luck. One of them is going to the washroom. That only leaves one of them."

"Let's get up the stairs," Cleotis said to Harry. He added to William, "You better stay here. I'm sure we can take care of the last of them. I don't want you or any of the other passengers to get hurt."

William would have nothing to do with that, and neither would Sandra, who was right behind him with Shawn in tow.

"Our daughter is up there," William said. "Besides, once you get into the flight deck, who do you think is going to fly the plane?" That was a thought that had never entered Cleotis's mind.

"First things first," Cleotis said. "OK, stay at the top of the stairs and wait for me to give you the all-clear signal."

Like that's going to happen, William thought. He needed to get his daughter back, and he needed to get into the flight deck.

* * *

Hilary caught sight of Cleotis coming up the stairs and made her move. She walked among the hostages towards the terrorist. He immediately ordered her back. She pretended not to hear him and kept on attending to the hostages. This agitated the terrorist even more. Women were supposed to take orders from men and not disobey. He walked towards her. That was a big mistake. Hilary was well versed in martial arts after being raped years ago. *All of my training better pay off,* she thought as the terrorist reached out and grabbed her arm. In an instinctive move, she wrapped her arm under his and pulled him up, catching him off guard. With her other hand, she punched him in the throat. It took the wind out of him as he buckled to the floor. Cleotis, Nigel, Harry, William, and Sandra took their cue and ran up the stairs.

It was a good thing for the terrorist. Hilary now had him on the floor with her foot on his head. She was pulling his arm almost out of its socket. Cleotis, Nigel, and Harry quickly took control of the terrorist.

William felt like his heart stopped beating when he came to the top of the stairs and saw Marcel and his first officer lying on the floor, dead. Sandra walked right past them and went straight to the hostages.

She reached through them and pulled Zoë from her seat with tears rolling down both of their faces.

"What's happening, Mommy?" Zoë asked, crying.

"I'll explain it all to you when we get back to your brother." Sandra was relieved to see her freckle-faced redhead alive and well.

Cleotis and Harry moved to the front of the cabin as Nigel held the terrorist. Hilary put her finger to her lips and motioned the hostages to move down the stairs into the arms of their waiting loved ones. Shawn was glad to see Zoë.

"Great to see ya, sis!" Shawn said to his sister as she walked past. The upper deck was clear.

Cleotis motioned Nigel to remove the terrorist. He was dragged down the stairs by Nigel and a few of the other passengers.

* * *

At the bottom of the stairs, Nigel let go and walked behind the passengers, dragging the terrorist. "Time to join your mates, fucker," Nigel said as the passengers pulled the terrorist to the back of the plane. As he was being dragged down the aisle, he was kicked and spat on by passengers who wanted a piece of the evil that had tried to take over the plane. For Nigel it was like he was walking on the rugby field with the winning ball. It was all cheers and high-fives for the burly man.

* * *

Back in the first class upper deck, the terrorist who was in the lavatory was concerned about the noise and came out to investigate. He didn't expect to find a gun barrel stuck in his face or to be slammed into a bulkhead.

"What is this?" he asked Harry in Arabic, in a bit of shock.

"We took the plane back, asshole," Harry answered in his mother tongue.

"But why are you helping the infidels?" the very surprised terrorist asked.

"Because I'm one of them, and you are going to help us get into the cockpit," Harry said with years of built-up anger. Harry was often the target of anti-Arab comments and prejudice. He was looking at the source of his anger.

"You're not a Muslim; you're a victim of mind control. Your masters have told you about a twisted version of the Qur'an to justify their hatred of other people. That is not the message of Allah," Harry said as he looked into the young man's face.

"You're going to get us in the flight deck, or I will personally rip your head off; it's your choice. Either cooperate, or die right here!" All of his anger was boiling over. Harry was making an impression on this lost young man.

"But our mission is not complete," the terrorist said.

Harry took the young terrorist by the face and said in a quiet whisper, "Your mission is over." The terrorist looked around and then into Harry's eyes. He meant business.

"OK, OK, I'll get the door open, but you have to do the rest," the terrorist said.

"Ask him how many people are in the flight deck," Cleotis said, pushing the gun harder into the terrorist's head.

"How many are in there?" Harry asked in Arabic.

"Two," the terrorist said in English.

"Good, now tell them you need to get inside. No funny stuff, or I'm sure he'd like to put a bullet in your head," Harry said. The terrorist looked at the gun and then back at Harry. He reached over and knocked on the door. There was a pause.

"What is it?" was the annoyed reply.

"It's me; let me in, please."

* * *

The terrorists in the flight deck looked at each other with confusion. The plan was that once the door was shut, there was to be no one let in.

"We cannot open the door; you know that. Is there a problem?" the terrorist in the first officer's seat asked.

* * *

Back outside the door to the flight deck, Harry translated.

Cleotis nudged the gun under the terrorist's throat as Nigel made his return to the upper deck.

"All secure," Nigel reported.

The terrorist nodded his head and took a deep breath. "No problem, I just have something to show you that is important." He was sweating bullets.

"What is it?" he was asked by one of the terrorists on the other side of the door. He seemed annoyed.

"Tell him one of the passengers is rich and there are a few million dollars of diamonds in the cargo hold. Tell him the passenger wants to buy his freedom. Tell him you want to show him some of the diamonds." Harry was fast on his feet. He then told William and Cleotis what he had just told the terrorist.

The terrorist repeated what he was told to say to his comrades in the flight deck. There was a three-second pause, and then the lock on the door clicked open. Nigel took the cue and pulled the door wide open. The terrorist in the flight deck had armed himself with an ax, and he swung it at Nigel's head. He missed him and embedded it in the hinge of the door. Nigel reached out for the terrorist and pulled him out of the flight deck by the scruff of the neck.

His fellow terrorist sitting in the captain's seat hadn't expected this to happen. He knew it was over, and in a desperate act, he took a bottle of water that he had been drinking from and started to pour it all over the controls. At the same time, he pushed the controls of the 747 forward, putting it into a dive.

49.

For each of the missions, targets had been chosen for their strategic and symbolic effect. Monuments of America were also chosen for their symbolic significance. Other targets that were chosen would ensure the collapse of infrastructure, thus causing the collapse of the American economy.

Since 9/11, there had been an active plan to strike at the heart of Hollywood. Some of Rafi's strike force would place their bombs in downtown Los Angeles. The others would place bombs up high in the mountains. One target was on Mount Lee in Griffith Park, the location of the famous Hollywood sign. Rafi's early morning drive to his target was without any incident. He parked the van full of explosives on the road as close to the sign as he could. Not only would his bomb take out the sign as a symbolic target, it would also take out a large communications array just behind the sign.

Rafi emerged from his truck in the early hours on this glorious day. He pulled out his radio and looked at his watch. The attacks all over North America would soon be well underway.

Rafi looked to the other member of his team and reminded him to keep his eye out for security or the police. His time in America was only a few months before this assignment, so he was a little nervous about law enforcement. Once Rafi arrived from the United Kingdom, he had worked nonstop, planning and setting up a strike that would change Hollywood and LA forever.

As Rafi was checking the location of the other teams, he received a call over the radio. "There is someone approaching in a police car!" the caller said with a bit of panic in his voice.

"Don't worry; let them come," Rafi said, putting the radio back in his jacket.

* * *

Officer Ken Wilson started his shift as usual—early and cranky. Without his morning cup of coffee, he was like a lion in a cage. He was about to enjoy his morning cup of joe when he received a call about a suspicious van parked where it wasn't supposed to be.

The police officer pulled up to see a van with media markings all over it and one man standing close by. Officer Wilson noted the Arabic man as he typed the license plate number in his mobile data terminal.

The MDT chimed back, saying, "Negative. All clear." Officer Wilson got out of the car and had started to walk toward the man when he noticed another man emerge from the side of the van. Wilson instinctively had his hand on the butt of his gun as he always did when he was dealing with an unknown situation.

"Good morning, gentlemen," he said, keeping his distance.

"Good morning," Rafi replied, trying to hide his British accent. The officer looked at the van that appeared to be a media van with its logo and satellite dish on the roof.

"Are you aware that this is a no stopping zone?" he asked as he continued to look around the area for anything suspicious.

"Yes," Rafi replied, "we are just about to take a few pictures for a story we are covering. When we are done, we will be on our way." He tried to imitate the voice of the anchorman of the late night news to conceal his accent. He didn't want to tip off the officer that he was a foreigner because his papers were not in order.

Some cops would have accepted that and turned a blind eye—too much paperwork if they found something. Not

Officer Wilson. In all his years of service, his gut had never let him down. His gut was telling him something was wrong with these guys. Officer Wilson needed to be sure he was right. He didn't know what it was about these guys that stuck in his gut, but he needed to find out. He knew they weren't gang members, but they weren't angels either. He could feel it.

Officer Wilson wanted to live in a safe city. The streets were tough in LA, and he didn't enjoy telling mothers that their sons had been killed by senseless violence. That part of his job he would never get used to.

It pained Officer Wilson when he noticed the other man beside the truck was Arabic as well. *Race doesn't matter,* he told himself over and over when seeing a group of youths hanging out. Race shouldn't matter here, either. The fact that the other man was Arabic normally wouldn't be a sign of any problems. That was before 9/11. This morning, however, during roll call, the captain mentioned to keep an eye out for suspicious activity as they were tipped off by the FBI of a possible attack in the LA area.

Officer Wilson knew he didn't have probable cause to search the van. He also knew that if he found something in the van, a high-priced lawyer could get it tossed out in court.

"If you don't mind, I'd like to take a quick look in the back of your van. It's just routine," he said, trying to make his investigation sound innocuous.

Rafi had been a soldier for many years. He started to go into offensive mode. There was no video equipment in the van as it had all been removed to make room for a bomb. Rafi had tried to avoid this as much as possible.

"We will leave, then," he said, sounding frustrated. However, in his frustration, his American accent sounded rather British.

Officer Wilson caught on to his mistake. "It will only take a second," he said, trying to think of how he could call for backup without spooking his suspects. He wanted to see what they were hiding.

"We'll just leave," Rafi said again as he and the other member of the team got back into the van.

"Hold it right there!" Officer Wilson said as he pulled out his gun and radioed for backup. He pointed the gun right at Rafi's head. Rafi had had a gun pointed at his head more times than he could count. If this was meant to scare him, it didn't. He just turned the key, smiled, and drove away. Rafi loved America; he knew that a cop could not just shoot a person for any reason. In the Middle East, his van would be full of bullets by now, but not in America.

Officer Wilson's heart was beating fast. He made his way back to his car, calling in the details as he ran. This was not what Officer Wilson had in mind when he received a call about a suspicious van. His first thought had been of teenage kids doing it under the Hollywood sign. It wouldn't be the first time he had caught some kids buck naked there. He never thought in his entire career he would come across terrorists, if that's what they were.

* * *

They started to race away down the winding roads in Griffith Park. "Why are we running away?" Umar asked. "Why don't we just shoot him? Why don't we just set off the bomb?" he asked with surprise in his voice.

"It's too early. We need to hear from our other team that all is ready. This is not like Afghanistan where you shoot first and ask questions later," Rafi explained as he was trying to keep his van on the road.

All his short life, Umar never ran from anything. This boy-soldier of twenty-two years was not about to run away from one cop. He unbuckled his seatbelt and cocked his AK-47.

"What are you doing?" Rafi asked.

"I'm going to show that infidel he messed with the wrong person."

Rafi didn't reply as he was concentrating on driving the van down the winding road.

* * *

Officer Wilson was right on the tail of the van, calling in his position.

"I'm on Mount Lee Drive, and I'm heading toward Mulholland Highway. We aren't going too fast because of the roads, but he won't stop."

Officer Wilson was about to give the description of the driver and the passenger when the back door was flung open. He had never dreamed he would see what was in front of him. It was like slow motion as the door swung open and out came the barrel of a gun. As the door opened up wide, a man emerged holding the gun with one hand and extending it in the direction of Officer Wilson. He recognized the automatic weapon as an AK-47. He then realized that it was about to fire on his squad car. In a move that was instinctive, Officer Wilson slammed on the brakes at the same time bullets peppered his police car. Officer Wilson had his thumb on the microphone button as bullets ripped his car apart. Police all over the county who thought they had a simple chase now realized that this was more, much more, as they heard the gunfire at Officer Wilson's car.

"*Get me some help up here, right now!*" he yelled into the microphone. Officer Wilson's police car was sideways at a dead stop with the engine still running. *You dickheads think you're just going to come to my country and start a war? You better think twice,* he thought to himself as he slammed on the gas and headed toward the escaping van.

* * *

"Ha, ha, I shot that pig up good!" Umar yelled as he waved his gun in the air.

There was quite a distance between the van and the pursuing police car. Because of the winding roads, Rafi could not gain much speed, and the police car was getting closer. "Come on, a little closer…" Umar was waiting for the right time to unleash another round of lead.

"Just a little more." Umar wasn't a patient person, so he didn't wait for the police car to get into optimum position. He reached out of the van and opened fire with a new barrage of bullets. It was bad timing as Rafi was trying to make a steep turn when Umar lost his grip and fell out of the van, still firing his gun.

* * *

Officer Wilson aimed his car to make sure the man firing a gun at him wouldn't be able to get up and shoot more bullets. He didn't realize how fast he was going and ran right over the man. He looked in his rearview mirror to make sure the man was not about to get away. He mumbled sarcastically, "Next time, put your seatbelt on."

* * *

Rafi was now headed towards a straight highway, and he put the pedal to the floor and drove as fast as he could. He noticed a string of police cars at the end of the street waiting for him. The mission was a loss, and he was unsuccessful. He needed to at least set off the bomb. It may not take out the intended target, but it would kill infidels. He reached down to grab the trigger of his bomb and was not paying attention as he reached the highway on-ramp. The van was side-swiped by a semitrailer doing about eighty miles per hour. There were pieces of broken truck and explosives all over the highway.

Once all the dust settled, Rafi was lying on the ground, near death. *These infidels have so much luck, saved by the police that they all hate,* he thought as he started to slip into unconsciousness.

* * *

All traffic on the highway stopped as Officer Wilson drove up in his bullet-ridden car. He looked over the carnage and realized he had just stopped an attack on his home turf.

But is it over? he wondered as he called his wife to tell her to keep the kids home from school. He also thought maybe it was time he told her how much he loved her and how valuable she was and how life was so precious. *The Hollywood sign is safe—at least for now,* he thought.

* * *

From the time the first attack started in New York until it stopped in California, the same scene played out all over. Terrorists were going to bring down the biggest superpower one airport, train station, gas line, power grid, and water supply at a time.

In some cities the terrorists used conventional bombs, but in some selected cities the terrorists used dirty nukes. In a few cities they even used smuggled-in nuclear weapons. At the Sears Tower, they planned to detonate a nuclear weapon on top at an elevation of seventeen hundred feet; there would be little left of Chicago. Dams were also a target for the terrorists. The floods and the lack of water afterward to fight fires would ensure the destruction was widespread. This was not going to be just an average day in the big city; this was going to be all-out war.

The leaders of this Armageddon on America anticipated that their attack would be enough to take down the Great Satan. Were they effective enough? Only time would tell.

50.

The last of the passengers were out of the terminal. Randy walked down the hall, looking around. He had never experienced this before. In all of his years, he'd never seen an airport empty and quiet like this. His radio was busy with the calls from the security team checking in and letting Mike know what doors were secured and what still needed to be done.

Here he was in a situation that could get worse. Closing down and securing the grounds was one way he could ensure that the people who were left in the airport and those who were arriving would be safe.

Randy grabbed the microphone and called Mike in the command center.

"Everything OK up there?" Randy asked, wanting to make sure all bases were covered.

* * *

"So far so good," Mike replied as he was checking the latest information on securing the grounds. He looked over to Tim and asked, "How are the ground searches going?"

"Slow, but we'll have it all wrapped up in about an hour," he reported.

Mike was making sure they covered every angle. Nothing was going to be unchecked, and no stone was going to be left unturned. He had more men showing up for duty than was expected. He was proud that the men and women were so dedicated that they would show up even on their day off.

"Good to see you, Donna. Are the dogs ready to go?"

"You bet," Donna answered. "They're excited about going out and doing lots of sniffing," she added.

"I'll be about five minutes, and then we can go check the grounds," Mike said, knowing he had to make sure that the perimeter was secured.

* * *

Randy was checking the security doors to make sure that the sections that were not going to be watched were locked down so they could not be accessed.

He was pleased with the progress. All of the passengers who had been in the airport were gone. All they had to do now was prepare for the thousands of diverted passengers who would call Winnipeg home for a few days.

He headed to the command center to touch base with Mike one more time before all of their unexpected guests arrived. He was in better shape than he thought he was as all of this running around wasn't killing him. He reached the command center and used his access card to enter the room. He walked into the nerve center, the eyes and ears of the airport operation.

"Mike," Randy called.

Mike was on the phone and nodded in Randy's direction. Randy walked over to his desk as Mike hung up the phone.

"Any news about two-niner-one-five?" Randy asked.

"Well, they're scrambling CF-18s to intercept and shoot it down if they confirm it's hijacked," Mike said, not sounding too pleased at the outcome of shooting down a plane full of passengers.

"What's your next move?" Randy asked.

"We've secured the interior, all airplanes that were here are now parked wherever there was space to make room for more showing up, and we're getting ready to double-check the grounds," Mike said as he was attaching the last bit of his equipment for the outdoor search.

"You're doing it yourself?" Randy asked, a little surprised. "Don't you have some junior officer who can do that for you?

"I have a good knowledge of the grounds, and I can handle the dogs well. If there's something to find, I'll find it," Mike said, and he smiled while putting on his gloves and reaching for his helmet.

"Good luck. I'll catch you later, and keep in touch," Randy said as he walked out of the command center, feeling good that Mike would make the grounds secure.

51.

Cleotis put the gun to the back of the terrorist's head, but then William stopped him. "*Stop!*" William yelled. "If the bullet goes through his head, it could damage some of the instruments or a window and cause explosive decompression."

Cleotis smashed the butt of the gun into the terrorist's head instead. That knocked him out cold. Nigel stepped in and pulled him out of the captain's seat as William reached for the controls. Alarms were going off like crazy, and circuit breakers were snapping as the water caused electrical shorts; the plane was dropping like a rock. William had to pull back on the yoke to slow them down before the plane fell apart.

"*Pull up! Pull up!*" Cleotis yelled over the noise of alarms in the flight deck and the distant sound of the passengers screaming.

The 747's warning system was chiming, "Shrink rate; pull up. Shrink rate; pull up." William had to slow down the rate of descent.

"I can't pull up too fast, or it will take the wings off," William yelled through the noise. He gently pulled back on the yoke to ease the 747 out of its dive. He looked at the large displays that showed the flight information. All six of the computer flight displays were dead. He looked over to the standby analog airspeed indicator.

"We're at 420 knots…400 knots…still too fast," William said as he read the instruments. They were at twenty-eight thousand feet and descending. The 747 was shaking violently; William was reading off the airspeed as the 747 started to level off. "Now we're at 370 knots...350 knots..." William yelled. Once the speed indicator dropped below 330 knots the overspeed alarm stopped chiming. While it seemed smooth enough, the 747 was not designed to exceed 350 knots. The stress on the airframe went way beyond design parameters.

* * *

Down in the passenger area, all passengers without a seatbelt on found themselves flying out of their seats. Anything that wasn't secure was flying around the cabin. Hilary was trying to hold on to a seat as she helplessly watched passengers and loose items flying about.

"Hold on tight!" she shouted above the screams of the passengers. The 747 was in a dive, and Hilary knew it couldn't take much more before it was over. She looked around at the passengers, who were staring back at her looking for reassurance.

* * *

William pulled the yoke backward and centered the airplane on the artificial horizon gauge to level off the 747. He managed to level off just under twenty-six thousand feet and a little under 330 knots.

He held the yoke tightly as he looked again at the standby artificial horizon to make sure he was straight and level. Once he confirmed that he was, he looked hopefully at the computer screens to see if they had come back to life. All six of the computer flight displays were still dead.

"This is not good. *This is not good!*" William said. This was the understatement of the year. While the 747-400 had a computerized flight deck, it also had analog backup gauges in the event of display failure. And though William was used to using analog gauges in his Baron, he was not used to using them in an airplane this size.

"We need to get these displays back online," William said, but he was not sure how to do it. William looked around the flight deck and thought that the water on the controls may have tripped the circuit breakers.

"We need to clean this water up and find the circuit breakers and reset them." He added, "Get Hilary to get me some towels or something so I can get this cleaned up quickly. I need the autopilot on." William took a small hand towel and started to wipe up the water on the controls.

* * *

As soon as the airplane leveled off, Hilary was on her feet and attending to the injured passengers. "Everyone stay in your seat and put on your seatbelt, please!" she said, observing the state of the passengers and the mess in the cabin. There was stuff all over the place. *This is a hell of a mess,* she thought. She called one of the flight attendants. "Melissa, look at the manifest and see if you can find a doctor on board to help with the injured passengers." The smell of vomit soon filled the air. "When you get a chance, open up as many air vents as you can; we need some fresh air in here, too."

Hilary was walking by one of lavatories when the door opened and a rather ill passenger fell out into her arms. As she held the passenger up, she looked over his shoulder and noticed something odd discarded in the corner of the lavatory.

* * *

In the flight deck, Cleotis searched for blown circuit breakers. "Here are some breakers; I'll reset them." He carefully reset the circuit breakers. He reset a switch and looked to see if the CRT would come back to life. *Click.* Nothing. *Click.* Nothing. Cleotis looked at the circuit breaker panel and noticed that he was running out of tripped breakers. *Click.* The computer displays came to life. There was a sigh of relief from Cleotis. William had a big smile on his face as the computer screens came back to life.

"Now that we've got that going, we need to get the autopilot engaged and keep her straight and level." William was trying to stay calm. He reset the altitude to twenty-five thousand feet to comply with an easterly path, and he set the speed down to three hundred knots.

"Here goes," he said as he hit the autopilot switch; nothing happened. William hit the button again; still nothing.

Cleotis, not sure what to make of it, asked, "Did it work?"

"No, it won't engage. You need to find the circuit breaker and reset the switch," he told Cleotis as he looked around the flight deck. William also was trying to keep her straight and level as best he could.

"There aren't too many breakers left," Cleotis said as he found a few circuit breakers that were still tripped. Cleotis reset each breaker, and William tried to engage the autopilot.

"Did it work?" Cleotis asked William. There was a pause.

The 747 started to slow down and level out all by itself. William and Cleotis let out a sigh of relief. "That's your answer!" William said to Cleotis as he gave him a thumbs-up.

"It's working," Cleotis said, still trying to calm down. Now that he'd confirmed that the autopilot had taken control of the overstressed 747, William slowly took his hands off the yoke. What to do now was William's first concern. So many things had happened so fast that he wasn't thinking clearly. He wasn't focused.

Years ago William had started his fledgling business, and it was a constant, nonstop barrage on the brain. He was used to thinking under pressure and getting the job done on time and on budget. This was far worse than anything he had ever experienced.

He needed to slow down his thinking and concentrate on getting this job done, getting this bird safely on the ground.

"We still need more towels to dry off the controls," William said to Cleotis.

Nigel returned to the flight deck after being tossed down the aisle. "What the fuck was that all about, man?" Nigel said in his Cockney accent.

"They tried to ditch the plane," Cleotis explained just as Hilary entered the flight deck holding two nun outfits.

"We may still have a problem," she said as she explained how the crew was killed and that she had found nun outfits in the lavatory. The impostors were still somewhere on the plane.

This was another problem that William didn't need right now. He looked over his shoulder at Nigel and noticed the broken cabin door. "I need the flight deck secured. Can you take care of that?"

Nigel looked at Cleotis and then back at William.

Cleotis said to Nigel, "We need to make sure that under no circumstances anyone comes up those stairs. We need to protect the flight deck."

Cleotis looked over at Hilary holding the nun costumes.

"If they take the plane back, we're finished." It wouldn't be easy to protect the flight deck. They couldn't lock the door because it was damaged and no longer securable.

"Nigel, where are the terrorists being held?" Cleotis asked.

Nigel put on a smile. "Those bastards are hogtied in the back of the plane, and they're being watched by a few of my mates. If they move the wrong way, they're goners," he said.

"Good, keep them under wraps; we'll need to talk to them soon," Cleotis said, planning the best way to interrogate his prisoners.

William looked over to Hilary and asked, "Can my wife and children sit up in the first class section so I can keep an eye on them?"

"Promise me you can land this plane, and they can sit anywhere they want," Hilary said with relief in her voice. "You can land this plane, right?" she whispered up close to William, trying to sound upbeat.

"Well, it's the same principle as the plane I fly, just a little bigger—well, a lot bigger," William said, with some reservation in his voice.

"I have faith in you; good luck getting us home," she said, patting William on the shoulder before she turned around to leave the flight deck.

Cleotis stopped her with a question. "What about these nuns? We need to find them before they get a second chance."

"That's going to be a problem; our fake nuns aren't like the rest of the terrorists," Hilary said.

"What do you mean?"

"They may be Caucasian." Hilary didn't want to alarm Cleotis any more than she had to.

"Go through your manifest and see if you can find out who these two individuals are. We need to find them soon," he said. "I'll head downstairs and talk to the others and see if they can shed any light on their identity." Cleotis had started to walk out of the flight deck when he noticed Harry heading his way.

"Is everything all right?" Harry asked in a cautious tone.

"It's too early to tell; we've bought some time. Right now we have a bigger problem that needs to be addressed. I'll need your help interrogating the prisoners in the back of the plane," Cleotis said.

Harry looked past Cleotis. William continued to clean up the water and scan the instruments.

"We need to interrogate the prisoners and then search for a potential threat. I need you to translate for me." Cleotis motioned to Nigel to stand guard at the door.

"Nobody gets through, got it?"

Nigel smiled; this was the stuff he lived for. "No one gets past me."

52.

After 9/11, plans were put into place in the event of another attack. If buildings like the FBI Building were attacked, all surviving personnel were to meet at a nondescript building, a safe house. One of these buildings was a warehouse in an industrial area. Davis pulled up, hoping there would be other survivors that he had not found in the rubble of the FBI building.

There was no time to wipe off the dust; there was no time for congratulations; this was not a good thing to be right about. Monroe and Davis just looked at each other, still in shock as they walked to the building. It was empty. The warehouse workers had gone home to their loved ones. Davis tried to call his wife, but as he expected, the phone line was dead.

"We have a lot of work to do," Monroe said.

"You have no idea how right you are," Davis said as they opened the door with their special key.

Monroe walked over to a steel door hidden behind a skid of computer cases. This was the main entrance that went down a set of stairs to the control room. Monroe opened the door and then flipped the large power switch to activate the lights and equipment. The sound of the switch echoed in the room. As the equipment came alive, Monroe and Davis made their way to their stations as the giant computer screens came to life. It took a few minutes for all of the equipment to power up and come online. Davis noticed a few more technicians and agents showing up and heading to their stations and activating their computers.

"The Internet was invented to keep communications alive in the event of a nuclear disaster; let's see if we're still able to talk to other cities." Davis sounded optimistic.

The map of North America was front and center in the room. Davis scanned the map to see what stations were online and what stations were down. Red dots on the screen meant communications were lost. Green lights meant that there was a solid signal, and the yellow dots meant that communications were intermittent.

"Lots of red dots," Monroe mused as he was setting up the communications links.

Davis was multitasking, trying to establish the location of Air Force One and trying to check the status of NORAD. "Looks like Air Force One is in the air; there are many commercial and military planes in the sky, too," Davis said as he typed in search requests from his computer.

"I'll try to get you a list of the cities hit and the status of communications." Monroe was trying to quantify the damage as fast as he could.

"Can you bring up a live satellite picture?" Davis asked. Monroe complied, and the picture was on a smaller screen off to the left.

"Put it on the big screen," Davis said, sitting back in his chair. On the big screen for the first time was a live picture from their secure surveillance satellite. The room went silent as Davis, Monroe, and the a few other people in the room stopped typing to look at the screen. The picture was of North America from two thousand miles in space. The satellite was in real time with a resolution that could read a license plate on a moving vehicle. In almost every major city in every state, there was smoke. In some states they could see fire on the ground. The quietness in the room ended as the door to their command center opened up to a new visitor.

ACT III

53.

"It's important you understand that the danger is not over and understand this is not what it may appear to be," Harry said in a calming tone.

Cleotis was trying to be polite to the man who had saved the day by getting them access into the flight deck. "Can you give me the abbreviated form so I can concentrate on finding our nuns?" Too much was happening for Cleotis to digest at once.

"I'll give it to you as simply as I can as this is a complex problem." Harry paused, took a deep breath, and started to give Cleotis a lesson in history as they walked to the back of the plane. It was hard for Cleotis to hear Harry above the cheers of the passengers. He listened as Harry told him about things like MK-ULTRA, mind control, and the New World Order. All the things that Harry told Cleotis sounded like nothing more than a conspiracy theory.

Cleotis said, "The bottom line is that this is not over until we find the other people still on the plane. I'm sure they'll make their move and try to complete their mission. I'm not sure what tactics you use at Interpol, but we need to get answers soon, before it's too late. Can you speak to the prisoners in their own language and see if you can reach them for more information?"

Harry smiled. "I'll do my best."

* * *

Now that the flight deck was secured and most of the water cleaned up, William knew he should call someone on the ground who could help. He grabbed the headphones so he could call the nearest ATC and tell them what happened. He dialed in the emergency frequency of 121.5 MHz and paused. He was trying to get his heart to stop beating through his chest and his breathing to slow down so he could talk clearly. He looked at the frequency readout to make sure he had it right. Thanks to his background as a pilot, William knew that the frequency 121.50 MHz, the equivalent to CB radio's channel 9, was the aviation emergency frequency.

William listened to the frequency and could hear a carrier wave like a microphone being stuck open. William took another look at the controls to make sure he had dialed in the right frequency. Again, all he could hear was a carrier wave.

He adjusted the microphone on the headset, took a deep breath, and keyed the mic. He thought if someone was close enough, they could hear him.

"Mayday, mayday, mayday, this is Western Global Airlines flight two-niner-one-five 747 heavy; we are declaring an emergency. Is there anyone on this frequency?" There was a long pause, and then he tried again. "This is Western Global Airlines flight two-niner-one-five heavy; we are declaring an emergency. Is there anyone on this frequency?" Still no answer. *This isn't good,* he thought to himself. He then switched the radio back to the frequency he was on before. He tried to call again. There was still no response.

William thought perhaps he could get someone's attention by changing the transponder's squawk frequency. The transponder sends a signal out with a code so the ATC can match the plane's squawk code with its radar signature. Some codes are used to give the ATC an idea of what is happening on the aircraft without even talking to the pilot. Code 7700 was one of them. When that code is put in and received by an ATC, alarms go off as that is the squawk code to signal an emergency. William placed the transponder to standby mode and entered the code 7700. He paused and then closed his eyes and his fist, hoping this would work. He extended his hand and turned the switch from standby to TA/RA. This turned on the transponder and the equipment that would let the pilot know if the plane was getting too close to other aircraft.

With the transponder squawking 7700 and William calling mayday on the radio, it was only a matter of time before he got someone's attention.

Years had gone by since William took his first solo flight in a Cessna 172. He remembered that day as clearly as he remembered the day of his wedding and the birth of his children. How the world had changed since those days of innocence. Long before 9/11, William remembered living in a city that was safe and clean—a city where his children could grow up safe and enjoy life to its fullest, a place where they did not have to be concerned about a dirty nuke killing them all. How sad it was that he now lived in a different world.

William's digression into the past was interrupted by the crackle of the radio and a response to his call. "Aircraft calling, say your call sign again?" There was hope; there was someone on the ground who could still help them.

"This is Western Global Airlines flight two-niner-one-five heavy. We are a 747, and we are declaring an emergency." Up to this point, William had no idea what was happening on the ground below him.

"You and everyone else," was the reply from the voice on the radio. "I'm not sure what your status is, but I'll let you know what's happening on the ground. According to the radio and TV, most major cities and airports are under attack. Montréal, Toronto, and everything east of that is under attack here in

Canada. In the States, it's worse." William was taken aback by the agitated sound of the controller. Emotion in their voices was not normal.

William took a long pause before he asked, "Where are you, and could we land there?" He asked this because he knew that a 747 couldn't just land anywhere.

"Sorry, but we're just a small airport, and there's no way we could take a 747. As the eastern airports are being targeted, your best bet would be an airport out west. The nearest airport that may still be operational that could handle a heavy jet would be Winnipeg. My radar is out, so I can't tell where you are. You should head west and try to intercept another ATC when you get closer to Winnipeg, over." The controller sounded overwhelmed.

William didn't know what to do. He had never expected anything like this. While he was familiar with IFR flying, he had always done so under the control of an ATC.

He keyed the mic once again. "Can you give me some frequencies for Winnipeg Centre, over?"

"Roger, please stand by," the controller said.

William was looking around for a pen to mark down some frequencies when he noticed Marcel's travel bag. "*Bon par, mon ami*," William whispered as he took out pen and paper to mark down the frequencies.

William looked over at Nigel as he stood watching at the door. Cleotis had gone below with Hilary to make sure everything was under control and to see if they could find the nun imposters. Nigel gave a wink and a smile and stood as big as the door itself. Nothing was going to get by him. William was a little more assured of his safety with Nigel there. He needed some help in the flight deck, so he picked up the intercom phone to call Hilary. At the same time, the controller gave William the frequency information.

It's time to turn this bird around, William thought to himself. He had done this on his simulator a hundred times, but was it going to be the same? Was the 747 going to cooperate? William was hoping that the ten-thousand-foot dive and the water hadn't caused any damage that would be a problem during the turn. It was the first of many turns and twists that William knew he would have to take the 747 through. She was the best plane ever built, and William was sure she could do it. It was time to head back to Winnipeg. "I hope you guys are still in one piece," he said.

William turned the heading indicator to read 270 degrees. He wanted the big bird to head west. William was surprised as she slowly banked left and started to make a 180-degree turn. *Maybe this is going to be OK,* he thought to himself.

William dialed in the frequency for Winnipeg Centre. He was thinking of his children. While he'd had a long life, it was too early for his children to die. They deserved to have a long and wonderful life. It hadn't been easy for him in the past. William had made many wrong choices in some aspects of his life. His friends, his jobs, his girlfriends—all had been a hindrance in his life. He remembered being told by his guidance counselor in school that he would never amount to anything more than a worker in a warehouse. But now here he was, the owner of a successful business. He had a wonderful wife and children, and he was a pilot. Who could ask for more? *I am blessed,* he thought. Could he be blessed enough to bring this heavy jet home? Only time would tell.

"Nigel, can you get my wife here for me, please?" William asked, doing what he did best—multitasking. Nigel waved Sandra to the flight deck. She was sitting in the first few rows of the upper deck. Sandra soon appeared with a child under each arm.

"You didn't need to bring them, too," William said, even though he was glad to see their smiling faces. "Can you get my flight bag, Sandra? I need my portable GPS." William needed to get a bearing on Winnipeg, and just to make sure he was on the right track, he would use his portable GPS.

"*Wow*, look at all of these controls, sis," Shawn said to Zoë as his eyes scanned the controls. Zoë wasn't interested and left the flight deck with her mother. She was still traumatized by what had happened earlier. William motioned Shawn closer to him so he could give him a hug. Shawn was more interested in looking at all of the instruments.

"What do all of these buttons do, Dad?" Shawn asked with wide-open eyes. William smiled and motioned to Shawn to sit in the first officer's seat.

"Sit there, son, and let me explain to you what they do," William said with pride in his voice. With all that was going on, Shawn was in learning mode. He couldn't learn enough about flying. He was the type of boy who would grow up to be a great pilot. William only hoped Shawn would have that chance.

Sandra reemerged in the flight deck and handed William the GPS with Zoë under her arm and tears in her eyes. She bent down on her knees and moved close to her husband. "What's going to happen, Wil?" Sandra asked with a broken voice, choking back the tears. "Are you going to be able to land? This plane is so big," she added. Sandra never doubted William's determination, but she also knew that a 747 was not like a Baron. In fact, you could fit several Baron 58s in the cargo hold of a 747. It was all so overwhelming for Sandra—almost losing her daughter and the thought of William trying to land this monster of a plane. This was too much information for Sandra to process.

William looked his loving wife in the eyes and asked her a question. "Have I ever let you down? Have I ever broken a promise?" He reached around and took Sandra's face in his hands and used his thumbs to wipe away her tears.

"I will use every fiber in my being to get his plane on the ground; I promise this to you." William looked his wife right in the eyes to reassure her.

Sandra stared back at him, looking past his face and into his soul. She trusted him. He had never let her down when it counted.

"Wil, do it for the children. Do it for all of the people on this plane, *please*," she said as a new stream of tears ran down her face. Sandra turned away and took the children with her, even though Shawn protested. William looked back to the controls of the plane. He would keep what was happening on the ground a secret from Sandra and the rest of the passengers for now.

54.

Randy hadn't gotten too far out of the command center when he was called to the tower. "Randy, can you come up here? We have a situation." Randy made double-time to the elevator that went to the tower. He motioned to two security guards who were close by.

"Make sure this is secure. Nobody, and I mean nobody, gets in here without proper clearance. Got it?" Randy looked the men in the eyes. He was more serious than normal.

The ride in the elevator gave Randy a quick second to close his eyes and reflect on his experience. He had to focus on securing this airport and keeping the people safe; that was his job. His family would be safe at their cottage in Lake of the Woods. Randy wasn't worried about them. He was worried about the passengers and the people in the airport, and he was saying a special prayer for the people in the 747 making its way to Halifax.

The elevator doors opened to the tower of Winnipeg International Airport. The tower was abuzz with activity. Ever since the attacks started, the controllers had been planning for a way to help the many airplanes now stranded in the air all over America and Canada.

Chief Controller Phil Wayant was thinking to himself, *Could it get any worse?* Yes, it could, and he knew it. It was his worst nightmare come true. Randy walked over to Phil, who was watching his controllers.

"What's the latest update in the skies?" he asked, hoping it was not as bad as he assumed.

"I'm not sure what you know, but a lot of major airports in America are under attack. We're just getting word that Halifax and Mirabel are under attack, too," Phil said, scanning the room full of controllers gathering data.

"What about Pearson? Is it still up and running?" Randy asked. Phil looked around the room for his second in command.

"I need an update on airport status," he asked.

"Updates on the screen now," was the reply.

Phil and Randy looked at the screen. "Looks like Pearson is off the grid, too." Phil looked over to Randy. "Maybe we're next," he whispered.

Without hesitation, Randy grabbed the two-way radio microphone and called Mike. "Base calling patrol, this is base calling patrol. Mike, can you give me an update on your search, over?"

Mike responded, "So far so good, over."

Randy looked out of the windows of the tower to see the activity around him. "Let's make it through this day," he said.

55.

Davis was reassured that there were more survivors than he had seen at the FBI Building when Grace walked in. He put a smile on his face when he saw his personal assistant coming down the stairs with a few more survivors.

"Grace," he said, trying to hide his obvious affection. She walked toward him, covered in dust and looking worried.

Although she was typically not an affectionate person, she reached over and gave Davis a big hug. "I'm glad you made it out, Burton," she said in a soft tone. She looked over at Monroe and smiled. "Good to see you too, Ethan."

Davis, with a sarcastic grin on his face, looked over at Monroe and said, "Ethan? I didn't know you had a first name."

Davis looked around the room at the handful of arrivals and smiled, knowing the more survivors the better. "We have a lot of work ahead of us, people. We need to be focused on what's happening now, and we need to protect the assets we have left." Davis was in command mode. "I need two teams, one that's damage assessment, and one that will determine how to protect what we have left. Monroe, I need you to contact each field office, either at their primary or secondary locations. Let's see how many personnel we have left."

Davis knew he had been vindicated in a big way. He also knew his adopted country had taken a major hit today, and he was worried about his home and family. He was trying not to get ahead of himself and realized it would all work out and he would find out in time.

"What would you like me to do?" Grace asked, waiting for instructions from her boss. Davis paused and looked her in the eyes. He reached up and removed some insulation from her hair. "Perhaps I should freshen up a bit first," she said.

"It's OK, Grace. You look fine, all things considered," he said with affection in his voice. "You can do one thing for me, though—find out what the military response is and what they have in the air so we can keep track of who's who," he added.

Davis looked away from Grace. He had feelings that were not professional. In this business, he knew he had to keep business and personal feelings separate. Davis stood up and walked to the front of the room.

"Give me the information as it comes in. I want to know if the attacks have stopped and what damage has been caused. I also want to keep track of all airplanes in the air, from Cessnas to A380s. Nothing moves unless we know about it. See if you can keep track of Air Force One as well." Davis paused and then added, "Let's do this by the book, people. I'm sure more lives are at stake if we don't get in front of this."

Davis walked away from the front of the room over to Monroe and asked him, "What's the status of the other field offices?"

"Not good," was the reply. Monroe added, "Looks like most of them were hit, and they haven't brought their safe locations online as of yet."

"Keep me updated," Davis said in a monotone sounding voice. "I need to get in touch with Air Force One. See if you can get them on the secure sat phone," Davis asked Monroe. It was getting hard to hear as Davis was now getting information from all over the room.

"All right, people, settle down. Give me all of the important information as it comes in. We can meet in the boardroom in thirty minutes to formulate a game plan," he added as he looked over to Grace, who was gathering the information Davis had asked for.

Davis needed a rest. He hadn't been sleeping the last few weeks. It was catching up to him. For years, Davis had been sleep deprived. Every night his nightmares would return, 9/11 all over again. Each time he couldn't stop it. He carried the weight of the world on his shoulders, and it had taken its toll.

"Monroe," Davis called, "you're in charge of the floor. I'll be in the office. See you in thirty," Davis said, looking like he was on the verge of collapse. Grace noticed and helped him walk to the office.

"We'll make it, Burton. Trust me—we'll survive," Grace said as she helped her boss walk to the office. Grace always had a way of putting on a good smile when it was needed, and today was the day they all needed it the most.

56.

It was time for William to make the call to see if he was in range of Winnipeg Centre. He first paused, said a silent prayer, and then listened to the frequency to see if there was any activity. Nothing but dead air filled his ears. He tried anyway.

"Winnipeg Centre, this is Western Global Airlines flight two-niner-one-five heavy. Do you read me?" There was no response. "Is there anyone on this frequency? This is Western Global Airlines flight two-niner-one-five 747 heavy, declaring an emergency. Can anybody hear me?" Still nothing. William was trying to stay calm as he programmed his GPS to fly to Winnipeg at the same time. He was hoping they were just out of range. He told himself that they were still there and were going to help him get back on the ground any way they could.

The portable GPS came to life and pointed the way to Winnipeg. William set the heading to 280 degrees, and the 747 turned to the right. William watched his plane on the GPS point to Winnipeg. *All will be well,* he thought to himself, *I just have to stay calm and keep on trying to call Winnipeg Centre every five minutes or so.*

William looked behind him and was glad to see Nigel filling up the doorway. He reached over to the intercom and looked at it carefully and pushed a button. He wanted to talk to Cleotis to see if they'd had any luck finding the nun impostors.

"Hello," said the voice on the other end. William could tell the person who answered the phone had fear in her voice.

"Can you do me a favor and ask Hilary to come to the flight deck?" William asked, trying to use his calming voice, the same voice he had used to rock his children to sleep when they were babies.

"I'll send her right up," was the response. This time the voice sounded reassured that all was well.

William tried to call Winnipeg Centre once again, but still there was no response. The feeling of being out of control was overwhelming to William. He needed to land this plane, but he knew it was not like his trusty Baron. A 747 can't just land anywhere. He was starting to feel the weight and responsibility for the passengers on this plane. It was more than the eight hundred tons the aircraft weighed.

He was snapped out of his thoughts when Hilary walked into the flight deck. She had been putting on her happy face for the passengers. Now she could tell it was time to do so for William. He smiled at her and said, "Thanks for the smile; I needed that." Hilary put her hand on his shoulder and gave it a squeeze. William needed her strength. Often in his life he looked to Sandra for her strength; she had never let him down. Hilary was a lot like Sandra. Hilary knelt on one knee, holding onto William's shoulder like a reassuring mother.

"Any news on the nuns?" William asked, trying not to show what effect Hilary's hand was having on him.

"So far, nothing—no little naked old ladies in their seats," Hilary said with a comedic tone.

"We'll have to keep an eye out for them; they may still pose a threat to us," William said.

"Cleotis has been up and down the aisles several times, talking to passengers and looking for them, but so far no luck," Hilary said with more of a professional tone. "What's new up here?" It was time for Hilary to ask the questions as she moved to the first officer's seat.

"Well," William said and then paused, not sure what to say. "We're heading back to Winnipeg, and I'm trying to contact someone on the ground to guide me there. So far, no luck; we're just out of range." William didn't want to give too many details as he was keeping secret what was going on twenty-six thousand feet below.

Hilary was puzzled. "Maybe the radio isn't working, because they're always in contact with someone," she said, looking at the controls.

"No, the radio is working. We're just out of range, that's all," William said, looking Hilary in the eyes and trying to give her that reassuring look.

Hilary looked back at him with a look that went past his eyes and deep into his soul. "Is there something you're not telling me?" she asked in a concerned voice. William was not a good liar; he looked away and said nothing. Now Hilary was really concerned.

"Look, Mr. Maddock, if you want me to trust you, you have to trust me. I can't trust someone who's not telling me the truth." She implored, "What's going on?"

William was always truthful with Sandra. He felt a real relationship had no secrets. He told the truth all of the time. He paused, looked Hilary in the eyes, and said, "OK, I'll tell you the truth, but you have to promise me to keep this to yourself. You can't tell anyone, especially my wife."

Hilary leaned in a little closer and looked him deep in the eyes and said, "I promise." William reached over and grabbed Hilary by the hands. They were warm and reassuring, just like Sandra's.

"What has happened to us is part of a bigger plan. As I'm sure you have heard from the passengers texting and making calls, there are many cities under attack. What you may not know is that there are many airports in the United States and Canada that are under attack as well." Hilary started to pull away. She didn't want to hear more. William held her tightly. He knew it was time to reassure her.

"As far as I know, there's no response from Winnipeg because we're out of range—that's it." He added, "But there's a possibility that they're under attack as well. I'll keep trying to call them. We have a ton of fuel, and I know western Canada like the back of my hand. Trust me when I say I will land this plane. I'm not sure when or where, but we will land," William said, also trying to reassure himself.

Hilary smiled at William and said, "Thanks for being honest. I needed to hear the truth, no matter how bad it may be."

They gave each other one last reassuring look. Hilary reached over and gave him a hug. William returned the hug, wanting to give Hilary some strength. She got out of the chair to leave the flight deck. As she passed Nigel, she said, "It's time for me to get back to work."

Nigel smiled and winked, oblivious to what had been said due to the noise of the flight deck.

57.

Agent Burton Davis sat at the desk as Grace closed the door behind her. Years of pressure were now gone. He had been right, and today is when. He had been vindicated, and all of the sleepless nights had put a heavy burden on his system. Davis put his head in his hands. "I just need five minutes of sleep," he mumbled to himself, but he knew that was impossible. The adrenaline was flowing, and he knew they would all be up for days trying to sort out this mess.

He felt guilty for thinking of sleeping. A good sleep would be the relief he needed from all of the stress. But now was not the time. In time, he could sleep. He wondered if there would be no more sleepless nights thinking about when, no more little heart attacks every time the phone rang. Would the nightmare be over, or was this just the beginning? It had happened as he said it would, and now he needed to help in stopping any further attacks and protecting what was left undamaged.

"We're about to have the meeting," Grace said, offering Davis the latest reports from his team.

He blinked his eyes a few times to get them to focus. His eyes scanned the reports as Grace made him a cup of coffee. "I don't know how fresh it is. It's from a survival pack," she said, trying to break the ice.

"Any coffee is good coffee, no matter how old or stale it is," Davis said, trying to get the fog out of his head as he scanned the documents. It was far worse than even Davis had expected.

"Let's get the team in here, and let's get underway," Davis said, sipping on his coffee.

Grace was happy to see that Davis was now alert and ready for what lay ahead. Grace called the team leaders into the room.

They came in the room, trying to have optimistic looks on their faces. Davis picked up on their desolation as they sat at their seats around the boardroom table. He had to reassure them there was hope. He had to be a leader when one was needed. He had to review the information at hand, and he would have to sell them on the idea that it wasn't as bad as it was.

Davis addressed the boardroom full of people. He noticed a few new faces in the room of people who had recently arrived to the safe location. "People, listen up. Let's have a pragmatic look at our situation. Let's keep emotions out of this. Monroe, give us any news you have," Davis said, looking over to Monroe and giving him the floor.

Monroe started by nervously flipping through his notes and looking at all of the eyes staring back at him. "As you can imagine, the situation is bad. Every state has been attacked in some way. Most major cities have been attacked, with a few exceptions. It looks like infrastructure was their main target. From what we're learning, gas, hydro, and water systems are offline or limited. Some nuclear power plants have been attacked, as well as a few hydroelectric dams. Broadcast stations are also down— ABC, CBS, NBC, FOX, and CNN are all off the air on a network basis. Some local affiliates are still up and are switched over to the emergency network. There are plenty of AM radio stations that are still on the air as well, operating on reserve power."

A technical analyst chimed in, trying to ease the tension. "CNN is off the air. Is that a bad thing?" Everyone in the room laughed. It was what they needed. Davis smiled too at the effectiveness of the joke.

"What about the Emergency Broadcast System?" Davis asked.

"So far, they haven't been activated; it's still too early," Monroe answered.

"Make sure they get up and running, and make sure we have a link to the AM stations that are up and running as the people will want to hear that there's something being done to help them," Davis said, giving the floor back to Monroe.

"Aviation was hit hard as most major airports are either destroyed or unusable because the navigation systems were destroyed. It looks like they don't want the planes in the air to be able to land anywhere. The airports they didn't hit directly may not be operational because their navigation systems as well as voice communication systems are down," Monroe said with a tone of futility in his voice.

"What about Canada? Can we divert those planes there like before?" Davis asked.

"Our neighbors to the north are in just as much trouble as we are. They've had their share of attacks, and airports all across Canada have either been attacked or are unusable for the same reasons as ours are," Monroe said.

"Get me an updated list of which airports are open, both here and in Canada. We'll need to use them," Davis said, making notes. "How many aircraft are in the air right now?" Davis asked, not really wanting to hear the answer.

"About five thousand," Monroe said, looking Davis in the eyes and contemplating the horror that must be unfolding in the minds of the crews and passengers of those flights.

There was a pause as the inevitable questions had to be asked. Monroe looked at Davis as he scanned all of the faces looking at him, and then he looked back at Monroe.

"Do we know at this point how many are hijacked ones?" Davis asked.

Monroe looked down at his notes. "So far we have reports of fifteen to twenty hijacked airliners." There was a gasp in the room.

"Any idea what their targets are?" Davis asked.

"We are speculating, the targets will be either buildings of symbolic value or infrastructure. So far one crashed into a dam and did little damage, and there's one unconfirmed report that an A-320 Airbus was hijacked and crashed into a nuclear power plant in Ohio."

"Are we in contact with the FAA?"

"No."

"Can we see their radar screens now?"

"That's up, but the link to the FAA is slow; it may not be in real time." He added, "They're hard to read; there is about five thousand flights on the screen. How many are legit and how many more will turn out to be hijacked is anyone's guess."

"Let's assume there are some that are and treat them one at a time. What about our military?"

"They're off the grid," Monroe replied.

"What do you mean, off the grid?" Davis asked with an annoyed tone in his voice.

"Once the shit hit the fan, they went into stealth mode. We can't contact them, and they're not keeping us in the loop. We know they're in the air and active on the ground, but we have no idea what they're up to."

"What else do you have to report?" Davis asked.

"We also have reports of civil unrest; looting is going on. The police aren't stopping any crime because they're too overwhelmed. We're trying to establish communications with the National Guard, but as you know, most of them are overseas. It looks like a few local civilian militias have called out the volunteers to help with local law enforcement."

"What about the border?" Davis asked.

"As of now, the border is unsecured. We have no idea what's going on down there, but it can't be good." Monroe was feeling the futility of the situation.

"What about Homeland Security?" Davis asked.

"We're in contact with other agencies and getting other bureaus online. That's looking good, but so far we haven't been able to contact DHS," Monroe added.

"We have our work cut out for us," Davis said. He looked around the room at all of the eyes looking back at him. "Step one, we need to get in contact with the White House. Step two, let's keep an eye on the planes have been hijacked and where their targets are. Step three, secure the infrastructure that we have left. Step four, let's figure out a way to get the airplanes in the air that haven't been hijacked on the ground." Davis paused and looked around the room. "If I don't get a chance to say this in the future, I want to say it now. It's good that you survived; let's take that as a sign that we're needed to get some work done. Let's get to work, people; don't let the other survivors down." The people in the room were full of energy. Davis pushed his chair back and stood up to dismiss them. "Make me proud, people."

Monroe stood up and looked up at Davis. "Make sure you contact the Canadians and see how many airports they have open and how many planes we can send their way. I'll bet that a lot of the pilots are instinctively heading that way already," Davis said.

"You got it, boss!" Monroe said as he walked out of the office, leaving Davis with Grace.

The door closed, and the room went back to silence. "How are we going to get those people down?" she asked.

"Now there's the question of the century," Davis replied, and he looked out the window at his team.

58.

Hilary always knew how to make the passengers happy. She was as professional as they came. She did her job with passion and dedication. The passengers had no idea how lucky they were that they had her on that flight. They all looked to her tall frame for support. Some of the passengers were crying and in shock, some were praying, and some were texting notes to loved ones below. The younger children were playing as they were oblivious to what was going on.

Sandra held Zoë tightly as she sat in the aisle seat, listening to who was coming up the stairs. Nigel was passing back and forth between the flight deck door and the top of the stairs, keeping guard.

He stopped by and knelt down. "You don't worry; they won't get past me. I've never lost a fight, and I'm not going to start now," he said.

Sandra believed him and felt safer knowing he was there. Zoë sat in the seat to her right, and Shawn was in the window seat keeping an eye out.

William was looking over the controls of the 747, trying to familiarize himself with the real buttons, dials, and gauges versus the ones on the simulator. *This is not happening,* he kept thinking to himself. How was he going to get this plane on the ground? This was the real thing in real size and not on some computer monitor. He knew one thing for sure: he had to remain calm. He wouldn't be much use if he was hyperventilating.

The autopilot was giving him cause for concern. It had disengaged three times, presumably because of the water. He could fly by hand, but these heavy birds were meant to fly by autopilot.

William opened up his flight bag and pulled out his *Canadian Flight Supplement* for all of the radio information between where they were and Winnipeg. He knew that his track would take him toward Winnipeg, but without ATC or VOR guidance, he would have to rely on his GPS. William wanted to have as many backup navigation systems as he could. When he flew his Baron, he used three navigation systems. There was his GPS—they were a must in the flight deck in any long flight. He always used the VOR radio beacons to confirm the readings from the GPS. William, who was a VFR pilot by heart, also always brought navigation maps along and would often follow his course along the maps using the coordinates of longitude and latitude from his GPS. Now in the 747 at twenty-six thousand feet, he couldn't be looking out the window for landmarks. If the GPS was out or not programmed correctly, tuning in the VOR beacons was a must.

William programmed in the VOR beacon for the Winnipeg International Airport. Soon he would be in range and would be able to pick it up as he had so many times flying to Winnipeg.

What was happening on the ground was not good. He wondered if he would have an airport to land at by the time he got there. All of the cities under attack, all the hijacked airplanes, all of the dead people. *This is way worse than 9/11,* William thought. He wondered what they were going to call this infamous day. He was in deep thought when all of a sudden the autopilot alarm went off and the plane started to descend.

59.

Mike Harper had worked in law enforcement in some way most of his life. His father had been the chief of police on his reserve for many years, and Mike had always wanted to be a cop just like his dad. Mike, however, took a different route as he went into the military to train in special ops.

He did his time in the military and considered his future with the local police department. He liked to look at things in the big picture. He decided to take law enforcement to the next level and become an airport police officer. Mike not only wanted to catch the bad guy, he wanted to catch the international bad guy.

He had started working at Winnipeg International Airport several years ago with the goal of one day being the head of airport police in a larger centre like Toronto or Chicago. He had trained for a lot of different scenarios, and looking for explosives was one of them.

Mike and his team of three and their German shepherd/ husky cross named Rusty were checking out the grounds when they received a call from a neighbor of the airport reporting a van parked in his yard that shouldn't be there. The van was parked northwest of the airport, just off Sturgeon Road, in a yard a few hundred meters northwest of runway three-one.

Mike and his team pulled up to the yard and noticed the van parked behind some bushes. "Control, can you get me a CPIC check on the following license plate," Mike said with the microphone close to his mouth and his eyes on the van. Just as he was about to give the plate number to the dispatcher, one of his team used a hand signal that told the rest of the team that he had an eye on someone in the van.

"Dispatch, stand by," Mike said as he tried to get closer to Roger, the member of the team who had spotted the van. "What do you have?" Mike whispered to him.

"It looks like one male slumped over in the passenger seat," he said, looking through his binoculars. Mike motioned to the other team members to get into position. He pointed to the dog handler to get the dog closer so she could sniff for explosives.

Mike and Roger kept their distance from the van as Larry walked Rusty over to it. The dog didn't let out a sound but pointed in as it was trained to do when there were explosives. Mike saw Rusty point and then motioned Larry to move away from the van.

Just as they were going to back up and call for the bomb squad, the man slumped over in the passenger seat sat up and looked out the window. "Help me!" he yelled.

Mike looked at Roger and paused for a second. The man couldn't have seen them, so he might be in some distress, or this might be a decoy to get them in closer before he set off the bomb. Larry was now away from the van, and Roger moved to a new position for a better shot.

"Person in the van, put your hands on top of the dash!" Mike said through a bullhorn. The man in the van complied immediately, placing his hands on the dash with his fingers wide open.

"Help me, please. I'm shot, and I'm bleeding. The bomb is disabled; please hurry before I die!" the man pleaded. All Mike heard was "bomb." He was starting to sweat, and the adrenaline was flowing. Mike motioned to Larry to open the door and pull the man out. Rusty would rip the man to shreds if he made the wrong move.

Larry had his left hand out toward the handle on the door as he kept the man in range of his MP5. The man didn't even see him coming. It was in one motion; the door in the van opened, the man was pulled to the ground, and Rusty grabbed his pant leg. The man was covered in blood.

"Stop the dog! I won't resist; stop the dog!" the man pleaded. Larry called Rusty off of the man once Larry made sure he was not a threat and didn't have a trigger or a gun. Mike and Roger came over with their MP5s aimed at the man lying on the ground.

"Don't shoot, don't shoot!" the man said with a thick Arabic accent. "I've disabled the bomb, and I killed the other men," he said, breathing heavily and holding his side.

Roger looked in the van and saw no movement. He pulled open the door to the back of the van to find two dead men and a very large box in the middle.

The man on the ground started to explain what had happened while Mike called in for an ambulance.

"We were supposed to detonate the bomb, but I couldn't do it. These people twist the Qur'an. They are full of hate; that is not the message of Allah."

Larry leaned over the man, who was dying right in front of him.

"Does the bomb have a backup? Can it go off by itself?" he asked, not caring about his pleas for medical attention at the moment.

"It has a manual trigger; that is destroyed. And then there is a timer; it's destroyed as well. It is harmless, I can assure you," he said, trying to regain some composure.

"The ambulance is on the way," Mike said as he walked over to the van and took a quick look inside.

"What kind of bomb is this, conventional or dirty nuke?" he asked.

The man took a few quick breaths and replied, "Just a conventional bomb, but it has enough C4 to take out the airport." The man started to weep. "I was forced into this by people who have kidnapped my family back home. They killed my brother and have my family hostage. They will die, but I will not kill innocent people. I will not do to innocent people what they will do to my family," he said with tears streaming down his face. Mike felt sorry for the man and asked for the ambulance to get there as soon as possible.

Mike looked up to the sky as a 737 flew overhead, landing on runway one-three. Mike thought, *It looks like we missed a bullet. At least we can land airplanes here that couldn't land at other airports.* Mike looked at the man, and their eyes met. Mike could see the sorrow in his eyes. Thanks to the compassion of this man, hundreds of people would be able to land safely. *Maybe there's hope for the world yet,* Mike thought as he reached out his hand and placed it on the man's shoulder. "The ambulance is almost here; just hang on."

60.

William felt his stomach sink as the plane started to descend, slowly at first, and then she took a steep dive. He also heard the screams of passengers in the cabin below. The circuit breaker for the autopilot controls had kicked out again, and the alarm rang in William's ears. Luckily William had fast reflexes, and he reached out and grabbed the yoke to keep the 747 from descending too fast. He pulled back on the yoke to slow the dive and level out, trying not to put too much stress on the airframe. Even in a panic, William managed to think about his childhood. All his life he had dreamed of flying the Boeing 747; now here he was with his hands on the controls of the greatest achievement in aviation history. His father, who never had much faith in William, would be proud. If only his father were here to see him now.

If the circumstances were different, he would have loved to fly her by stick, but with a plane full of passengers and possibly an overstressed airframe, he was going to let the autopilot fly her. If only he could get it to work properly.

William leveled off the aircraft with only a small increase in G forces. All was well as the 747 leveled back off. Nigel, who was still in the doorway, asked, "Problems, mate?"

"No, it's just the autopilot circuit breaker pops out once in a while because the console got wet and the water is shorting out the connections," William explained. "Can you do me a favor and reach over there and push that button on the panel, the one that's popped?"

Without hesitation, Nigel walked over to the panel, leaned down, pushed the button, and went back to the doorway. William reached over to the autopilot button on the console, paused, and pushed the button. The light on the panel lit up. William could feel the aircraft lift her nose up a bit to regain some lost altitude. William let loose his grip on the yoke and relaxed in the captain's seat.

* * *

In the deck below, there were some very nervous passengers. It's not often a person is faced with the possibility of death; it's not often a person has his life pass before his eyes. To say it was nerve-racking is an understatement. One of the passengers who was feeling the stress more than most was a passenger sitting in seat 28A. He was on a trip to England to visit friends and see the sights. As the plane took its last dive, he looked out the window for the hundredth time, concentrating on engine number two.

This passenger had a unique perspective as he was a structural engineer for a firm in Calgary. He noticed after the initial dive that engine number two looked like it was not in the position it was supposed to be. Being that he hadn't looked before the first dive, he didn't have anything to visually compare it to. But now with this second dive and the associated G forces, he could tell that the engine was not secure on the pylon, and he was concerned it was going to fall off. He didn't want to panic any other passengers, so he calmly pushed the attendant button and waited for a reply.

61.

Davis was pulling out all the resources he had at his disposal. They still hadn't been able to get a hold of Homeland Security to see what response they were planning. Davis hoped there were other survivors of higher rank than he had. He didn't want the survival of America on his shoulders. But until they found someone, he would take the responsibility.

"Monroe," Davis called, "give me an update."

"We've established contact with some states and confirmed that they called out the National Guard to patrol the streets to stop looting and any unrest," Monroe read from his damage assessment computer screen.

"Any nuclear or biological attacks?" Davis asked, hoping there were none.

Monroe paused and said, "Looks like at least three cities have been hit by dirty bombs, and two have been hit by full-blown nuclear weapons."

"What cities?"

"Denver, for sure. We're still trying to confirm LA and San Francisco. But we're waiting for confirmation; it's still too early."

"Biological?" Davis asked.

"That's too early to tell. I'm sure we'll know that in a few days," Monroe said, looking at a row of monitors.

Davis could imagine nuclear weapons being shipped in from one of the millions of containers that come into the country unchecked on a daily basis.

"We also have several reports of firefights going on along the southern border—militias protecting the border perhaps," Monroe speculated.

"Do we have the Emergency Broadcasting System up yet?" Davis asked as he scanned his computer screens, looking for information.

"We have the link here, and they're confirming the link in all states. It will be ready for a broadcast in about twenty minutes. Hopefully there are radio stations to broadcast the message and people to hear it," Monroe said with a pessimistic tone.

"Let's keep it positive, Ethan," Davis said with a grin as he seldom called Agent Monroe by his first name. Monroe just smiled and went back to work.

Davis walked back to the quiet office and sat back in the big, comfy leather chair. He opened the blind on the window and looked out at all of the dedicated people scurrying about getting their jobs done. These people were now on their own. There was no more America, they had no boss, and they would not receive a paycheck for who knows how long, if ever. Yet here they were, dedicated people doing what was right, not just doing it because it was their job. They were doing it because they wanted to save lives.

Davis typed on his keyboard and began to chew on a pencil. It was a nervous habit he'd had since he was a child back in the United Kingdom.

Davis thought about the message he was going to broadcast to the nation. There was a prepared message they were supposed to play. After listening to the prerecorded tape, Davis realized that this was not some lame high school fire drill. Davis was going to redo the script and re-tape the message himself. He would have Grace read it as she had a very reassuring voice.

It would be best if the president read it, if only they could get a hold of Air Force One.

Davis grew angry as the events that had happened that day could have been prevented if only people would not put politics before safety. Davis thought about what he was going to write. He was a big fan of *Monty Python*, and his first thoughts were thoughts of sarcasm.

"America, thanks to your apathy, your country has been destroyed." No, that would be too blunt. How about a shot at the FBI? "Ladies and gentlemen, the destruction of your nation is brought to you by the politically correct morons at the FBI and Homeland Security." Enough sarcasm. It wasn't their fault that they were sheep. Americans were a trusting, caring, compassionate people who trusted their government to keep them safe. Those attributes had been used against them. The enemy took the strength of a great people and made it into a weakness and used it against them. Davis thought, *Those people need my help. I'll keep my anger for the people in government who got them into this mess.* Davis had started to type on his keyboard when Monroe called him on the intercom.

"We have a link to the Emergency Broadcast System, but we're not sure how long it will last. We need to get a message out now while we can."

Davis paused and looked out at the people in the room once again. He was looking to them for strength. He needed inspiration, he needed to think, and he needed to pray. He hadn't done that in a long time. He had to say something positive.

He printed out his message and walked over to the studio designed for this purpose. He looked over at Grace, who was busy at her desk. He decided to give the message himself.

Davis sat in the chair and put on the headphones. He adjusted the microphone, took a deep breath, and clicked the "On the Air" button.

"Fellow Americans, this is Special Agent Burton Davis of the FBI. If you are hearing my voice, that means you have survived another attack on us, on our way of life. Please remain calm and be reassured—we may have been hit hard, but we have survived. Help will be on the way as soon as possible."

Davis paused and thought that if he were out there, he would want the truth and not some sugar-coated bullshit. He took a deep breath and continued. "As you can tell from my voice, my native country is the United Kingdom. I immigrated to America years ago just as many of you have. I came here because America was, as I was told, the land of opportunity. I also came here to help stop these types of events from happening. We failed to stop it, but that doesn't mean we're dead. What I have learned being here in America is that Americans don't give up. Here in America, there is no stopping even if you are up five runs in the ninth inning of the Word Series. Well, people, we're in the ninth inning, we have two out, and we may be down a few runs, but we're not out yet, and we have our best hitter coming to the plate. And that hitter is you, America. You are the best chance we have to defeat this enemy and win the most important World Series in your life—your freedom!"

On the streets, people all over America were looking for direction. They felt abandoned. By some instinct, they turned to AM radio stations as they had after earthquakes, tornados, hurricanes, and floods. AM radio was a format that had been left behind as FM and cable dominated the market. The source that was still on the air and the beacon of hope was AM radio. As the speech began, they all stopped what they were doing, sat close to the radio, and listened intently. It was a breath of fresh air. Now they had hope.

Monroe reached over and turned on the speakers in the room so everyone in the FBI's control room could hear. They stopped what they were doing and listened to Davis. He was saying what they all needed to hear.

Davis was getting excited as he looked out the window of the studio and saw all of the smiling faces looking back at him. He continued. "I'm going to be honest with you, America. You may be on your own for several days, maybe even weeks, as this is a bad attack. But we are America; we've been through a lot, and I know we can get thought this, too." Davis decided not to finish by saying, "God bless you, and God bless America," as would the president. He would leave that up to him. He then turned over the headphones to the coordination team that was going to broadcast the locations of safe harbor and information updates. They would be live 24/7 until further notice, or until the signal failed.

Davis had always been proud of being an American. He was proud that he could help the people of his adopted home. He walked out of the room to a round of applause. Davis wasn't used to this and smiled and waved his hand in the air for some quiet. The room went silent. "We have a job to finish, people. Let's get to it." He paused, and then he finished off by saying, "And people...thanks for being here."

Davis went back to his office with Grace on his heels. She closed the door behind her, reached out, grabbed Davis by the arm, and spun him around. This caught Davis by surprise. What was even more surprising was Grace pulling him closer for a hug. The hug lasted a few seconds, and then Grace pulled back only to reach up at Davis to pull his head down so she could give him the kiss she had always wanted to give him. Davis was surprised and tried to pull away, but Grace held tight. Davis relaxed and gave in for a long time; he wanted to hold Grace in his arms and kiss her deeply as well.

62.

Some passengers who were able to text or call loved ones on the ground had a bit of an idea what was going on. The information was sketchy with the service not being at its best. The messages helped people know they were alive, but the speculation just added to the fear. For those passengers who had no information, they looked to the tall flight attendant who was in charge.

As Hilary walked down the aisle, the passengers kept asking the same questions over and over again. She could see the fear in their eyes. Hilary decided to tell them something, a general announcement over the intercom about what had happened and that there was a pilot flying the aircraft back to Winnipeg. She knew she couldn't conceal the fate of the flight crew as many of the passengers who were held hostage in the upper decks had seen the bodies of the captain and the first officer. Hilary prided herself on her honesty; to her, omitting something was just like lying, so it was the whole truth and nothing but the truth. Well, almost all of it. She knew that there was some idea of what had gone on below because people were talking about the text messages and cell phone calls. She decided not to let them in on the fact that there may be no airports left to land at as she had promised William.

Hilary focused on getting the job done. She wasn't going to think about the fact that she could die today never having met her soul mate. She was a positive thinker, and she knew that one day she would meet the man of her dreams.

She was interrupted in her thoughts and rounds when the passenger in seat 28A grabbed her by the arm. She tried to remain calm and reached up to turn off the attendant button.

"How may I help you?" she asked.

The passenger pointed out the window and motioned for her to lean closer. Hilary was hesitant as she was still looking for her nun impostors. She leaned a little closer.

"I didn't want to alarm the other passengers," he whispered, "but it looks like that engine is about to fall off." He pointed out the window again.

In all her years of flying, she'd had hundreds of passengers point out windows in fear, alerting her to engine flaps and even wings that were about to fall off. One of the most common reasons why passengers pointed out the window was because they thought gas was leaking out of the tank and that the plane was going to explode. Passengers often confused condensation rolling off the wing for fuel.

Hilary, thinking the engine was fine, leaned over and looked out the window to humor the passenger and keep him calm. Her eyes froze and her heart skipped a beat as she looked out at engine number two. It *was* about to fall off. She leaned a little closer, trying to get a better look. After all that had happened today, she thought she was imagining things. She looked at engines number one and number two, back and forth, to compare the moorings. Sure enough, engine number two was ready to fall off.

She looked at the passenger, not knowing what to say. He smiled and said, "I'm an engineer. I sort of notice things like that." He paused. "The G forces from the first dive did a lot of damage to the airframe; they're not designed to take that kind of force. The second lesser dive made it worse. One more dive, and it'll be gone," he said as he looked back out the window.

Hilary patted him on the shoulder, said thank you, and headed up the stairs to the flight deck. She smiled at Nigel on the way, trying to cover up her fear, and made a beeline right to the lavatory. She closed and locked the door, sat down, and started to cry. *This is it,* she thought. *We're going to crash, and we're all going to die.*

I'm never going to meet anyone, and I'm going to die alone, she thought to herself, trying to choke back the tears.

I have to tell William. I have to do my job. This is not like me. Why am I doing this? I never lose control like this. She just couldn't sit there; she had to do something about it. She had to tell William.

After a few minutes of collecting her thoughts, she stood up and looked into the mirror. Her eyes were red, and her cheeks were covered in tears. She wiped them away as best as she could, and she unlocked the door to the lavatory. She walked into the flight deck and did something she thought she would never do; she sat in the first officer's seat and looked out the window, trying not to make eye contact with William. This took William by surprise.

"Hilary?" he said, with curiosity in his voice. She didn't respond. William said it a little louder. *Hilary's tall frame fits nicely in the first officer's seat,* William thought as he looked toward this amazing woman.

She was trying to avoid the inevitable. She raised her left hand and slowly traced the outside of the yoke. When she was done, she put her hands firmly on her lap and put her head down. She took a deep breath and turned to him, and their eyes met. Hilary looked away and looked at the panel instead. In the second that they made eye contact, William knew she was under a lot of stress.

"What's wrong?" he asked, knowing something must be very wrong if she was this distressed. Hilary slowly looked over to him and started to tell him the bad news. She didn't know how to break it to him gently.

"It appears that the plane was damaged in the initial dive. One of the engines, engine number two, is about to fall off, Wil," she said in a desperate voice as she choked back the tears.

This isn't good, he thought. He tried to look out the window to see for himself, but the wing was too far back. William knew that he could not leave the flight deck because of the erratic autopilot. If it disengaged while he was out, it would be all over. He would have to take her word for it.

"Are you sure?" he asked, knowing she was probably right.

"I wish I wasn't, Wil. I've seen this before going to Heathrow once in a 747 just like this one. The weather was bad, and the captain made a hard landing. One of the engines almost fell off on the runway. We all had a good look at it the next day once the weather was clear. Rivets missing—it was a mess. I know what an engine should and shouldn't look like," she said, sounding offended. "This one is about to fall off—trust me," she added, giving him the stare of confidence.

This was not what he wanted to hear. Engines falling off, terrorists still on the plane, half of North America in smoldering ash—this was too much.

"Hilary, Sandra has been my rock for many years. I have never depended on another person like I depend on her. In this situation, I need you to be my rock. I need you to be my eyes and ears on this plane," William said as he reached out to touch Hilary's hand. She tried to look him in the eyes without too much success.

"Look at me," William said. Hilary wasn't making eye contact. "Hilary, look at me, please." William was trying to reassure her. "I know this is a lot for the both of us to digest all at once, but I need you to be strong. I need the passengers to remain calm, and I need you to keep an eye out for any other potential problem." William reached out with his other hand and lifted Hilary's head with his finger under her chin. She put on a smile, choking back the tears.

"Stiff upper lip, eh?" William added, putting a grin on Hilary's face. She hadn't heard anyone say that with sincerity in years. Sure, some smartass passenger would say that, making fun of her British accent, but William said it like her father did when she was young and had fallen off her bike and scraped her knee. Even with a Canadian twist, it was good to hear.

The moment of serenity ended when the sound of the radio broke the silence. William turned his attention back to the plane.

"We must be in range for Winnipeg Centre. I'll give them a call and hope we can get this bird on the ground before the engine falls off. We may need to slowly shut that engine down to decrease the stress," William said.

William grabbed the microphone of the headset and pulled it closer to his mouth. This was just as much for Hilary as it was for him. He keyed the mic. "Winnipeg Centre, this is Western Global Airlines flight two-niner-one-five heavy. Do you copy?"

There is hope, William thought.

This put a smile on Hilary's face as she jumped out of the first officer's seat. "I'll head back to work, Wil. Thank you," she said as she was on her way.

William listened to the radio and all the chatter from Winnipeg Centre. It sounded like there were a lot of airplanes heading their way. He remembered how many planes had come to Canada on 9/11 and how busy the radio was back then. He tried to call them again.

"Winnipeg Centre, this is Western Global Airlines flight two-niner-one-five heavy. Do you copy?" William said it like a pro.

There was a short pause and then a reply. "Western Global Airlines flight two-niner-one-five heavy, we do copy you. Squawk ident," said the voice over the radio. William pushed the identification button on the transponder that would flash on the controller's screen so the controller could tell them apart. *This is great news,* William thought to himself. Then the controller replied. "Western Global Airlines flight two-niner-one-five heavy, we have you on radar contact. What is your status?" the controller asked.

William took a deep breath, keyed the mic, and began to tell the controller the story. He knew there were a lot of other aircraft on the frequency, so he kept it short.

"Winnipeg Centre, this is Western Global Airlines flight two-niner-one-five heavy. There's been an attempted hijacking on board; the flight crew is dead." William paused so the controller could absorb what he had just said, and then he continued. "We took back the plane from the hijackers, and we're currently heading your way, hoping to be able to land at your airport."

There was a long pause. Then the silence was broken by the controller's voice: "Western Global Airlines flight two-niner-one-five heavy, please stand by."

63.

Randy's cell phone and radio had been going nonstop ever since this nightmare began. Running up the stairs to the control tower, he had his phone to his ear and the radio microphone in the other hand. He knew it was going to be a long day. As he approached the top of the stairs, he could see controllers running around the room. When he reached the top, he called for Phil Wayant, the main controller.

"Phil, I have some good news!"

"Good news is what I need right now," he said, looking for some hope.

"It looks like we were a target, but one of the terrorists decided not to go along and stopped the bomb," Randy said with satisfaction that the airport should remain safe.

"So we're secure then?" Phil asked.

"Yes, we have a perimeter set up all around the airport. We've finished evacuating the complex and locking it down. We should be safe," Randy said with a voice of confidence. He added, "What's your operating status?" He was still trying to catch his breath.

"All navigation systems are up and operating, and communications are all functioning. We've received a phone call from the FAA; there are a lot of airplanes heading our way. All runaways are clear, and we're ready to receive any heading this way." Phil was normally a calm man, but Randy could see he was under a lot of pressure.

"You land 'em any way you can; I'll keep the airport running, and Mike will keep us secure," Randy stated as he walked back toward the stairs.

Phil was glad to hear some good news and thought it couldn't get any worse until a controller called him over to a console. "Phil, you're not going to believe this. I've just been in contact with Western Global Airlines flight two-niner-one-five that left here a few hours ago. She's been hijacked, and the flight crew has been killed." Phil didn't like the sound of this.

"If the plane has been hijacked, then who are you talking to?" he asked.

"One of the passengers."

"What's he doing in the flight deck?" Phil asked.

"Sounds like he's flying the plane."

"One of the passengers?" Phil couldn't believe his ears. It was 9/11 all over again. Not only were there hijacked airplanes crashing all over the place, but now they had one that was being flown by one of the passengers.

"Are you sure it's a passenger, or is it a terrorist?" Phil asked.

"I can't be sure as I just talked to him for a few seconds before I called you over."

"OK, let's talk to this guy and see if he's for real." Phil walked over to the console with the other controller and plugged in his headset and paused. All that had happened today and now this. He was expecting at least a hundred airplanes carrying passengers coming his way from the various parts of the United States. He needed to make as much room as he could at his airport to fit all of those airplanes and people. He didn't need to deal with some clown terrorist.

"Western Global Airlines two-niner-one-five heavy, this is Winnipeg Centre. Do you read me?" Phil said, almost expecting not to hear a reply.

There was some static on the speaker, and then he heard, "Winnipeg Centre, this is Western Global Airlines two-niner-one-five heavy. Yes, I can hear you; go ahead."

"Western Global Airlines two-niner-one-five heavy, this is Phil Wayant, the main controller here at Winnipeg Centre. To whom am I speaking?" Phil was trying to listen to the voice to see if he could pick out an accent.

"Winnipeg Centre, my name is William Maddock. I'm a passenger on this flight. We've now retaken the plane, and we're heading your way, over."

Phil didn't hear any accent that would say the person he was talking to was anything other than Canadian or American. The voice sounded alarmed, but that would be understandable if this was legit.

"What happened to the flight crew, over?" Phil asked.

"The crew was killed by a group of people who tried to take over the plane," William said, trying to remain calm.

"What do you mean, tried? And how did you get it back?" Phil still thought he may be getting jerked around.

"Some of the passengers got together and attacked the hijackers before they could crash the plane."

"Is there any damage to the plane or the flight deck?" Phil started to realize that this guy sounded real.

"Before we took control back, one of the terrorists in a panic took a bottle of water and started to pour it on the controls. The autopilot is acting up, and a bunch of circuit breakers snapped. They also put the plane into a dive, and it looks like one of the engines is about to fall off because of it." William scanned the controls to see if there were any other instruments not working. He wasn't sure what all of the controls did, and he was trying to go by memory from the flight simulator.

Phil thought he was in a dream. This couldn't be real. Who was this guy flying this plane? How were they going to get it down? How many more acts of terrorism were they going to see this dreadful day? Phil paused, took his microphone, and keyed the mic.

"Western Global Airlines two-niner-one-five heavy, this is Phil Wayant again here at Winnipeg Centre—or should I call you William?"

There was a pause. "William is fine," was the response from the Boeing 747.

"OK, William, let's start from the top," Phil said. "Are the terrorists still a threat?"

"No—well, sort of," William said, trying to put his thoughts in order. "It's a long story, but we have all the terrorists accounted for except two potential collaborators." William didn't know how to break it to him that the plane wasn't one hundred percent secure.

This is a problem, Phil was thinking to himself. For all he knew, he was directing this plane toward a city so he could crash the plane right in the middle of it.

Complications were something that Phil didn't need. It was bad enough already, and he didn't need to have it get any worse. The airport had already survived one attempted attack, and they didn't need to have another one.

"We need to know if this guy is legit. We need to know if this guy can fly a plane, and not like the other terrorists, he better know how to land one." Phil was talking to himself but loudly enough to have Bill come over to the radar screen that Phil was looking at.

Now looking out the window at the latest arrival of a plane diverted from the United States, Bill said, "Welcome to Canada. Enjoy your stay."

Phil let out a heavy sigh and rubbed his eyes. *It's going to be a very long day,* he thought to himself. *A long day, indeed.*

64.

The kiss seemed to last an eternity for Grace. She let loose of Burton's lips and looked back at him. He was surprised but looked happy.

"You didn't know?" Grace asked him as they still embraced.

"I had my suspicions," he said with a grin.

Grace leaned in and tilted her head and closed her eyes. Davis did the same, and they kissed again. It was the second kiss, and Davis hoped it wasn't going to be their last. This time the kiss was more intense for both of them. Davis had felt this way about Grace for a while, but he never wanted to cross the line. He was always professional, and so was Grace. But now the rules had changed, and Davis felt lucky to be in Grace's arms, especially at a time like this.

Davis broke off the kiss and embrace.

"We should finish this later; we have a lot to talk about and a lot of catching up to do," he said.

Grace smiled back at him. "Yes, Burton, we do have a lot to talk about. Now go do what you're best at—catching the bad guy," she said as she walked out of the office with a big smile.

Things are bad, but it just got a little better, he thought. He'd had feelings for Grace for some time, and he was glad she had made the first move so he wouldn't do so and make a fool out of himself. In all the destruction and all the hate, there was still some love in the world.

Davis knew that the people needed help; they needed action now. He tapped on his window and waved Monroe into his office. Monroe left his desk with a quick pace and headed into the office.

"Give me some good news," Davis said.

"Well, we have established communications with almost all surviving bureaus, and we are ascertaining damage in each state. The power grid will take some time coming back online, and FEMA is activated. The National Guard is being called out, and so far the looting is limited." Ethan was sounding optimistic.

"The major looting will start tonight, but it should be put down quickly as we've learned a thing or two since New Orleans," Davis said with more of a relaxed tone. "What about communications?" Davis asked.

"Looks like most that are running are on generators. There are also lots of CB and ham radio clubs helping with communications. They're helping evacuees, reporting looting, stuff like that. I think our speech gave everybody something to look forward to," Ethan said, leaning back in his chair.

Davis looked at Ethan. "We spoke to the FAA, and they've spoken to the Canadians; there are four major airports in western Canada that are still open. They'll take as many flights as they can."

Davis paused, looking over some of the notes that Ethan had put on his desk focusing on aircraft currently in the air. "Looks like there are over sixty thousand people in the air as we speak. We need to get them down safely. Make that your new number-one priority." Ethan gave Davis the thumbs-up as he pushed the chair back and walked out of the room.

65.

"William, it's obvious you know how to operate the radio. Tell me you know how to fly a plane." Phil was trying to make light of an obviously bad situation. He was also trying to discern if William was the real thing or just another hijacker.

"I hold a private pilot's license, multiengine IFR rated. I have about a thousand hours VFR and about the same IFR," he said with pride.

This is looking up, Phil thought, but the next question was make-or-break.

"What's the biggest size plane you've qualified in?" Phil held his breath.

There was a pause. William swallowed a bit of pride, keyed the microphone, and said, "Twin engine Beechcraft Baron 58P."

All of Phil's hope that this day would turn out a little better died with that last statement. While it was true that both a Baron and a 747 were airplanes, that's where the similarities ended. To put it mildly, a 747 was to a Baron what a rowing boat was to the *Titanic.* Phil knew that there had never been a case where an untrained civilian had landed a large airliner. While William had more experience and know-how than someone who had never flown a plane, Phil knew that there was still a lot that he didn't know. Getting him to land an airplane of that size in one piece would be a miracle.

"Tell me you have a little knowledge of the inner workings of a 747," Phil asked, not expecting to hear any good news.

"Well, I'm not too sure if this means anything, but I've logged a few hundred hours flying a 747 in a simulator," William said.

"*Yes*, that's good. What type of simulator? Mock-up or full version?" There was a long pause.

"Sorry if you got the wrong idea; I mean flight simulator as in *Microsoft Flight Simulator*," William said.

Phil's heart skipped a beat. "What the hell did he just say?" Phil asked, looking around the room. "Did he just say *Microsoft Flight Simulator?*" Phil couldn't believe his ears. "He's going to fly a 747 based on his time playing a fuckin' video game?"

Bill piped up and said, "Well, it's not really a video game, per se." Bill smirked as he realized that Phil wouldn't catch his drift that *Flight Simulator* was more of a teaching tool and not a game.

"This guy has terrorist written all over him," Phil said, thinking to himself that it was over, anyway. Even if he was legit, they couldn't walk a Baron pilot through landing a 747. Phil wasn't a pilot, and there were no 747 pilots nearby. The aircraft was damaged and could fall out of the sky at any time. Phil thought about having to inform the relatives of the flight that their loved ones became statistics on this awful day.

Since the attacks began, the control room was as busy as a bee-hive in midsummer. Now, the room was dead silent. All eyes were on Chief Controller Phil Wayant. His next move would set the tone for the rest of the day. Phil could feel the weight on his shoulders. With all of the death this day, he didn't want to add the people who were on this flight. There had to be a way to get them down.

Just as Phil thought all was lost, he jumped to his feet and scanned the room for his second in command.

"Bill, find me the best 747 pilot we have; get him here, no matter what it takes." Phil's years of experience kicked in.

"But the FAA has issued a no-fly order and so has Transport Canada. The only aircraft that are allowed in the air are the ones that are currently in flight and military; anything else will be shot down by CF-18s," Bill said.

"Call all of the airlines to see if they have a pilot on layover. If not, see if we can find someone close by; we can ask for permission to fly him in." Phil's outlook went from bleak to hopeful.

* * *

Bill Tate had been a controller at Winnipeg International Airport for many years. He had seen many things happen, from a few crashes, to major renovation and expansion. He even remembered a few unexpected guests like the Beatles in August of 1964. He also remembered tales from long before Bill's time from controllers talking about the time Howard Hughes was supposed to land in Winnipeg on his record-setting, around the world in ninety-one hours trip back in 1938. Hughes didn't land because of a prairie storm. Even after 9/11, Bill never imagined this would happen again, and this was a controller's worst nightmare. *It's time to retire,* he thought.

Bill picked up the phone and started calling the airlines in the airport to see if they had a pilot who was qualified in the city. If not, he was going to call other open airports to see if they had someone in mind. It was fortunate for Bill that the internal secure phone system was still in operation and not down like the public system.

* * *

Phil returned back to his console and keyed the mic. "William, we're going to get you some help from a qualified 747 pilot as soon as we find one. Keep the autopilot on, and do some praying; this might take a while."

Phil looked over at another controller and said, "Get me the passenger manifest for that flight. I want to confirm this guy's name. Once we get that, talk to the RCMP, CSIS, and Transport Canada. I want to know everything about this guy—what he does for a living, what his political beliefs are, and what he ate for breakfast." Phil looked back at the radar screen and noticed a group of planes getting closer to the airport.

66.

William was always an honest person. He attributed the fact that he was not a billionaire to the fact that he was too honest and not ruthless enough. He treated everyone with respect, dignity, and honesty. He was, in fact, honest to a fault. He would never lie to a client, and he would never sell a client something he or she didn't need. He lived an honest and comfortable life, and he could sleep at night. His peace of mind was important to him.

William was optimistic about getting a hold of Winnipeg Centre and that they were going to get a pilot to talk him down. He picked up the intercom and paged Hilary. He told her the good news, and he asked her to tell the passengers.

"That's good news. I'll just forget to tell them about the engine," she said in typical British sarcasm. William was trying to forget about the engine, too.

The news put a smile on Hilary's face. She had been looking for the imposters and keeping an eye out the window at the engine. She looked over at Cleotis, who was also talking to the passengers and trying to find the nuns. Hilary walked over to the galley and picked up the intercom and pressed the announcement button. There was the paging *bing-bong*, and the aircraft went silent.

Hilary was a little nervous. In all of her career, she had never had the complete attention of the cabin. Passengers often talked during the announcements, so to have complete silence was odd. All she could hear was the sound of the engines purring like little kittens.

"Ladies and gentlemen, may I have your attention please." She paused, realizing that she already had their attention. "We have an update for you. We are now in contact with Winnipeg. They are going to get a pilot to help our pilot land the airplane. We are in good hands now, and we should be back soon. Thank you for your cooperation in these trying times; I'm sure we will get there safely." Hilary smiled as she realized that all eyes were on her, too. It was good for Hilary to see the passengers begin to smile.

For Hilary to see the passengers smiling and happy again made her feel good, too; even if it was for only a moment, she felt alive again. She looked down the aisle and noticed Cleotis motioning her to the back of the cabin. The sinking feeling entered her stomach again. *This can't be good,* she thought.

Cleotis led Hilary to the very back of the plane to the lavatory. He opened the door and removed a panel that had been loose in the baby changing station. Behind the panel were two wigs and what looked like the remains of plastic face masks. Hilary looked at Cleotis, and her look said she was going to die right on the spot. Cleotis looked back, and his eyes were filled with worry.

"One of the passengers noticed this and called me over," Cleotis said as he held the masks and showed the hole in the lavatory to Hilary. "Looks like this just got a whole lot more complicated, doesn't it?" he asked.

67.

In the control room of Winnipeg International Airport, the wheels were in motion. All of the controllers were there; even the ones who had the day off either were called in to work or just showed up. There weren't enough seats or screens, but having two sets of eyes on a screen filled with dots made a big difference.

Phil had the passenger manifest and was confirming who William Maddock was with Transport Canada and the RCMP.

Phil looked over to Bill Tate and asked in a demanding tone, "How is it going on finding me a qualified 747 pilot, Bill? I don't care what it takes or how you do it; I need a pilot here, now. Don't let me down, Bill."

Bill was rubbing his chin and trying to think of how he was going to pull a rabbit out of a hat this time. In all his years of being an air traffic controller, Bill had never failed in a mission. He had made several phone calls to the local airlines, with no luck.

"What about the planes that are on their way here?" Phil asked, grasping at straws. "Any 747s?"

Bill looked over at the radar screen full of dots. "We have Speedbird two-six-niner heading this way. They were on their way to LAX, but they are still several hours away."

"That's no good to us." Phil was looking for solutions in a world full of problems.

Bill had turned to his computer to help him find a pilot when the light bulb in the back of his head turned on.

"Wait," Bill yelled, remembering reading a story in the news.

"You found someone?" Phil asked.

"Not yet, but we may have cut a break." Bill was trying to find the story he had read on Google. "Ah, yes, Spencer Hammond—a famous pilot is in Canada on a speaking tour. I'll have to see where he is, and I hope he's in the west and not out east," Bill said as he looked up Spencer's Web site. It felt like all eyes in the control room were on him.

"Well, Bill, we haven't got all day, man. Where is he?" Phil said with a frustrated sound in his voice.

Bill moved over to the second computer on his desk to look up more information. "According to the schedule on his Web site, he was to speak in Toronto tonight at seven."

"Shit!" Phil exclaimed.

"Just hang on a second, Phil. He was scheduled to speak last night in Vancouver, and it was supposed to go on for two hours, according to his Web site."

"What are you trying to say, Bill?" Phil asked as he kept his eyes on the screens and the action outside his window.

Bill paused as he looked at the information on his computer screen. "Phil, it looks like he has a private jet, a Gulfstream," Bill said as he moved over to another computer and typed in more information. "I just looked up the tail number of Spencer's Gulfstream. He didn't leave until seven this morning, Pacific time."

"That means he hadn't gotten very far when all hell broke loose," Phil added. "Can you see how far he went?"

"I'm looking on the tracking Web site now to see where he ended up," Bill said, looking at his computer. The room went silent as Bill stood at his desk and yelled, "*He's been diverted to Regina!*"

That's good news, Phil thought after Bill scared him half to death.

"His Gulfstream was diverted to Regina. He landed there a while ago." Bill thought to himself that they had the break they needed.

Phil was in the dark as to who Spencer Hammond was. "By the way, Bill, who is this Spencer again, and why does he have his own Web site?" Phil asked.

"Phil, Spencer Hammond was the top 747 captain and 747 pilot instructor for twenty-plus years. If anyone can talk him down, it's Spencer," Bill said with excitement.

"How do we get him from Regina to here with a no-fly order?" Phil asked, hoping the answer was obtainable and fast.

Randy Bergen was still in the control tower when he overheard the news. "We don't," Randy said, butting into the conversation. It was just what Phil didn't need to hear. It was a day of problems, and not just the ordinary ones like a burnt-out light on a runway. Phil was in charge because he could sort through problems like a child sorting through a candy bowl. This, however, was getting complicated.

"Why is that, Randy?" Phil asked without understanding the predicament.

Randy said, "We have about a hundred commercial aircraft coming this way, don't we?"

Phil nodded.

"We're trying to make room to park as many as we can around the complex and taxiways. Once we've done that, we'll park as many as we can on the inactive runways. After that, that's all she wrote; we're out of space. What we don't need is a possibly hijacked 747 that's eight hundred thousand pounds of steel and fuel rolling down a runway and crashing into half a dozen parked aircraft. Can you imagine the fireball that would cause?" Randy asked.

Randy was right, but Phil was running out of options. In conversations with other airports, anything east of Winnipeg was either full or closed down. West there were only a few airports that could take a 747, and they were or would be full of planes diverted north from the United States.

"OK, here's what we do. The 747 won't be here for about an hour, so let's see if we can get a hold of this Spencer fellow. In the meantime, we can see if we can find them a place to land. Once we do that, we can see about getting Spencer to the airport," Phil said, looking at Bill and Randy.

Bill piped up, saying, "We know Regina and Edmonton will be full, and Calgary is closed because navigation is down, but north of Regina is Saskatoon. They can handle a 747, and they'll have some room left since only a few remaining jets that don't land in Regina will be landing there." Bill had the attention of all in the room. He continued. "We can get permission to get Hammond to Saskatoon; it's only a thirty-minute hop in the Gulfstream. He'll be there and ready long before two-niner-one-five flies past us," Bill said. Phil smiled and gave Bill a nod, knowing he had come through again.

"Set the wheels in motion. Get a hold of Spencer, make the calls, and get the clearance for the flight from Regina to Saskatoon. Tell them the urgency, and if you need to patch it into the control room, I'll talk to them." Phil was in top form with his assertive voice and hand gestures. This day might end on a positive note yet.

68.

"Looks like our imposters are not only fake nuns, they may not even be female," Cleotis said, showing the wigs and masks to Hilary.

Hilary seldom felt rage, but this was it; it was her boiling point. She was tired of being oppressed by men. She grabbed a wig out of Cleotis's hand and walked over to the terrorists tied up on the floor. She grabbed the nearest one by the hair and pulled his head over so he could see the wig. "Who does this belong to?" she said, demanding an answer. He didn't understand what she was saying, or he was pretending not to.

"Get Harry over here," Cleotis said to one of the men from the rugby team.

"Hilary," Cleotis started to say as he pulled her away from the prisoner. "They can't hide, and it's only a matter of time. We'll find them," Cleotis said, trying to calm her down.

This can't be happening, Hilary thought to herself. We need to find these imposters before they get another chance to either take over the plane or crash it. She reached over to the intercom, but then she changed her mind as this was too important for her to let someone else do it. She made a dash from back of the plane to the front, sidestepping passengers' questions and keeping an eye out for the nuns. All of this was happening too fast—first the nuns, then the hijacking, and then the engine. Now she had to worry about two men somewhere on the plane who would be planning a way to complete their mission. She wasn't going to give them another chance to kill an entire plane load of innocent people.

What had she missed? Hilary was trying to remember all of the faces boarding the plane. All of the men she was first concerned about were all accounted for. She remembered the nuns, and she remembered where they sat. But there were other faces and none that stood out. She looked at the faces as she passed by on her way to the stairs to the upper deck. They all looked the same—scared half to death and looking for answers.

At the top of the stairs, a strong hand reached down to assist her. She reached up and grabbed Nigel's hand. He pulled her close, and with his strength and momentum, she stumbled into him. They embraced; this took them both by surprise. She enjoyed the feeling of being held again. She felt like she was going to break down and cry. She broke the embrace and the bliss of the moment and looked up at Nigel.

"Sorry, we'll have to finish this later. I have some bad news; we're not looking for two women," she said. "We're looking for two men. Get everyone down from here except William's family. Tell them they need to be moved downstairs *now!*"

She stopped for a second, took a deep breath, and looked into Nigel's eyes. "Nobody, and I mean nobody except Cleotis and me, gets up these stairs. Anybody else comes up here, do whatever it takes to take them down. Especially if it's a man you don't know. They'll be trying to get up here and take over the plane again." Hilary was feeling a rage that she hadn't in a long time.

"The only way they get in here is by getting past me, and the only way that's going to happen is over me dead body." Nigel looked Hilary in the eyes and then looked down the aisle toward the flight deck and then back at her. "My mate Willy is safe, and don't you worry." Hilary never believed much that came out of the mouth of a man, but she not only believed Nigel, she trusted him, too.

"Just to be sure, I'll get one of me mates up here that are watching the wankers in the back," he said as Hilary walked back down the stairs.

"I'll tell one to come up here; you just clear out the upper deck." Hilary felt a little better knowing that there was a six-foot-four wall protecting the flight deck.

69.

Spencer Hammond was what most pilots dreamed of—a captain of a Boeing 747. Until the Airbus A380 took to the skies years ago, the 747 was irrefutably the queen of the skies. From its maiden flight on February 9, 1969, the 747 was the largest and the best jet airliner in the business. Spencer was just a child when he witnessed his first 747 taking to the skies. He remembered thinking that the bird would never get off the ground. It went down the runway, picking up speed, then lift-off. Spencer used his hand to trace the 747 as she climbed in the air. As she climbed, he knew it was his destiny to fly one.

Like most pilots, Spencer started off learning how to fly in a Cessna 172. It was like second nature to him. He didn't just fly the plane, he felt the plane. He knew every noise she made and every rotation of the engine. When he placed his hand on the yoke, his touch became the extension of the wings. It was like he could feel how the air was flowing over them.

He was only sixteen when he received his wings with a round of applause from his instructors. Flying was in his blood; flying was his future. He knew that he was one step closer to living his dream.

After many hours flying his little Cessna, he said good-bye and moved on to the bigger aircraft once he received his commercial license. He spent many hours training and gaining hours in various aircraft, moving closer to his dream.

One of his instructors had kept an eye on him since he was a young pilot and was astonished by his accomplishments. He contacted a friend who worked as a recruiter for Pan Am and told him about this rising star pilot. The day after, he was hired; Spencer started to fly for Pan American when he was only twenty-one.

He started off as a flight engineer in the classic Boeing 707. All the time he was dreaming about the day he would be flying the 747. Spencer took a lot of flak from the much older pilots. He soon earned their respect with his professionalism and sense of humor.

The first time he stepped into the flight deck of a 747 was as a flight engineer in the older 200 series. He walked in, paused, and looked where the captain sat. He knew that it was only a matter of time before he sat in the left seat and took command.

Spencer took pride in the fact that he not only knew his job, but he also knew the jobs of the first officer and the captain. He studied every move made by the flight crew. He knew every checklist by heart. He graduated from flight engineer to first officer in record time.

When he graduated to first officer, the senior captains wanted him in the right seat as he was a natural pilot. The fact that he did most of the work was another reason, as well. He was so well respected that Pan Am's senior 747 pilot, who had a reputation of being not the most patient teacher, took Spencer under his wing. Also in record time, he earned his fourth stripe as a captain of a 747 after many hours as first officer. Spencer was recognized as having been one of the youngest 747 pilots to take the left seat in the history of civilian aviation.

His first flight as a captain was a day that made many people proud. His parents and a dozen or so other pilots came along for his first flight. Pan Am's senior 747 pilot had sat in the right seat and bragged tongue in cheek that he taught Spencer everything he knew. The flight was from LAX to Heathrow. Spencer thought he would tear up as the controller gave him clearance to roll into position and hold on runway two-five right.

As the controller gave Spencer clearance for takeoff, there was a little pause and a smile on his face. He reached over to the thrust levers and placed his hands on the levers of engines one and two. His mentor's hands were on the levers for engines three and four. They gently pushed the levers forward, and the engines rolled up to full power. The 747 started down the runway as Spencer anticipated the command from the right seat.

"Eighty knots."

Spencer squeezed the yoke, and on cue, he heard, "Rotate." He gently pulled back the yoke, and the nose lifted off the runway on their way into the heavens. The smile never left his face.

Over the years of flying the 747, Spencer had made a name for himself as a captain who was firm but fair with his crew. Flight attendants and other crewmembers fought for positions on one of Spencer's flights. He truly was a great captain to the crew, passengers, and the company. He always decided whether to fly or abort the flight on the side of caution. He would not ever take a chance flying a bird that he didn't have one hundred percent confidence in. On a few occasions, Spencer got into a verbal sparring match with a few mechanics over problems that seemed minor to the crew chief. To Spencer, it was more than a part that might malfunction at thirty-five thousand feet. It was the passengers who had entrusted him to get them to their destination safely. Those passengers had families that depended on the decision he was about to make. He never wanted to put the families through the pain and suffering of losing a loved one because he felt pressured to keep flying a plane that should not be in the air.

He soon became famous among pilots after he managed to land a crippled 747 through a major thunderstorm. While en route to Los Angeles, contaminated fuel had taken out two of his engines and started to take out a third. A 747 could fly on two engines, but if it lost the third engine, it would be next to impossible to control the plane. Both nonfunctioning engines were on the same side of the airplane, and that was bad. What made it worse was that he was forced to divert the plane and land through a major thunderstorm. Any other pilot in any other plane may not have made it. Not Spencer, and not in his favorite 747. He had a personal relationship with each plane he flew. He knew every noise she made, and he knew every rivet on her. Much to the surprise of his sweating first officer—whose only words were "oh shit, oh shit"—Spencer coaxed her down to a landing that would rival many landings by the best pilots in the best weather with all four engines. He made it look easy, and he had done it all by stick—no autopilot or ILS on this landing.

After landing the crippled 747, Spencer patted the dashboard. He looked over to his first officer, who was as white as a sheet and ready to pass out, smiled, and said over the cheers of the passengers, "Send the people at Boeing my regards. Tell the passengers we'll be a little late to LA, and welcome them to Vancouver." Spencer was grinning from ear to ear.

He moved on to the new 747-800 when it was unveiled, leaving his favorite 747-400 behind. For him, flying a few million miles around the world several times was enough. Spencer was missing his wife and children as they were getting older. He made the choice that family came before flying, and he retired as chief 747 captain. He still kept his foot on the rudder and started a consulting business as a 747 flight instructor. His hours were better, and he was able to spend more time with his family.

His passion for flying 747s made him the number one instructor for his clients. He was sought after by every airline that flew 747s for his teaching skills and his expertise. His consulting firm kept him busy year-round, making DVDs and going on an occasional speaking tour. Not only was Spencer a great teacher, he was also a great motivational speaker.

Spencer had been on his way to Toronto when he was diverted to Regina amidst all of the chaos. Spencer was in high agitation mode. He was a highly structured individual who didn't like to be diverted from a schedule. Years of flying made him a by-the-book kind of guy. He was not only agitated about being diverted, he was agitated that the country he loved was again being attacked.

Spencer had been training a group of pilots that September morning. The class was interrupted by the news of the events that would change the world. He was a man who liked to be in control. That day, he had never felt so out of control. He couldn't help, he couldn't fly, and he couldn't do anything. All he could do was sit and watch the events unfold.

Spencer stood by his Gulfstream in Regina, trying to get his BlackBerry to work. "All lines are dead," he said, putting it back in the holster. Out of the corner of his eye, he noticed an airport ramp worker walk over to him.

"Are you Spencer Hammond?" Spencer was caught off guard, thinking the man had seen his picture in a magazine or on TV.

"Yes, that's me," he replied, looking at him.

"You must be an important guy. All of the phones are down, and you get a call on the secure emergency system," the ramp worker said as he pointed up to the tower and gave a thumbs-up. The ramp worker and Spencer walked over to a bank of airport security phones on a wall. The ramp worker picked up the red phone, punched in a code, and handed the receiver to Spencer.

"Hammond here," Spencer said, covering his other ear as it was hard to hear with all of the outside noise.

"Spencer? Spencer Hammond?" the voice on the other side of the phone asked.

"How can I help you? What do you need?" Spencer replied, sounding annoyed as he looked through the window at the TV screen in the waiting room, watching the carnage.

"Are you sitting down, Mr. Hammond?" the voice on the other end of the phone said.

Bill Tate started to explain to Spencer the situation that was in front of them. The wheels in Spencer's head were spinning.

"You're telling me that a hijacked 747 is being flown by a passenger?" Spencer had a million scenarios going through his head. "Does he have any flying experience? Where is the airplane now, and where are you going to try to land her?"

Bill told Spencer of the situation in Winnipeg and that the plane would have to go to Saskatoon, which was only a thirty-minute flight from Regina in the Gulfstream.

"You can't land it here instead?" Spencer asked. Bill explained that Regina would soon be filled with many planes heading from the United States and that their only hope was Saskatoon.

"So what's the plan?" Spencer asked. Bill explained that he would need to get special clearance so Spencer could fly to Saskatoon. Once in Saskatoon, Spencer would coordinate with the control tower there, and he could talk down the 747 being flown by the neophyte jumbo-jet pilot.

Spencer hung up the phone and motioned to his copilot to head to the Gulfstream. He picked up his BlackBerry out of its holster to see if he had signal. No change. Spencer met up with his copilot and explained the situation to him. Spencer thought to himself, *This time I can make a difference; this time I can save lives. This time, I am in control.*

70.

Over the years if there was one thing that Davis had learned, it was to always document everything. Since 9/11, the hair on Davis's neck had stood up on more than one occasion. In the back of his mind, he knew that 9/11 was a part of a bigger picture. He knew that the "weapons of mass destruction" were a fabrication to justify the "War on Terror." Since then he made notes, he kept files, and he kept it secret. He told no one about the files and in fact kept all of them on a portable memory stick. This was not easy to do as all ports on every computer at the FBI were locked down in order to prevent someone from stealing secrets. He remembered the young IT technician leaving him an older computer with a grin on his face, saying he would leave the "old computer" for the "old-school agent." Davis had used this to his advantage.

In the safe location, he took out the memory stick and held it in his hand. He stared at it for a minute, hoping that all of the information it contained could unlock the key to the how and the why of this day. Just like the Kennedy assassination, there were questions that would never be answered. It was the same for 9/11, and so it would be for this day. The day wasn't even finished, and Davis knew the spin doctors would be working overtime to hide the truth.

He opened up his notebook and inserted the memory stick into the USB port. As the machine began to spring to life, Davis looked outside the window at the buzz of agents ascertaining the damage of this new attack. Ethan had made him proud as he took command and was getting all the agents to gather as much information as they could.

Why, Davis asked himself, why did his boss want him to take a vacation? Why did they want him to drop it and leave it alone? How far up the food chain did this go? Did it go right up to the office of the president? All he knew was that he had to anticipate what was going to happen next.

Many years had passed since 9/11. Davis wanted to live in a safe and free country. He loved his adopted home, and he would do whatever it took to make it safe. Even if it cost him his life, he would never do anything that would cost him his soul. Davis was looking at some of the files on the memory stick when one of the folders caught his eye; it was called MK-ULTRA.

71.

Spencer had finished his preflight checklist by the time he received the special clearance from Regina to Saskatoon. The airport was abuzz with people and planes as ground crews were preparing for the planes heading their way. All the small aircraft were put in hangars, on grass, or wherever they could put them. The larger aircraft that didn't fit in the hangars were put on fields along the ends of the runways. They needed to make as much room as possible to fit as many planes as they could.

Spencer was in reflective thought as the sound of the controller interrupted him.

"Gulfstream Sierra-Papa-zero-one, special clearance has been approved. Squawk five-five-zero-zero. Climb and maintain flight level one-two-zero." The controller paused and continued. "Ensure that you *do not* deviate from your flight plan as there are a few F-18s not too far away with itchy trigger fingers," he warned Spencer.

"Roger, Gulfstream Sierra-Papa-zero-one. I'll make sure I stick to the flight plan—no sightseeing on this trip." Spencer loved to fly the Gulfstream by stick, but not with a no-deviation order. He would have to sit back and let the autopilot do all of the work. That was fine with Spencer as he pulled out a pad and paper and started to go over the landing procedure for the 747 in his head.

Spencer was tough on people in his class who were not at the top of their game. He had a dislike for incompetence and even more of a dislike for people in his class who shouldn't have been there in the first place. Most of the pilots were dedicated and hardworking. However, there were a few who, although talented, were more ego-driven than driven by the passion of flying. He disliked people who had an enlarged ego. While ego was a good thing, it could also be detrimental in a crisis.

Spencer had to rewrite the procedure several times as he realized that the passenger flying the plane was nowhere near the quality of pilot he was used to from his program. Spencer was told on more than one occasion that when he taught, he expected his students to know what he was talking about before each class. He didn't spend too much time with pilots who were not up to grade. He wanted only the best of the best to graduate.

He knew that he had to start with the basics. How could he train a Baron pilot to fly a 747 in the time it took to fly from their present location to Saskatoon? Spencer had met many challenges in his time; this would be the challenge of a lifetime that would beat landing his crippled 747 many years ago.

"Check the status of navigation at YXE."

"Where?" John asked.

"Saskatoon, CYXE," Spencer said, showing John where on the map they were going. John was sometimes left in the dark by Spencer, who was always two steps ahead.

"Make sure their navigation and ILS are up and running," Spencer called out as John made notes.

"Also, when we switch to Winnipeg Centre, get the latest weather, winds—the whole lot. I want to know what we have now and what we can expect in the next few hours or so." Spencer looked over his notes as he gave his copilot further instructions.

"Gulfstream Sierra-Papa-zero-one, climb runway heading and contact Winnipeg Centre on one-two-four point three. Good luck; our prayers are with you. Good day." The controller was reasonably calm, considering there were about a hundred planes of various types heading his way. The day was going to be a long one for the controllers of airports that were still functional.

Spencer stopped writing long enough to key his microphone and reply, "Over to one-two-four point three; good day."

Spencer changed frequencies and checked in with Winnipeg Centre. That was typically the job of the copilot. Pilots flew the plane, and the copilots worked the radios. However, being the copilot for Spencer was an easy job as he did most of the work himself.

"Winnipeg Centre, this is Gulfstream Sierra-Papa-zero-one with you at flight level one-two-zero."

"Gulfstream Sierra-Papa-zero-one, this is Winnipeg Centre. We have you on radar. Maintain course and altitude." The pragmatic voice of the ATC was always calming for Spencer.

"Winnipeg Centre, what is the current location of the 747, please?"

"Gulfstream Sierra-Papa-zero-one, she is just east of Winnipeg, just over three hundred nautical miles from her destination at flight level two-six-zero. At their current speed, they will be at YXE in approximately one and a half hours," the controller replied.

"Good, that will give me time to get ready for them. Do you have any information on their operating status?" Spencer asked.

"According to the pilot, there was a last-ditch effort by the terrorists to damage the controls by pouring water on them, and they put the plane into a dive that may have caused some external damage. Looks like the primary systems are OK; however, the autopilot is acting up. We're not sure how much damage the water did," the controller reported.

"Roger, Sierra-Papa-zero-one. Let me know if there are any changes in their status," Spencer responded in true form, going back to writing on his makeshift checklist.

"OK, John," Spencer addressed his copilot, "let's rip the guts out of her and get us to Saskatoon. We have a plane to land." The Gulfstream soared through the air like a hot knife going through butter.

Just as Spencer thought he had a good idea of what he was in store for, his copilot gave him more bad news.

"Looks like the weather is not going to be good. YXE has had a low pressure system over them for the last twelve hours, and it's not expected to get any better any time soon—lots of low rain clouds and wind from the north," John said, reading the METAR to Spencer.

"What's their ILS runway?" Spencer asked.

"That's even more bad news; they only have one ILS runway, and it's runway niner, and two-seven is the back course. With the winds at three-one-zero at twenty knots gusting to thirty-five knots, his only choice for a runway is runway three-three." John knew it was bad news.

The instrument landing system, or ILS for short, could guide a plane toward the runway automatically. Without the use of the ILS system, it meant that the pilot would have to land by flying the plane himself in what is called a visual landing. Spencer knew that performing a visual landing in a 747 was not hard for a trained pilot. To have a civilian at the controls was bad enough, but then add low clouds, gusty winds, and thunderstorms to the mix, and that meant trouble.

"This is not looking good, John. Is this the only airport that's available to him?" Spencer was looking for alternatives. He had a simple philosophy: There was always an option. There was always another choice.

"Anything big enough to handle a 747 is either closed or full. This is his only choice. Even Regina will be full, and that storm that's heading to Saskatoon will be in Regina sooner."

John could see the futility of the situation. However, Spencer never gave up.

"OK, YXE it is. Let's get there and ascertain what our options are." A smile came back to Spencer's face. John thought that was a good sign.

72.

Davis clicked the folder named MK-ULTRA on his computer. With sophisticated software, the system interpreted intercepted information and automatically categorized it into subfolders. This folder had automatically updated itself in the last few days.

It had been a while since he had looked into or encountered anything to do with mind control. From the time of the end of the Second World War, mind control had been used to mold the minds of the masses. From simple things like what kind of hamburger people ate, to what type of shoe they wore, all of this was a more subversive form of mind control. A more direct form of mind control came in the form of a government program called MK-ULTRA. This ultra secret program involved controlling the minds of the masses. This was not the innocuous form of mind control that could sway people on how to dress or how to eat. This mind control was used in its worst form; it could be used to assassinate presidents. Davis knew that for most people, it was hard to imagine people being controlled, but it was a reality—a reality that Davis knew too well as he was an agent who had helped dismantle the UK version of MK-ULTRA years ago.

Here he was years later, and he was still fighting the evil of mind control. This time it was not about bringing in more gun control laws or taking out a president abroad; this time it was about bringing in the New World Order. What caught Davis's eye was the fact that some of the locations that terrorists had come from and the chatter that Monroe had brought to his attention were matching up.

It had been whispered that 9/11 was what was known in the business as a "black op." Those are operations that are off the books and not traceable to any agency or government. Shortly after 9/11, Davis had tried to look at files that would give him a clue if these rumors were true or just from the people in society who had their tin-foil hats on too tight. After looking at a few files, Davis's computer was locked out of the classified section on 9/11. He was told that because of security, all files on 9/11 were locked down.

In the back of his mind, he sometimes wondered who the bad guys were. Who were the real criminals—the terrorists or the government within a government that dispossesses governments? After all, it wasn't a terrorist who controlled the price of gas to the point that everyone would soon be driving scooters to work. The way Davis saw it, the difference between the good guy and the bad guy was who controlled the spin, who controlled the media.

MK-ULTRA was officially closed years ago. Or was it? Mind control could be used in an operation as big as this. Davis would have to take a closer look into this to see if there was any connection to the people on any of the hijacked planes.

73.

"Saskatoon approach, this is Gulfstream Sierra-Papa-zero-one. We need vectors to your active runway." Spencer was a pro, even in times like these.

"Gulfstream Sierra-Papa-zero-one, airport is fifteen miles north. Turn right, heading three-four-zero; descend and maintain three thousand feet. You are number one for landing on runway three-three. Call Saskatoon tower on one-one-eight point three. Good day, and good luck." The controller sounded professional even with the amount of stress that she must have been under.

"This is Gulfstream Sierra-Papa-zero-one, heading three-four-zero, three thousand feet, one-one-eight point three," Spencer replied as he punched in the coordinates into the Gulfstream's autopilot.

"You're going to get them down, right?" John asked with reservation in his voice. John knew that this was something that had never happened. A civilian had never landed a commercial airplane before. *What are the chances of success?* John thought to himself. While he admired Spencer for all of his accomplishments, this one would put him to the test.

"Let's look at the situation," Spencer said with a confident smile.

"We have a civilian flying a very sophisticated airplane; he has a few thousand hours in a small, twin engine Baron. He knows and understands most of the systems, and he's fully IFR qualified." Spencer paused, collected his thoughts, and continued.

"I think he stands a good chance of getting her on the ground. Now whether the landing gear and the tires withstand the landing, if he doesn't over flair and take the tail off, and if it doesn't splatter it into a million pieces like an egg—that's a different story. I'm sure he'll get it to the airport." John was hoping for more of a reassuring answer. "Keep in mind that the 747 is a sturdy bird with all of the most updated equipment on her. She can fly herself; he just needs to get her on the ground safely." Spencer said it like it was a given that they would land. This made John feel a little better.

"Time to land. Flaps and gear down, finish off the landing checklist, and call the tower; we have the runway in sight." He was imagining what the airport would look like to the neophyte commercial pilot in a few hours when he tried to land.

The wheels of the Gulfstream hardly made a noise as they touched the runway. Spencer turned right on the apron as he taxied to the tower. He would let John do the after-landing checklist and take care of all of the other little details.

Spencer was ready to jump out of the Gulfstream and head up to the tower when John said, "Are you going to wait until I stop, at least?" He admired his boss's ambition. He was a man on a mission.

Spencer just smiled as he walked down the Gulfstream's door as it opened. He was greeted by two nervous-looking controllers.

74.

The Boeing 747 was flying like it was just another flight, smooth and sleek. However, she was feeling her age, and her wounded wing was taking its toll on the old girl. She was one of the last 747-400s made before they went on to the new 747-800. Typically, the airframe for the 747 was good for at least thirty years; that was, however, assuming the airframe did not exceed established parameters. In this case, the 747 had been pushed way beyond the specifications. William was also being pushed way beyond the limits of the average human, and it was starting to show.

"How are you feeling, Wil?" the voice said, coming from behind the captain's seat. William was taken by surprise. He looked up and smiled at Sandra's reassuring face.

"Sorry I can't be with you and the kids right now, but as you can see, I'm needed here," William said in a soft tone to keep Sandra feeling safe.

"It's OK, Wil. This is the one time I understand that you're in a situation that's beyond your control," Sandra, said returning the smile.

"How are the kids?" William asked, looking into Sandra's eyes.

"They're fine," she said, holding back the tears. "William, are we going to be alright?" She was trying to keep in control of her emotions.

William could sense that Sandra needed to be reassured that all was going to be all right even though William was not sure if he could bring home the crippled bird. He turned to Sandra, and in the most convincing look and tone he could give, he reached out and caressed the side of his wife's face.

"We've been together for a long time, and I've made several promises to you." William paused as he felt the lump in his throat get bigger as he looked deep into his wife's eyes. "I've never broken any of those promises; you always have been my universe, and the kids will always be the center of it. I promise to you today, like the day of our wedding, I will bring us home safely; just trust in me," William said with certainty in his eyes and in his voice.

"Don't do it just for us, Wil; do it for all of the people on this airplane. Make it right," Sandra said as she broke down and left the flight deck to go back to the kids. William looked out the front of the 747 and looked into the skies with a determination that he had never felt before. He griped the yoke gently and looked at the instruments. "I know you're hurting, and I know you want to rest. Just a little more, girl, that's all I'm asking. Hold together just a little longer," William whispered, knowing he was asking a lot of the battered bird. He also knew the history of the 747. He knew over the years situations where there had been problems and they had been flown beyond specifications and stayed together. He just hoped this 747 knew that, too.

75.

"Welcome to Saskatoon, Mr. Hammond," the controller said as Spencer quickly shook his hand and walked past him to the control tower. Spencer was not the kind of person who spent a lot of time with small talk. Years of talking on the radio on commercial airlines had taught him to keep his words to the most pertinent information only.

Spencer and the controller entered the elevator that would take them to the floor below the control tower. Spencer realized he may have been abrupt, looked at the controller, and said, "I'm sorry, I'm not trying to be rude, but there's a lot going on right now."

The controller looked back and smiled. "No worries, I understand." He paused and then said, "Oh, Bill Tate from Winnipeg wanted me to tell you he got a hold of your wife. She and your children are safe and doing fine."

Spencer was surprised and very happy about this. He was wondering how they knew he was trying to get a hold of her when the controller added, "Bill assumed that since the phone lines aren't working correctly you may want to let her know you're alright."

This was news that motivated Spencer to make sure that other people's loved ones would get the same news that the people on that plane were OK, too.

Spencer walked out of the elevator and up the stairs of the control tower with a briefcase full of notes and a head full of ideas.

At the top of the stairs, he stopped and looked around as he walked to a station. He asked a controller, "Give me an update of the situation, please." Spencer stood tall, and his presence took over the control tower. The other men in the room stood for a second and didn't know what to make of this stranger in their control room. There was a pause. Spencer knew he had stepped on some toes; he scanned the faces in the control room.

Spencer knew that controllers are rarely pilots, and pilots are rarely controllers. There was a professional relationship between pilots and controllers, but in all structures there are egos and animosities. Controllers seldom stepped into a flight deck, and a pilot would never just walk into a control tower and take command. Spencer knew he had overstepped his boundaries in his rush to get to the control tower.

"Sorry, people, I don't want to intrude on your space. I'm sure you're aware of the situation, and we are all professionals who can put aside egos and animosities and work together. Our focus is on how we are going to get the three hundred and twenty-one people on that 747 safely on the ground." For Spencer, it was like being at one of his seminars. He was in control even if the controllers didn't know it.

"Can someone give me the latest information? I need to know your operating status, the ETA of the 747, and what the latest is on her condition." Spencer was looking around the room for a response when he heard the footsteps of someone coming up the stairs.

"Mr. Hammond, I presume?" asked the woman now at the top of the stairs.

"Yes, and you are…?" Spencer asked, trying to put on his "nice" face the best he could as he reached out his hand.

"I'm Chief Controller Jacky Foster," she replied as she mimicked him by put on her "nice" face too and shaking his hand.

"I was expecting your arrival, Mr. Hammond," she said with a sarcastic smile.

Jacky Foster wasn't the typical controller type. She was articulate, attractive, and everything that an alpha male was in the female package. She took no crap from anybody, male or female, but especially not from people who looked upon her as the "defenseless female" type. Defenseless she was not; she could handle herself not only in a control tower, but also in any bar. She had a fearless streak a mile wide, and she loved to put people in their place when it came to defeating the female stereotype.

She had quickly moved up the ranks at Nav Canada not because of her pretty face, but because of her sharp wit and her skills as a controller. She saw the screen of airplanes as a ballet without the music. To Jacky, every dot had its place, and every dot represented people's lives, something she never forgot. Jacky had worked all over Canada at small and large airports as a controller. She loved to be in control. Once the chief controller retired in Jacky's home city of Saskatoon, she applied and was surprised when she got the job and the respect that she deserved. Sure, Saskatoon wasn't the biggest airport she had ever worked in, but it was home, and she was a homebody. Here in her home city, and home tower, was a man she was unsure about.

"Please call me Spencer," he said, scanning the face of the chief controller, not sure what to make of her. Spencer was from the old school and was expecting the typical chief controller: white, older, maybe overweight, gray hair, and well, a man.

It took a lot to put Spencer off of his game, and that smile was like a flame-out at thirty-five thousand feet. He lowered his voice. "What's your status?" he asked in the most politically correct, professional manner he could.

Jacky felt the tension in his voice and tried to reassure him by lowering her voice and replying, "We are one hundred percent operational." She gave her reply with a smile of confidence.

"All systems are go…?" Spencer asked.

"Radar, navigation, runways, and taxiways are all up and fully operational," she replied with pride in her voice. She continued. "We've had no threats, the grounds have been searched, and the police and military have secured the perimeter. The only problem we may run into is a July storm and running out of space." She walked Spencer over to one of the radar screens and showed him the planes flying toward Saskatoon.

"Winnipeg will soon be closed—Regina too. Calgary is out of commission, and we have approximately twenty-five flights heading this way." Jacky was showing Spencer the latest radar screens.

"All aircraft check out? No 7500 or 7700 squawk codes?" Spencer asked.

"All squawk codes are normal, and there are no other reports of hijacked airplanes. We have several CF-18s in the air that will intercept anything that doesn't conform to our every command." Jacky's tone was one that Spencer could relate to.

"Good. What is the ETA of the 747, and will we have all of the other aircraft on the ground first?" Spencer asked as he pulled up a chair to the radar screens.

"We want the 747 to land last so if he takes out the runway or half of the airport, it won't affect anyone else as we're evacuating the facility," Jacky said, trying not to sound so cold. Spencer knew what she meant, and she was right. If the 747 crashed, the airport would be closed, and any other aircraft in the air would be out of luck.

"Let's make sure he makes it a good one," he said as he took notes and looked through his 747 study material. Typical of Spencer, the captain that he was, he was about to bark an order to the controller like he would to his first officer when he remembered where he was. He took a deep breath and asked politely, "Jacky, can you get me the METAR-TAF for the time you expect the 747 to arrive?" *Oh,* Spencer thought to himself, *I should have tossed in the word please.*

Jacky smiled, knowing Spencer was trying not to overextend his authority. "Sure, they're on the way. It looks like we have a storm on the way and strong winds from the north."

Spencer looked at a map of the airport in front of him. "Is this the same storm that closed down Regina?" he asked.

"No, this is a different system. The question is who will get here first, the 747 or the storm." She tapped on the radar screen showing the approaching storm. "With the winds from the north, that means he may have to land on runway three-three," Jacky said.

Spencer was concerned. "That's not your ILS runway. If he can't use your ILS runway, looks like landing on runway three-three will be a little tricky." Spencer was making notes and looking up information. "I see that runway is only 6200 feet long," he said.

"How long does he need to land her?" Jacky asked as there hadn't been a 747 land in Saskatoon in years.

"Oh, another 1350 feet," Spencer said, sounding almost unconcerned as he wrote his strategy on his notepad.

"That doesn't worry you?" Jacky asked, looking at Spencer.

"Sure it does," Spencer replied, looking up from his note taking. "But so does the amount of fuel he has, his speed, and the fact that he could stall over the city and crash on a bunch of houses. He could take the tail off if he doesn't flair right. All of these things are factors in the big picture," he said, trying not to sound too condescending.

Jacky was at a loss for words. She was looking into the eyes of this man who had intruded on her turf and took control of her space; her internal airspace intrusion alarms were going off.

"You worry about getting him down; I'll worry about getting the rest of the planes on the ground and out of the way," she said, trying to save face and show Spencer she was in control. Jacky didn't even wait for a reply. She just turned around to the other controllers and said, "People, we have a job to do. Let's get it done. Get 'em down as fast as you can, and get them out of the way. We have a 870,000-pound bowling ball coming, and I don't want any pins in the way." Her voice was demanding. Spencer was impressed.

"When will he be in range so I can talk to him?" Spencer asked, getting back to his note taking.

"He should be in range in a few minutes. We're going to patch you into the approach frequency so we can increase the range," Jacky said as she was punching the data into the computer.

"OK, we have a lot to cover once I get in contact with him, so I'll need some space. And can you spare someone to keep me updated on the status of the incoming flights as well as the WX?" Spencer said, looking Jacky right in the eyes. This made Jacky nervous as eye-to-eye contact was her weapon in showing someone who the boss was.

"I'll have a controller for you once things start to heat up," she said, giving Spencer her best stare. Spencer was enjoying this game they were playing. He kept it in the back of his mind that what was important was the people on the plane and not who won a pissing match.

"Thanks. Let's hope he gets here before that storm does," he said, turning away from Jacky and looking out the window as lightening flashed in the distance.

76.

Davis was trying to make sense out of all of the raw data that was stuffed into the MK-ULTRA folder. He kept thinking to himself, *Are the attacks over, or is what happened so far just the beginning?* Davis was working on his game plan when Monroe came into the room with a news update.

"Bursting into my room has become a habit of yours that has consequences, Mr. Monroe," Davis said in a quiet, serious tone. Monroe didn't get the joke and started talking.

"Looks like all fast response teams are in place at all key installations, nuclear power stations, conventional power stations, and anything that's considered essential. All remaining infrastructure is secure as best as can be. All agents who survived the attacks are manning Bureau offices or are at their safe houses," Monroe said, almost in one breath.

"It's good to know things are looking up. Any bad news?" Davis asked, still perusing the files on his computer.

"That's the good news on the ground; in the air, we still have several aircraft on the way to Canada. All of them are confirmed OK, and we have one flight that hasn't crashed that's a confirmed hijacking. It's on the way back to an airport, and it's being flown by a Cessna pilot or something like that..." Monroe was trying to digest so much information about all of the attacks, including what was going on in Canada. He was about to continue giving his report when Davis interrupted him.

"Get me the list of the names of the passengers and crew of that flight. And not just the Middle Eastern ones, either—I want all of them," Davis said as he rubbed his chin, still reading the files. Monroe didn't know what to make of the request.

"What's important about that flight that has you intrigued?" Monroe asked with a puzzled look on his face.

Davis looked up from his computer at the young man who was to inherit the mess they were now in. One day, Davis would leave the FBI while Monroe would be going on in what was left of America. Davis spoke in a reserved voice; this was the voice he had used on his children over the years when they were in need of some moral support.

"I think today is not as it looks," Davis said and then paused. He rubbed his eyes, shook his head, and then looked back at Monroe. "I think something deep and dark is going on here. I want to check a few leads I have and compare some names that keep coming up," Davis said. "You keep everything running smoothly as best you can; we can use this safe house as forward command until Washington is back online." Davis sounded like his old self.

"There is another problem I was going to tell you about. It looks like every group and whack job who has a problem with Uncle Sam is out on the streets fighting, looting, burning, and preaching that the end is near. It looks like the next few nights are going make the LA riots look like a church picnic," Monroe said, waving his notes around.

"Let them burn off some steam. Just make sure all of the important infrastructure is protected—power plants, water supplies, and hospitals need to be secure. We can worry about the looters later. Your top priority is getting me that list of names on that flight, A-SAP," Davis said as he turned away and went back to his notes. Monroe was feeling good as Davis was back in command.

77.

In the control tower of Winnipeg International Airport, Chief Controller Phil Wayant was watching the last airplane land at his airport. *I've never seen it this full before,* he thought to himself as he sipped his coffee. He looked over to Bill and smiled.

"There's something you don't see every day," Phil said as he pointed out the window with the coffee cup in hand. Bill stopped his typing, stood up, and looked out at the sea of airplanes. There were airplanes as far as the eye could see.

"I hope we never see it again—at least not for the same reason," Bill said in a pragmatic tone.

"Any news on two-niner-one-five?" Phil asked.

"They're getting closer to YXE—so far, so good," Bill said, looking back at his computer screen.

"Now that we're done here, bring up the radar and the audio so we can listen in," Phil said.

"Give me a second and it'll be up," Bill said, and he flipped a few switches and pushed a few buttons.

"Maybe get Randy and Mike up here so they can listen in," Phil said. "Keep the coffee coming, too," he added as he took a sip.

78.

"Are we about to make contact?" Spencer asked, looking at the dot on the radar screen.

"He should be in range any time. As soon as Winnipeg Centre switches him over, he'll be yours," Jacky said, scanning the radar screens and listening to the radio chatter.

"Give it a try now," Jacky said, giving Spencer the go-ahead.

"Western Global Airlines two-niner-one-five heavy, this is Saskatoon tower. Do you copy?" Spencer held his breath. There was no reply. Spencer seldom doubted anything he did; he never let the odds stack against him. This was the first time in his life he felt the weight of the world on his shoulders. He had to make this work.

"Western Global Airlines two-niner-one-five heavy, this is Saskatoon tower. Are you on the frequency?" The quietness in the room was deafening. Then there was a spark of hope.

"Saskatoon tower, this is Western Global Airlines two-niner-one-five. Go ahead." Spencer listened to the sound of the voice from the speaker intently. Given all that had happened today, Spencer was suspicious of who was behind the microphone.

"Western Global Airlines two-niner-one-five heavy, this is Saskatoon tower. We have you on radar. Squawk ident." Spencer looked at the radar screen to see if he would get the right response. The squawk code for the dot on the screen lit up as it was supposed to. *That's a good sign,* Spencer thought.

"OK, let's give you a new squawk code so I can tell you apart from the few planes that are still in the air." Spencer looked at the screen and put on a bit of a grin. "Squawk seven-five-zero-zero," he said, waiting for a response. This was the first of many tests that Spencer was going to put to the neophyte 747 pilot.

In the flight deck of the 747, William had his hand on the control to set the new squawk code when he paused.

"Seven-five-zero-zero?" he said. He knew that was the international squawk code for hijacking. *We're not being hijacked anymore,* William thought. He needed to clarify the code.

"Did you mean seven-seven-zero-zero?" William asked

The grin on Spencer's face turned into a smile as he was becoming reassured that the person on the other end of the radio was indeed a pilot and not a hijacker.

"Yes, I said seven-five-zero-zero." Spencer was playing a game, and Jacky was looking unimpressed.

"But seven-five-zero-zero is the code for hijacking, and we're not being hijacked anymore, over." William was trying to explain, not understanding what Spencer was up to.

"You're right; I was just checking. Your squawk code is seven-seven-zero-zero." Spencer looked at Jacky and said, "I just had to be sure he was for real."

"Got it, seven-seven-zero-zero it is," was the response on the radio.

"We have a lot to cover in a short amount of time, so I'll bring you up to speed on what we need to do to get you and your passengers on the ground safely." Spencer was looking at his notes and his 747 checklist when Jacky walked over to him.

"Let him know in a few minutes he will have an escort into the city. A CF-18 will be off each wing for the duration of the flight. If he deviates one degree from the flight course, they've been given orders to shoot him down." Jacky didn't look at Spencer at all; she didn't want to see his reaction.

"I'll let him know in a few seconds. I just need to confirm if his autopilot is indeed working or not." Spencer was trying not to get ahead of himself, realizing that this was not one of his courses where the pilots were all seasoned commercial pilots. He was speaking to a recreational pilot, someone who flew for fun. He would have to keep that in mind.

"The autopilot is erratic at best," William said.

"OK, keep your hands on the yoke just in case and your eyes on the instruments. We need to go through some of the checklist to make sure you're configured for landing." Spencer added, "I hope you're good on visual landing because it looks like that will be the approach you'll be taking." He wanted to break it to William gently.

This took William by surprise; he had assumed he would be doing an ILS landing. While he had done hundreds of visual landings in his Baron, the thought of doing a visual landing in a 747 was something he had never contemplated.

"What is the visibility like, over?" William asked, hoping for some good news.

"We're expecting cloud cover about the same time you're scheduled to land. We're hoping to get you in before a big storm hits," Spencer said, looking at the weather radar.

"What's the ceiling?" William asked with a nervous tone.

"We're expecting about three thousand feet." Spencer was trying to sound upbeat.

"How long is this supposed to last? Can we not circle the airport for a while?" William was trying not to sound too afraid.

"We need to get you down ASAP; we don't know what might happen if we keep you up too long." Spencer wanted to give William the whole story, but that would only add fuel to William's fire.

There was a long pause. "OK," William said.

Spencer and William went through a shortened checklist in order to prepare the 747 for landing. What was important, Spencer knew, was weight, speed, and altitude. Spencer needed to slow down the 747 and dump fuel so William could still fly her and it would not stall. At the same time, he had to get William to drop flaps and the landing gear.

Spencer was hoping this was not too much for William. It reminded him of some of his students in his advanced 747 course. Even seasoned 747 pilots with thousands of hours in a 747 couldn't handle too much all at once. He had to spoon-feed his latest student information that takes most pilots years to adapt to instinct. The difference was this student couldn't make any mistakes because that could cost the lives of every person on board and many on the ground.

"William, you're about forty nautical miles out. Descend to four thousand feet and turn right, heading thee-zero-five, over." Spencer was looking at the radar screen as there was no way of seeing the 747 out of the window. He could see the 747's speed and altitude on the radar screen, but that was it. The storm was getting closer, and the winds were picking up.

Jacky looked at Spencer and asked the question that needed to be asked. "What are his chances? And give it to me straight, no bullshit, professional to professional." Jacky looked at Spencer as intensely as she could.

"OK, professional to professional." Spencer was looking out the window; he then turned to Jacky and gave her the same look back. "First, the bad news; never in the history of aviation has a civilian landed a commercial airliner. The good news is he's a pilot, and he has a good understanding of flight and flight controls. He has a better chance than someone with no experience at all. With our help and a lot of help from above, he just might make it. That's the truth," Spencer said, giving Jacky his best poker face.

Jacky didn't know looking at Spencer if he was telling the truth or if he was, as she put it, "full of shit."

"I'm an optimist, and I hope you're correct. I don't need him taking out my control tower and half this airport because you think he might make it," Jacky said, using her fingers as quotation signs emphasizing "might." "We need to evacuate this airport and get the thousands of American passengers a safe distance away from here."

Spencer went into control mode. "Get a contingency plan together to evacuate the facility. Keep only essential personnel, fire department, EMTs, and police to keep the airport secure. We don't need any local fanatics getting in on the act. All of the rest of the nonessential personnel, get them out of here and lock this place down." Spencer looked at his watch. "We have twenty minutes. Can you get it done by then?" Spencer said, trying to be diplomatic by giving Jacky the last word in her control tower.

Jacky was trying to keep it in perspective. She hadn't been given an order in her control tower in years; she was used to giving the orders.

"The evacuation plan is already in action. I'll make sure the airport is evacuated and secure. You do what you need to do to get him down," Jacky said as she turned to head for her office.

79.

In all her years of flying, Hilary never missed a face. Each person that she greeted at the door she remembered. She played a memory game that helped her place passengers with their seats as they entered the aircraft. She had this uncanny sense to be able to tell if a passenger was going to be a pain or a pleasure, and on more than one occasion she was right. The problem she was having now was placing faces with seat numbers. But with all of the mayhem, many passengers were not where they were supposed to be.

Hilary was also having a hard time concentrating as she kept thinking about the plane losing an engine at any time from the stress on the airframe. She was seeing all of these people with their worried faces, and their fate was in the hands of a private pilot who had never flown a commercial airliner. And to top it off, she was looking for two imposters who may again try to crash the plane. After a while, all of the faces started to look the same. Her heart was beating faster and faster; she knew the plane was getting closer to landing as it was starting to slow down and descend.

She was looking at all of the faces in the forward section of the airplane for the third time when something caught her ear and not her eye. It was a voice with a distinctive accent—a distinctive Russian accent. She didn't remember where she had heard it before, and she was trying to remember passengers with Russian accents. There were none that she could think of; there were lots of English, French, Northern European, and even some Middle Eastern accents, but none from Russia. Yet she could remember hearing one and not too long ago. She was trying to concentrate on the voice as the plane was starting to rock back and forth in the lower lever turbulence when Cleotis interrupted her.

"Hilary, we need your help in the back. One of the prisoners is sick; he's choking on something." Cleotis was waving Hilary to the back as she was still trying to put a face to the voice.

"I'll be right there," she said, taking one last scan of the faces in the section. "What's the problem?" she asked with an annoyed tone as she walked to the back of the plane.

"One of the prisoners is starting to puke all over, and we don't know what to give him. Maybe you have something he could take," Cleotis said, looking at the prisoners on the floor. "Do we have anything that would make him better?" he asked.

"How about a bullet to the bloody head?" Hilary said in a sarcastic tone.

"We'll save that for later," Cleotis said, trying to get control of the situation. "For now, we need these assholes alive; they might have some valuable information for us." Cleotis was always three steps ahead.

The rocking of the plane was starting to get everyone a little on edge. One of the prisoners, who was lying on the floor with his hands tied behind his back, was trying to speak.

"I can help you. Please don't have my family killed," he begged.

One of the men from the rugby team guarding the prisoners yelled, "Shut up, man, before I smash your face in."

Cleotis, smelling a lead, went over to the man and motioned the makeshift security guard to move out of the way.

Cleotis was a man of compassion. Even though an hour ago this prisoner was going to kill all the people on the plane and as many as possible on the ground, Cleotis knew there was more to this man than the monster he may be now. Cleotis reached down to the man lying on his stomach and sat him up.

"How can you help us?" Cleotis asked

"Please, make sure the others don't have my family killed," he said with fear in his voice. "I don't want to be here, but my brother, who was supposed to be here, was arrested. So these men said I had to take his place, or they would kill our family back home," he said as Cleotis sat the man in a seat near the back.

"Please, we don't have much time. How can you help us?" Cleotis looked the man in the eyes and saw that the man was under a lot of stress. "Tell me who the other men are. Who are the men who were in disguise?" Cleotis got right to the point.

"They are not Arab," he said, gasping for breath.

"We assumed that. Do you know what they look like?"

"They are white, from Europe," he started to say, and then he paused as he was searching for the right words.

"Are they Russian?" Hilary asked, leaning in from the seat in front of Cleotis.

"Yes, yes, they are," the man added, nodding his head with excitement.

"Do you know where they're sitting, what they look like?" Cleotis asked.

"No, I just heard their voices the other day at a meeting, and I know they came on the plane in a disguise," he said, thinking about any other information he might have.

Hilary had heard enough. She started to bolt down the aisle toward the front of the plane. She had to match a voice to a face before they made another move.

But maybe it was too late. As soon as Hilary turned to leave Cleotis, passengers in a forward section of the plane started to scream. Something was happening, and Hilary ran towards the screams beyond the curtain to find out why.

80.

Spencer and William were going through the approach and landing checklist, making sure the 747 was configured for landing.

"Set the altimeter to two-niner point two-one," Spencer said.

"Two-niner point two-one, set," William replied.

"Set auto brake to max."

"Set to max."

"Arm auto spoilers."

"They are armed."

"Flaps, set ten degrees."

"Setting the flaps to ten." William did it like he had done in the simulator a hundred times.

"Make sure you're slowed down to two hundred knots."

"Two hundred it is."

"You're looking good, Wil. You're about fifteen nautical miles out. Descend to thirty-seven hundred feet. Turn to heading three-three-zero. Are you ready for your final checks?"

William closed his eyes, did a quick, silent prayer, and answered, "As ready as I'll ever be."

Spencer took that as a yes and started to read off the final checks from the checklist.

"Landing lights on."

"On."

"Slow up to one hundred and eighty knots." William reached over to the speed indicator on the autopilot and turned to dial.

"Landing gear down." William pulled the lever down and watched the light on the monitor indicate they were down.

"Gear down," he responded.

"OK, you're on final approach. Set flaps to twenty-five degrees."

"Flaps set." William was perspiring and feeling a little sick from all of the adrenaline rushing through him.

"Set speed to one hundred and seventy knots." Spencer looked up from his checklist out the window in a vain attempt to see the 747.

"The airport is at your twelve o'clock. Your speed is good. Let me know when you can see the airport, and keep an eye on the left for the PAPI—the precision approach path indicator." Spencer looked between his notes and the window for the big bird.

"How is it going up there, Wil? Is everything under control?" Spencer was getting ready for the landing of his career.

"Well, it's rough at this altitude; it's very bumpy. How is the visibility in Saskatoon?" William was trying to conceal his concern as he couldn't see a thing out his window.

"No change; you'll be home soon and on solid ground. Just get ready to disengage the autopilot and auto throttle. Keep your hands on the yoke just in case, and keep your scan going between the instruments and the window." Spencer never doubted that the 747 would be able to make it; he was concerned how much he could push William.

William was taking a quick look around the flight deck to make sure that all of the instruments were functioning when an alarm when off. He then turned around to see if Nigel was at his post. He was not. William called out to him. "Nigel!" There was no answer. William tried to look to see if he could see Sandra and the kids. They were out of sight. William looked back at the front of plane, gripping the yoke and trying not to panic but wondering where they all were.

William keyed the microphone. "Spencer, I need to do something. I'll be right back," he said as he took off the headphones and pushed his seat back.

Those words were not the words that Spencer or the pilots of the CF-18s wanted to hear.

"William, what's going on?" Spencer said with a loud tone. There was a long pause. "William, can you hear me?" Spencer squeezed the microphone tighter. "William, can you hear me?" Spencer repeated the question. "You just can't leave the flight deck, man; the F-18s will shoot you down." Spencer was loud enough to be heard all over the control tower.

There was no response.

"Damn it." Spencer slammed his fist on the desk and stared intently at the radar screen.

"He's going to be over the city in a few minutes. We need to act fast," Jacky said.

"Keep the F-18s at bay. Give it a few minutes," Spencer said as he was trying to think of how to regain control. *What's going wrong up there?* he was thinking to himself.

"Saskatoon tower, this is Night Hawk. We have orders to shoot him down if he deviates from his flight plan, over."

"Deviates from the *flight* plan are your orders, and he has not done that. Please stand down." Spencer was not optimistic about the situation.

"We have our orders, sir," the captain of the CF-18 said. "We'll get ready and in position. If he's not back in the flight deck in a few minutes, we will assume the worst and shoot it down before he gets too close to the city." The reality of the situation was hitting home, and Spencer didn't like the sound of it. Hell, if he was the captain of that CF-18, he would be doing the exact same thing.

"I'm sure all is OK; he's just checking something," Spencer said, grasping at straws.

"For their sake, I hope you're right," the captain replied.

"Trust me, I am. Besides, I don't think you want to kill all those people, do you, captain?" Spencer said trying to give the captain the grim reality of the situation.

"No more than you do, but I do have my orders, and I *will* shoot down that plane. Now if you don't want that to happen, you better pray that he gets back in the flight deck A-SAP, as we are now in position and ready to fire." The captain didn't like the situation he was in, but the reality of a 747 crashing into a city full of people was a grim one.

81.

Monroe was taking care of most things in stride. He was doing well considering he was under an enormous amount of pressure. Davis was busy looking for clues to see if the worst was over and to see if he could help identify the bad guys on the hijacked airplane still in the sky. He was having some luck deciphering some of the data, but it was all too much for him. He looked out his window to see Grace at her terminal checking the status of the power grid. It was slowly coming back online in some cities, but in some it would take many more days to get it up and running.

Davis took another look at some of the chatter logs so he could see if there was any connection. He fed the files into the computer and hoped it would come up with some connections in the terabytes of data it had to search through.

Davis reflected on the day's events and the work that would need to be done; it was going to be a long haul. This time they were going to do it right and get to the bottom of today's events. But first Davis needed to keep an eye on what was going on in America, Canada, and the rest of the world, for that matter.

Bong. The computer sounded a chime; it had an answer.

Davis sat back in his chair and looked at his screen. He scanned the information for a few minutes before his eyes almost popped outside of his head.

"*Monroe!*" Davis called almost at the top of his lungs. "We have some suspects!"

82.

"Nigel!" William yelled as he walked to the back of the passenger section of the upper floor of the 747, looking for his new best friend. On his way towards the back of the plane, William could hear the screams from the passengers. As he approached the top of the stairs down to the lower level, he could see Sandra and the children huddled in the back. Sandra had Zoë and Shawn behind her like a mother bear protecting her cubs. She was crying, and she gave William a look that said, "Make this all go away." William could also see Nigel halfway down the stairs.

"Nigel, where are you going, man?" William asked.

"I heard screaming, and I can smell smoke. My mates might be in trouble; I need to help them," he said, taking another step down the stairs.

"I need you here, Nigel. We *all* need you up here protecting the flight deck. Nigel, if we don't land this thing, we are all dead, and that includes your mates. Trust me; I'm sure Hilary will take care of it, and they are all OK. I need you up here, Nigel, and I need you up here *now!*"

William was taking a chance getting loud with a guy as big as Nigel. In all his years of working with people, William had a way of getting people's attention; he figured Nigel needed some reassurance that his mates were OK.

Nigel looked back up the stairs and said, "You better be right about this one, man. My mates mean a lot to me, and it's hard to just leave them there." He turned around, trying to put the screaming passengers out of his head, and went back up the stairs. William bolted back toward the flight deck. He could hear Spencer on the radio calling him.

"William, can you hear me?" Spencer said, and there was a long pause. William looked at the circuit breaker panel and pulled the bathroom smoke detector alarm so it would stop chiming. He was hoping they would take care of that before too much smoke filled the flight deck.

"Spencer, I hope you have the fire department and a lot of cops there, too, as we have a situation that will need their attention," William said as he adjusted his headphones and his seat.

"They're standing by," Spencer said with a bit of relief and a smile on his face. "What the status up there, Wil?" Spencer asked, not really wanting to hear the answer. There was another pause.

William was not much of a liar. He was, in fact, honest to a fault. He keyed the microphone. "Some passengers are concerned about the turbulence, that's all." Spencer could tell that William was not being entirely truthful, but he didn't push it as he also didn't want to give the CF-18 pilots a reason to shoot the plane down.

"We're almost home, Wil. Let's do the last few checks on the list." Spencer was going to do as little as possible as far as checks were concerned. He knew that William was being pushed beyond his limits, and Spencer didn't want to put him over the edge.

"Check that the landing gear are down."

"Down, and I have a green light."

"Turn off the autopilot. Make sure they are all off, and keep one hand on the yoke at all times. It's going to be all up to you, Wil."

William paused and made sure that his hand was firmly on the yoke. He didn't know how firm it would be as his hand was very sweaty. He then turned off the autopilot. "Autopilot disengaged," he announced.

"Turn off the auto throttle."

"Auto throttle off." William kept trying to see the airport out the window.

"Set landing speed one hundred and sixty knots." William pulled the thrust levers back, and the plane slowed down a little more.

"One hundred and sixty it is."

"OK, once you touch down, apply reverse thrust."

"Reverse thrust on touchdown," William said as he looked over to Nigel. William was also trying to keep the sound of what was going on below out of his mind.

"Keep it secure for a few more minutes, and then you can kick all the ass you want. Just hang tough," William said to Nigel.

Nigel smiled and said, "I can't wait to get me hands on those fuckin' wankers." Nigel stood tall and rubbed his hands together as he filled the doorframe in the flight deck.

83.

Agent Monroe was sitting in front of his computer looking at the information he was receiving. At the same time, he was keeping an eye on several live satellite video feeds of the remainders of many cities. Once great cities now lay in ruin; a once great nation was no more.

Monroe was in deep thought when he heard Davis call his name. He leaped from his desk and headed up the stairs, wondering what Davis was excited about.

"Close the door on your way in," Davis said to Monroe, and he removed his glasses and leaned back in his chair with a grin on his face.

"What do you have?" Monroe asked as he pulled up a chair to get closer to the desk.

"I'll say this," Davis started to say. "They even had me fooled. Those dirty sons of bitches had me fooled like I was some greenhorn who rolled in on the last watermelon truck." Davis wasn't speaking English, as far as Monroe was concerned. Davis knew this was going to take some explaining. He said, "Before your time, governments and covert agencies experimented with control of the masses through the use of mind control. The program was called—"

"MK-ULTRA," Monroe interrupted.

"You know of it?" Davis asked, a little surprised by his colleague's knowledge.

"From the time of the Second World War, there's been experimentation in controlling the masses through various ways of mind control." Monroe was trying to remember what he had read about MK-ULTRA years back. He continued. "The program was supposed to be banned back in the late sixties or early seventies, but there are rumors of its existence to this day."

Davis smiled. "Well, lad, let me tell you, MK-ULTRA is alive and well." He paused so he could swing the monitor so Monroe could see it as well.

"Remember the chatter we've been monitoring?" Davis asked. Monroe just nodded.

"We could see that most of the chatter came from several areas of the Middle East and the States. We could also see that some of the people we've been watching for a few years all came from the same region. What we didn't look at was where these men came from before they ended up in the Middle East," Davis said, trying not to get ahead of himself.

"Where did they come from?" Monroe asked, not really knowing what to think.

"Russia," Davis said, looking back at the information on the screen. He then added, "Not that I've been snooping through some classified files, but back in the late seventies and into the eighties, during the Russian war in Afghanistan, thousands of Afghanistan men, women, and children went missing. Officially, they were killed in the war; unofficially, we've always thought that they were kidnapped and taken back to Russia as slaves, just like a lot of missing Vietnam soldiers were."

"If they were taken as slaves, what does this have to do with the situation today?" Monroe asked, not understanding what he was hearing.

"MK-ULTRA," Davis said in a somber voice.

"I'm sorry if I don't sound like I understand, but..."

"Don't worry, Ethan. I find it hard to believe it too, but it makes all the sense in the world," Davis added. "What we see and what we are told is not always what the truth is," Davis said in a quiet voice.

"Back in the war, the Russians took men, women, and children out of Afghanistan and moved them to Russia. They took the hard-core fundamentalists and brainwashed them. They had them train the children to be soldiers for Allah. A few generations of brainwashing, and they would willingly go and kill people by flying planes into buildings, blowing themselves up in a crowd of people, and committing other acts of terrorism. They do that, and they are bona fide soldiers for Allah. All of the suspected passengers on the list you gave me came from the Middle East, as we know, but according to my files, they didn't exist until a few years ago, and at the same time they all appeared in the Middle East emigrating from Europe." Davis added, "Now that I look further back, I see that they're all from Mashhad in the northern part of Iran. They all trained at a camp in the area, and they all left from there several months ago at the same time, ending up in Germany, the United Kingdom, Canada, and the United States."

"That's why they didn't show up; we didn't go back far enough. I bet if we did, we would find that they all came from Northern Europe before, right?" Monroe asked.

"Russia, to be more precise. I'm sure most of them were born as children of slaves, indoctrinated to be used one day as tools for the New World Order."

"I've heard a lot of stuff over the years, but I've always discounted that New World Order stuff as just crazy talk," Monroe said, trying to comprehend the bigger picture.

"This is the beauty of MK-ULTRA. Now it looks like Muslims are behind this, just like they were supposed to be behind 9/11. The outcome is that people will hate Muslims, and this will justify bombing them back into the stone age.

That's something we're going to have to worry about another day. Let's get through this day, and we can worry about the big picture some other time," Davis said as he knew he couldn't overwhelm Monroe with too much information.

"What next, then?" Monroe asked, getting down to the task of the day.

"Give me an onscreen live shot of that hijacked airliner heading toward—where did you say, Saskatoon? Get a message to them and warn them about terrorists who maybe European, Russian in particular, and to not just concentrate on every brown face they see," Davis said, giving Monroe his orders as he got back to reading more files on his computer.

"I'll call them and let them know. I don't know if I can get radar that far up north, but we may be able to patch into the ATC audio and listen in," Monroe stated.

"Put it on the big screen, and let's hope and pray for them," Davis said, adding under his breath, "and for the rest of the world."

84.

Hilary was racing down the aisle as the screams of the passengers became louder and louder. As she flew through the aisle from one section to the next, not only could she hear the screaming, but she could smell smoke. Smoke on an airplane is not good in the first place, never mind a plane that was in the middle of an emergency landing. *What other problems do we have in store?* Hilary was thinking to herself as she was trying to place the source of the smoke. She couldn't tell as it was thick and all over the front of the cabin. The passengers were moving about in their seats, trying to get away from the smoke.

"*It's in the bathroom!*" a passenger yelled.

"*Clear the way! Clear the way!*" Hilary yelled as she made her way toward the lavatory, grabbing a fire extinguisher from the galley.

Hilary knew this was not just someone who had snuck off for a fag. Over her years of flying, she had encountered a few passengers smoking in the lavatory. When this happened, the smoke mostly stayed in the lavatory and did not pour out of it. This smoke was different as it was thick and black; something else was on fire besides toilet paper in a washroom.

* * *

At the top of the stairs, Nigel was having a panic attack as he could hear the commotion and see that the smoke was getting thicker.

"William!" Nigel yelled. "You better get us down soon, mate, or we'll all be goners."

William was having problems of his own keeping his eyes out the window for the airport when smoke started to fill the flight deck. *This isn't happening,* William thought to himself. *We are so close to landing; we need to hold on just a few more minutes.*

Just as William was about to call out to Nigel, he received word that there may be a potential problem from passengers other than ones from the Middle East. "Russian?" William said in confusion. "I don't need this right now," he said with frustration. He turned in his seat. "Nigel!" he called out. There was no response. William was again staring at an empty doorway where Nigel was supposed to be. The smoke was getting thicker, and the screams of the passengers were getting louder as he looked out the window in hopes he could see the airport.

"Twenty-five hundred," came out of the speakers in the flight deck, scaring William half to death.

"What the hell was that?" William asked himself. Then he realized it was the ground proximity warning system, the system that warns pilots how high they are from the ground. William didn't need any more distractions at this time. Enough was going on in his mind; he didn't need more to worry about. He again called out to Nigel.

* * *

Back on the main level, Hilary was having problems of her own. It looked like the fire was in the lavatory right next to the stairs going to the upper level. Hilary and another passenger used fire extinguishers to put out the fire. She aimed the extinguisher towards the source of the smoke and blasted away.

Just as she started to do this, two men brushed past her and headed for the stairs to the upper level. They were two short, European-looking men, she noted. A chill went up her spine.

Hilary assumed the worst as they were going up the stairs. "Nigel!" she yelled. Hilary heard a thud and a tumble at the bottom of the stairs.

* * *

William was trying to keep as calm as possible while trying to see through the smoke and follow Spencer's directions. He was keeping an eye on the speed and didn't notice the two men entering the flight deck.

"OK, William, you're looking great. You should be out of the clouds soon," Spencer said with growing optimism.

William keyed the microphone and responded. "All looks good on this end—" William started to say, and then the next sound Spencer heard was a loud *bang!* Spencer knew the sound of gunfire when he heard it. So did the captain of the CF-18.

"That's it; he's under fire. We have to take that plane down before it's over the city," the captain said, repositioning his CF-18 for a kill shot.

"Stand by, Captain; that may not have been gunfire." Spencer knew it was, and he was just trying to buy time.

"William, if you can hear me, key the mic and let us know you're alright." Spencer kept his eye on the radar screen to see if the plane diverted from course or lost any altitude. There was a long pause that seemed like it went on forever.

"We have the authority to shoot it down, and we're taking the shot," the captain of the CF-18 said. "Hawk twenty-two, reposition yourself off my wing. If I miss, you take the next shot."

Spencer was frantic to get a hold of William. *"Wil, key the mic and let us know you're alright, damn it!"* Spencer was loud enough to be heard all throughout the control tower. All eyes were on the speaker in the control tower.

"We're OK…and we're still in control," William responded on the radio. The control tower erupted into cheering. Spencer had a mile-wide smile on his face.

"It's good to hear you again, William. We can all start to breathe again. What happened?" Spencer asked.

"It's a long story, but it looks like we have all of the terrorists under control."

* * *

Back in the flight deck, William had been sitting in the captain's chair when the two terrorists came up the stairs to finish the job they had started.

Thankfully, Cleotis's instincts kicked in, and he knew the fire was a distraction, so he headed toward the flight deck and hid, waiting for the imposters. Because of the smoke, one made it past him, but the second one wasn't so lucky. Air Marshal Cleotis Johnson took one shot into the head of the terrorist who was now wearing a crew uniform for Western Global Airlines.

The first man leaped for William in the flight deck. Sandra flew past Cleotis and leaped on the back of the terrorist, bringing him to the ground and subduing him. "I've just about had enough of you assholes!" Sandra screamed as she pulled him back enough so Cleotis could smack him in the head with his gun, knocking him out. Cleotis put out his hand and picked Sandra up. She went back to the children, passing Nigel on the way.

Nigel was rubbing the back of his neck. "They came to the stairs and sucker-punched me, the bastards. I saw the uniforms and didn't put it together," Nigel said as he shook his head, trying to regain full control of his senses.

After Hilary and the passenger put out the fire, she ran up the stairs to see if all was OK. Cleotis dragged the last terrorist on his back to get him out of the flight deck and ask him some questions. The terrorist looked up and saw Hilary coming up to him. He asked her through a cough of blood, "All up to your specifications, ma'am?" and then he died. Hilary now remembered where she'd heard that distinct accent before. It was in the cargo hold before they left Winnipeg. She finally matched the voice to the face.

"What the hell?" Nigel said as the three of them looked at the former terrorist.

"Most likely cyanide pills; they didn't want to get caught," Cleotis said, remembering from his years of police work.

"The fire is out, the smoke is clearing, and the passengers are getting settled back in their seats," Hilary announced.

"OK, get them all ready for landing. We're almost there," William said taking command of the situation.

"Aye, aye, Captain," Hilary said with a salute and a smile as she turned and walked away from the flight deck, a woman on a mission.

William turned to Cleotis and gave him a smile. "Thank you for saving my life," he said, reaching out to shake his hand.

"You can pay me back by getting this plane on the ground in one piece," Cleotis said as he shook William's hand. Cleotis then started to move one of the dead terrorists out of the flight deck.

Nigel grabbed the second terrorist and pulled him behind the first one, stopping long enough to say, "Sorry, mate. I let you down."

William smiled and said, "Once you get rid of him, I'll need you to become part of that door frame again, just in case."

"You got it, mate," Nigel said as he pulled the terrorist into the business class section.

William leaned back enough so he could see into business class. His eyes met with Sandra's red eyes. He had never seen that side of her, after all these years. She gave him a smile, and he blew her a kiss and mouthed the words, "I love you!" It was like a million pounds of weight came off of William's shoulders. All he had to battle now was some turbulence and land this wounded bird. *This will be a lot easier than fighting terrorists,* William thought to himself.

85.

To Spencer, it was important that he get the plane on the ground. While he had accomplished a lot in his career, he always loved giving back, and this would be giving all the families a second chance.

The control tower was full of optimistic professionals who were focused on the task at hand. Spencer was trying to keep his emotions in while making sure he covered every item on the checklist that William could set and that was necessary. Jacky was busy with the last few 737s that had just landed from the diversion.

"Southwest two-niner-three-two, turn right and follow the Jet Blue down runway zero-nine. Contact ground one-two-one point niner." She turned to Spencer and said, "That's it. All that are coming this way are here, and the last one is up to you." She looked at him, trying to see if he was cracking under the pressure. He didn't even break a sweat. He was like a kid in a candy store. Pressure was something he obviously relished.

Jacky turned to the rest of the controllers and said to them, "Make sure all of the planes on the ground are evacuated and the terminal is empty. We've done our jobs; now let's hope that the last one makes it here OK." She turned and looked at Spencer one more time as if it may be the last time she would see him. "Good luck," she said as she picked up her binoculars to look out the window for the 747.

Spencer keyed the microphone. "Flight two-niner-one-five, winds are three-four-zero at fifteen, gusts to twenty. You're about five miles out, and cleared to land runway three-three. You're looking great, Wil."

* * *

William thought for sure his heart was going to pound through his chest. This was it, all of the flying in real life and all of the hours spent on the simulator flying his favorite airplane. His mind was full of thoughts of the people onboard and his family. He knew he must land safely if only to see the smiling faces of his children once again. He reached over to the intercom and called downstairs.

"This is it. Are you all ready for landing?" William asked it like he was a real captain.

"Yes, Captain, all is well down here. The passengers are still a bit nervous, but all is well, otherwise," Hilary said, watching the crew do their thing.

William looked back at Nigel, who was still in the doorway of the flight deck. "We're almost home, mate. Sit yourself down and buckle up." William tried to sound as confident as possible.

William returned to looking out the window at the clouds and rain. He thought this was futile; the clouds were so low and so dense. *No, wait a second,* he thought to himself when he thought he saw a little red light towards the ground. Was it really there, or was it just his wishful thinking? "Yes," William said out loud. The red light went from one to two lights. That was what he was looking for. These lights gave the pilot a way to guide the plane to the runway. There were four lights; he should have two white and two red to be in perfect position in the glide slope. William saw three red lights as he got closer; that meant he was too low. He had to climb, or he would land short of the runway.

"Come on, baby, pull up a little. Almost home, girl." William was trying not to overcorrect the 747. The lights changed to two white and two red. He leveled off and tried to stay on the glide slope. His concentration was interrupted by radio chatter.

* * *

"Time to slow her down a little more, Wil. Slow down to one hundred and seventy knots. You're three miles from touchdown; you're doing great," Spencer said, knowing that this was going to be the one and only approach. She was coming home.

Spencer kept looking out the window when he spotted the landing lights from the 747. *"There she is!"* Spencer shouted almost at the same time Jacky did. "Confirm all emergency equipment on the field and ready?" he asked.

"All are ready and waiting," Jacky replied with excitement in her voice.

The field at Saskatoon International Airport was abuzz with emergency vehicles and aircraft being moved. The 747 would have one chance to land and get down safely. The weather was closing in, and the airframe of the 747 was under a lot of stress.

"I have the field in sight," William said proudly on the radio.

"You look good, Wil. How is the plane holding out?" Spencer asked.

"All is well, and there are no abnormalities to report," William stated, still not wanting to tell Spencer about the engine that was about to fall off.

"Confirm that flaps are down and wheels are locked," Spencer asked.

"Flaps at full, and the gear is down and locked," William reported.

Jacky called over to Spencer and said, "Tell him the winds are picking up, and the thunderstorms are closing in."

"What are the winds?" Spencer asked, still looking out the window.

"They are now three-zero-zero at twenty-five, gusting to thirty knots," Jacky said with pessimism in her voice.

"That's thirty degrees off the center line of the runway at twenty-five to thirty-knot wind speed. That's going to be a hard landing with that wind and a short runway. That would be tough for a seasoned 747 pilot, never mind someone who has never flown one before," Jacky said to Spencer, trying to be as pragmatic as possible.

"William, you're looking good." Spencer paused, ignoring Jacky for the moment. "How are your crosswind landing skills?" Spencer asked.

There was a pause. William remembered his training and landing a Cessna 172 many times in a strong crosswind. He remembered being told by many seasoned pilots that a crosswind landing was an art unto itself.

"If that's what I need to do, that will be what I have to do." William was ready for this as he could tell the 747 was being pushed to the right side of the runway.

"That's what it looks like. Two miles to touchdown. Looking good, Wil. Keep an eye on the PAPI." Spencer was confident this was going to be better than he had expected.

The 747 sailed through the air like the graceful girl she was designed to be many years ago. This 747-400 had flown a few million miles and had a flawless safety record. If it landed in one piece, it would be her last flight. The airframe was flown way beyond what it was designed to do. She would be stripped for parts, and the airframe would be sold for scrap. It was a sad ending to such an elegant aircraft. But for now, the task at hand was getting her on the ground.

William had faith in the old bird and was feeling the effects of the crosswind. He was impressed how eight hundred tons felt flying in thirty-knot winds.

"Prepare to cut power and flair," Spencer said, giving William another command. William could hear the sounds of his heartbeat, the wind, and the engines. Suddenly the wind picked up from the west, alarming the normally calm Jacky.

"Winds are two-eight-zero at thirty-five knots!" Jacky called across the control tower as Spencer looked outside to see what effect it had on the 747. The right wing dipped very low.

"One thousand," the GPWS sounded. William's heart was beating so fast he didn't know how much he could take.

"Five hundred feet," the alarm sounded. William had all his attention on the runway lights.

Hilary in the lower level was making sure the passengers were secure. She yelled on the intercom, "Passengers, brace for a hard landing."

"Approaching minimums." The rain began to pick up; it was making it harder for William to see.

"Minimums," chimed the GWPS. At that point, William knew, if he couldn't see the runway, he would have to go around and do what's called a missed approach. William strained his eyes to make out the runway and PAPI lights in the rain. If he couldn't see them, he would have to pull up and go around for another try. With that kind of stress, the damaged engine would surely fall off.

William was trying to compensate for the crosswind.

"William, don't overcompensate, *don't overcompensate!*" Spencer shouted into the microphone. William felt the effects of the wind as he had a hundred times in his Baron. He turned the yoke to the right to bring the one-hundred-foot wing back up in the air as the winglet came close to the ground. It was just in time. As the plane came level, the wheels came over the fence just a few feet away from the tarmac.

"Four hundred. Three hundred. Two hundred. One hundred." *This is taking forever,* William thought.

"Cut power and flair," Spencer said as he watched the 747 reach the tarmac.

"Fifty, forty, thirty, twenty, ten."

The wheels touched the ground with a lot of smoke from the heavy landing.

"Reverse thrust, reverse thrust!" Spencer yelled.

William was shocked that he landed as well as he did and that it was close to the center of the runway. He engaged the reverse thrust seconds before the nose gear touched the ground, and he put his feet on the brakes to help. He looked out the front window to see how much runway he had left. The end of runway three-three was coming fast. He took a look at the speed indicator as it dropped below eighty knots. William knew he shouldn't use reverse thrust under sixty knots or risk damaging the engines, but at this point, avoiding damage to the engines wasn't at the top of his list of priorities. He was still going too fast, and the end of the runway was getting bigger in the window.

"He can't stop in time!" Jacky said, looking past Spencer.

Spencer was staring out the window with a smile on his face, whispering, "C'mon girl, show us how you can do it. C'mon, stop in time." Spencer looked down and saw the 747 slowing down with billows of smoke pouring out of the undercarriage.

Just as everyone held their collective breath waiting for the 747 to run off the end of the runway, it slowed and came to a graceful stop under a lot of smoke, dust, and rain.

The 747 stopped just feet from the end of the runway. This was much to the surprise of everyone, including William, who was sitting in the captain's chair waiting for the big crash off the end of the runway. *If there's any damage to the engines, they can send me the bill,* he thought to himself. He reached under the thrust levers and turned off the engines, set the parking brakes, and took his feet off the rudders. Then he heard the sound of the cheering passengers.

* * *

Cheering and high-fives erupted in the control towers, both in Saskatoon and in Winnipeg where they had been tuned in to the radio. Randy, Mike, and Phil all cheered and high-fived as if they had won the big hockey game.

"He did it!" Randy screamed.

In all of the madness, there was hope that this day would not end as bad as it could have been, Mike thought.

* * *

At the FBI safe house, the cheering was loud. Agents Monroe and Davis shook hands and smiled as they heard the news that the 747 was safely on the ground. Davis looked around at the cheering people and thought to himself, *We will make it through this day.*

* * *

Jacky and Spencer made it around the room with plenty of congratulations and high-fives until they finally met in the middle of the room. They were two professionals at the top of their respective fields, facing each other as if in a mirror. Who would make the first move to congratulate the other? They both looked at each other with anticipation.

Spencer spoke first. "Well, looks like we *did it!*" He ended his sentence loudly and reached around and grabbed Jacky, who had a big smile on her face and her arms wide open. They hugged for what seemed like an eternity. Truly this was a day that would be remembered as both a tragic one, and one in which all of the men and women who had trained for years made all of the training worth it.

Spencer, a man who was not normally emotional, pulled away from Jacky's embrace and looked up to all of the people in the room.

"Can I have your attention, please. Please, everybody, can I have your attention," Spencer said, raising his hand to get everyone's attention. The room went silent, and all eyes were on Spencer. He was choking back the tears.

"I'm normally good at public speaking because I sometimes do that for a living," he started to say, coughing back the tears.

"All I want to say, people, is that in all of my time in this industry, I've never been so proud to work with a group of people as I am right now. We pulled off something that was said to be impossible. Thank you for making this day a little brighter. I don't know what will happen now; all I can say is that, with people like you, the future looks great!" Spencer was showing a side of himself that he didn't often show.

Jacky didn't want to be outdone by Spencer, so she decided to make a speech as well. She raised her hand to silence the cheering crowd. "To say I'm proud of you all is an understatement," she began, fighting back the lump in her throat. She paused and then continued, saying, "We have shown right here today that people can overcome adversity by pooling together our skills. We need to remember that the most important thing is the love of life, living, and serving others. We are not the center of the universe as we may think we are. We are in this together, and together we stand, or divided we fall. So let's stick together and make sure that the world we live in is a world worth living for!" Jacky was surprised by her emotional outburst. Spencer and the rest of the people were too. They all gave her a round of applause as she sheepishly waved them off.

Spencer looked to Jacky and pointed to the stairs. "Shall we go and meet my latest graduate?" he said with a big smile.

"After you," she replied with sarcasm.

"This is your tower, Jacky. I insist—after you." Spencer was gently handing control of the tower back to Jacky. She saw through Spencer and just smiled and led the way.

86.

The sound of the engines wound down for the last time. William could hear the faint sound of cheering passengers and the sound of rain on the windshield. He then heard someone call his name. It was a voice he had longed to hear. It was Sandra's voice. She had come in the flight deck and came up behind the captain's chair, children in tow. William got up from the chair and reached over to his wife.

"Is it finally over?" Sandra asked.

William just pulled her head and rested it on his chest. He didn't tell her all about what had been going on while they were coming home. He would leave that for later.

As he held Sandra, Zoë and Shawn's familiar smiles looked up proudly at their father. Zoë was still upset and clung onto her mom, and Shawn was still curious. "Dad," Shawn asked, looking at all of the controls, "will I have to challenge Zoë to rock-paper-scissors to sit in the first officer's seat?" William and Sandra just hugged and laughed.

"Let's go, Wil," Sandra said, motioning the children out of the flight deck and heading towards the stairs.

On the way to the back of business class, Sandra and William met Hilary at the top of the stairs. Hilary had a big smile and gave Sandra a much-needed hug. Hilary reached out her arms to hug William and looked at Sandra for approval.

Sandra smiled and said, "Go ahead; we'll meet you at the bottom of the stairs." Sandra grabbed each child by the hand and headed down the stairs. She held them extra tightly, not ever wanting to live the moment of losing a child and feeling so helpless ever again.

Hilary was about to cry as she reached out her arms to William. William reached up and grabbed Hilary's shoulders to give her a well-deserved hug. He felt so thankful to have been on a plane with this wonderful woman. He could not repay her for what she had done, not in a million years. Hilary started to cry, but she tried to hold back the tears.

"It's OK," William said, trying to comfort Hilary.

"Yes, stiff upper lip and all that British stuff, *eh*," Hilary said, picking up on and teasing William about his Canadian accent. "You kept your promise," she said in more of a serious tone and with admiration as few men had ever kept promises in her life.

"I always have, and I always will keep my promises," William said, hiding his emotions by trying to sound macho.

"I could hug you all day, but I'm sure Sandra would have something to say about that, and you better not keep your fan club waiting," Hilary said as she broke off the embrace.

"Fan club?" William asked.

"Yes, you now have a little over three hundred new best friends. It's going to be a few minutes before they get stairs here, and we're not going to use the slides, so everyone is still on the plane," Hilary explained as they walked down from the upper deck.

"There he is," Nigel said as all of the passengers looked over to William and cheered. The sound of applause was something that William was unfamiliar with. He looked on sheepishly as Hilary joined in the applause. William was overwhelmed as he looked around for Sandra and the kids.

"There it is," said a passenger, "here comes the stairs." At the top of the stairs were police officers as well as some emergency personnel to take care of any injured passengers.

A few minutes later, Nigel looked over to Harry, who had already begun filling in the police with the details about the terrorists.

"Do you need my help, mate?" Nigel asked Harry.

Harry reached out his hand to Nigel and said, "You did well, for a rugby player."

Nigel shook his hand. "You're not such a bad bloke yourself," he said.

"I'll be fine. I'll just help get them off the plane and then start on all of the paperwork," Harry said with a smile.

"Take care, man. We couldn't have done it without you." Nigel said as he let Harry get back to it.

With the stairs at the door and the emergency personnel inside, the passengers started to leave the plane, all of them thanking William before they left.

With all the handshakes, congratulations, and hugs over with, William pulled out his BlackBerry to take down a few e-mail addresses of his new friends. Sandra grabbed it out of his hands with some embarrassment and put it in her purse. "We'll have time for that later, Wil," she said, trying to make him feel not so nervous in the crowd. William was relieved when people started to exit the plane as it was getting a bit claustrophobic for him.

Hilary let the other girls help the passengers down the stairs as she made her way toward Nigel. He smiled and said, "Well, I'll call that a match then."

Hilary didn't know what came over her, but she had to hug him one more time. The feeling of being held by such strong arms was a reassuring feeling. *This is something I could get used to,* she thought. "I owe you a lot," she said as she broke off the hug.

He smiled and looked her in the eyes. "We can talk about that over dinner, then?" he asked.

She just smiled and hugged him one more time. They were still hugging as they walked toward the stairs. *This could be the start of something good,* she thought.

William was talking to some of his new friends when Sandra walked towards the door and the stairs, holding the children's hands tightly. He wasn't ever going to let them get too far away from him again, he thought as he smiled at Shawn, who looked back.

"See you in the bus, Dad," Shawn said, not too happy about being held by the hand as he was a big kid and not a baby.

"I'm right behind you, guys," William said, trying not to be rude to his new friends.

* * *

Spencer and Jacky approached the bottom of the stairs, sharing an umbrella. Spencer admired his favorite bird; even in the rain she was glamorous. He had to look twice at engine number two and wondered how close it was to falling off.

"I wonder what he looks like?" Jacky asked.

"Who?" Spencer asked, still in wonder of it all.

"William," Jacky said, giving Spencer a dirty look.

"Oh, yes, well look for the guy who needs to change his shorts," Spencer said, looking up the ladder at the stream of passengers. Jacky was not impressed.

As the passengers left the airplane and boarded buses, Spencer looked at the top and saw a man who looked like he had just saved the world.

"That's him," Spencer said to Jacky, pointing to the man at the top of the stairs.

"How do you know?" Jacky asked, looking up at the man on the stairs.

"It's a pilot thing; he looks like a pilot." Spencer was pretty sure the man was William, his new graduate. He was also showing off to Jacky.

Spencer looked up at the man on the stairs, and their eyes met. The man smiled back; Spencer knew he was right.

The line of people moved down the stairs quickly. They all looked the same no matter where they were from. They all looked like they'd been given a second chance at life.

The two men met at the bottom of the stairs. William reached out his hand. "Spencer, I presume," William said.

Spencer paused to look at the man who had done the impossible, the man who had done what was said could not be done. Spencer admired this Baron pilot who in one day had eclipsed his whole career by landing a 747 on a short runway, in a crosswind, and in a thunderstorm. Spencer brushed off William's hand and reached around to give him a hug. This caught him by surprise, but he welcomed it.

"You did it, man. You brought them home safe," Spencer said, ignoring the summer rain. As he gave William a hug, he looked at the 747 one more time. "You did it too, girl; you did it too," he said as a tribute to the greatest commercial aircraft ever built.

"Thanks to you," William said as they broke their hug. "I couldn't have done it without you," he said with sincerity in his voice, looking Spencer in the eyes.

"Let's go inside where it's dry," Spencer said, leading William back to the tower with his arm around his shoulder.

"Let me get one last look at her, first," William said as he walked over to the undercarriage of the mammoth 747. He looked at the landing gear that was hot and steaming from the landing in the cold rain. It would be over for this bird. It would be its last flight except maybe one to Nevada where they retire old and outdated aircraft. *Maybe she'll get a second chance at a museum,* William thought as he admired her beauty. "Enjoy your retirement; you deserve it," William said, giving this gracious craft a few parting words. He then looked over to see Spencer smiling under an umbrella. He knew that Spencer understood. William then joined Spencer and Jacky as they walked over to the tower.

"Is it as bad as I hear it is?" William asked, not knowing the full story of what had been happening on the ground.

Spencer looked at William and then looked away. Spencer, trying to keep that bit of information between him and William, leaned in and in almost a whisper said, "It's a lot worse, Wil; it's a lot worse."

87.

A smoldering United States of America was all that remained of a once great nation, a nation built on the traditions of a great many people. As the happy people departed the 747 in a wet, warm Saskatoon summer afternoon, happy to be alive, the president of the United States prepared to make a speech on the emergency network.

This attack upon this once great nation put America back into the early twentieth century with little power, communications, or transportation. America and the rest of Western civilization would never be the same. It was ironic that for the most part the only people who would be able to receive the president's speech broadcasted on every broadcast medium were the rural people who had either old, battery-operated AM radios or, if there was power, they could watch the broadcast on their TVs with rabbit ears. America had truly been blasted back to another time.

The radio sounded fuzzy as the announcer stated, "Ladies and gentlemen, the President of the United States."

"Fellow citizens of America and all free nations, I bring you this message of hope. There is still an America, and no matter how hard the terrorists have hit us, there will always be an America as long as we breathe the breath of liberty. The terrorists have struck a mighty blow to our way of life, but like many times before, we have survived, and we will live to see another day. We have seen the determination of the terrorists to eradicate our way of life, but they have also seen the resolve of a people to defend a way of life that is envied all over the world.

"To the remaining people in the cities and in the oil patches and in the wheat fields, we will not forsake you. We will deliver you from the evil that has sunk into this once great nation.

"I have ordered, effective immediately, that all troops, deployed anywhere outside of the United States and possessions be recalled to seal the southern border and defend the west coast from possible invasion. People of America, our boys are coming home.

"I regret to announce that in desperate times, desperate measures must come into effect. For the first time since the Constitution took effect in 1789, I signed an executive order that has suspended the Constitution of the United States of America. We must do this so we can fight this new war on terrorism."

The president looked long and deep into the camera even though he knew that most people would be hearing his broadcast over the radio. He said his final words of the broadcast: "May God bless you, and may God bless the United States of America."

Made in the USA
Charleston, SC
28 March 2010